FOUR
DOORS
DOWN

a novel

emma
doherty

Cover by Murphy Rae at www.murphyrae.net
Editing by Megan at www.murphyrae.net
Proofed by Laura at www.facebook.com/editingforyou/?fref=ts
Formatted by Stacey at www.champagneformats.com

ISBN-13:978-1533664419
ISBN-10:1533664412

do I remember that I've spent the last hour drawing an elaborate sketch of the classroom in front of me rather than taking notes on his class. He takes one look at it and sighs again. "Impressive, Miss McKenzie. However, this will not help you pass English. You'll come back after school and we'll go through it again."

I slump in my chair. *Great. Fan-freaking-tastic!*

The bell rings and my friend Sam looks over at me, smiling in sympathy. I gather my things and head toward the door catching up with her. Ryan comes up behind me and I glare at him as he passes, which only adds to his smirk.

"Ignore him. He's just trying to wind you up," Sam tells me and I nod. No point in wasting words on him. We start working our way down the hallway of MacAllister High as it begins to fill up.

Sam glances sideways at me. "Still on for tomorrow night?" I grin and nod. She doesn't even have to ask. There's no way I'd miss tomorrow tonight. Charlie will be there, and even the thought of him makes my heart beat slightly faster.

Charlie is the guy I've been seeing for the last couple of months, and he is the sexiest, sweetest, most talented guy I've ever met. Just thinking about him makes me smile. Forget detention. I'm seeing Charlie tomorrow.

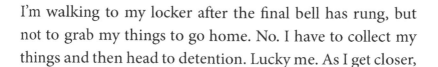

I'm walking to my locker after the final bell has rung, but not to grab my things to go home. No. I have to collect my things and then head to detention. Lucky me. As I get closer,

I see the familiar crowd gathered, and there he is, right in the middle, holding court—Ryan Jackson.

Ryan Jackson might be the bane of my existence, but apparently not everyone feels that way. Yes, he might be over six foot tall with shiny dark hair, bright blue eyes and with the broad build that's made him the star of the school's football team and formerly it's basketball team. But trust me, looks don't count for everything and the guy's arrogance knows no bounds. Seriously, Ryan Jackson is the ultimate jock, ultimate big man on campus, ultimate player and the ultimate pain in my ass. And I can say that as someone who's known him for years, like literally, since we were babies. Our moms are best friends and we live four doors down from each other. We were actually best friends up until middle school when he suddenly started acting like I didn't exist. We've barely spoken since. Well, apart from when he's bored and feels like annoying the hell out of me. And now, here when I have like two minutes to grab my things before making it back to Henderson's class, his fan club of skanks and tagalongs are spread out around his locker, and therefore blocking mine which is just a few further down.

"Excuse me," I say to Bianca Gallagher, who doesn't even acknowledge that I've spoken. "Excuse me." Again, nothing. No one even looks at me. "God, would you move!" I snap, and everyone turns silent and looks over.

Bianca turns her nose up at me. "Rude much," she says with disdain but does step aside.

I roll my eyes and open my locker.

"Ignore her, B. She's just pissed 'cause she has to go back

3

to Henderson's room now," Ryan explains. I shoot him a dirty look. He just grins back at me. He opens his mouth to say something else but is interrupted when Jake runs into him from behind. Ryan turns to greet him, and they bump fists, or whatever it is guys do now. I roll my eyes and turn back to my locker.

The chatter continues around me like I'm invisible, and once again I'm reminded of how over high school I am. Especially this particular high school in Maxwell, Southern California. I don't know who it was that said senior year is the best time of your life, but I'm already counting down to graduation and when I don't have to deal with these people anymore. Seriously, you'd think in this day and age the divide between the popular kids and the rest of the school would cease to exist and be of no importance whatsoever. But nope. Not here at McAllister High. I swear it's like something out of a cheesy teen film, and I, for one, cannot wait to get out.

Jake appears next to me. "Hey, Becca."

I look over at him and can't stop a smile from etching onto my face. Jake might be Ryan's best friend but I've known him forever too, and although Ryan and I barely speak anymore, Jake's always been the same with me. We might run in completely different circles these days, but we're still good friends and he always makes sure to say hi when he sees me.

"Hey."

"So I just came from art class with Miss Smith, and she showed me the piece you've been working on for your final project."

"She's showing people that?"

"Just me, and only 'cause I asked. She knows we're friends. Pretty amazing, Becca. Like seriously."

I allow a small smile to slip free. Jake doesn't bullshit and it was nice of him to ask to see it. "Thanks."

"Jake, come on!" Bianca's irritated voice calls from the group behind. He turns to look at her. "We're going back to my house to chill by the pool."

I look up and must admit I get a small, satisfied feeling watching her. She's clearly annoyed that Jake is talking to me and not her. Ryan's watching us too, probably incredibly confused as to why Jake would waste his time on me.

Jake turns to me. "Wanna come too, Becca?" I nearly laugh out loud at the look of horror on Bianca's face. I'm clearly not on the guest list.

"Nah. Thanks to your buddy Ryan over there, I've got detention with Henderson," I tell him. Jake looks at Ryan and then back at me while shaking his head with an amused smile on his face. "Although, otherwise, obviously I'd be there." I finish grabbing my things and closing my locker. "Don't let yourself be dumbed down too much by the masses," I say, and Jake laughs as I walk away.

I try not to think about the fact that school's over and I've got at least another hour here.

I arrive home from school and I'm annoyed. Henderson couldn't give me a full hour's detention, so he decided to give me a morning detention instead. I have to get there at the crack of dawn tomorrow and in his words, "show a drastic improvement in my attitude," as I am currently "wasting all my potential." God, he's annoying. All I did was not know the answer to his stupid question. This is all Ryan's fault.

Stupid, stupid, Ryan. Always there to annoy me. Ryan and I have known each other since we were babies. We were inseparable when we were children, our moms were always together so we were always together. We used to play soccer together, go to parties together, and do homework together. To be honest, we were pretty cliquey, never really bothering with anyone else. It was just Ryan and me. I mean, we were friends with Jake too and hung around with him at school, but it was Ryan who was my best friend and I was his.

Then we started middle school and at first, everything was great. We walked to school together every morning, spent all our breaks and lunches with one another and walked home side by side at night. But we weren't in the same homerooms, and when Ryan made the basketball and football teams, I started noticing that a lot of his friends from the teams would all of a sudden be eating lunch with us and some of their friends from their grade schools. Suddenly, it wasn't just Ryan and me anymore. Other girls would be around too, girls that weren't like me. Girls that were interested in boys and wore makeup to school (I mean come on, we were twelve!). Anyway, I got the impression that Ryan's new friends, especially the girls, didn't really like me. I soon realized that our table was the popular table at school and these kids were the most popular kids in our grade. Somehow, Ryan had become their ringleader. I told myself I was just being stupid, but things were definitely changing, and even when Jake was there and laughing and joking with everyone, I still didn't feel comfortable.

Then one Monday I left my house to walk to school and just had a feeling something was off. I hadn't seen Ryan all weekend, which was the first time that had happened in a long time. I was surprised when I got to his house and he wasn't there waiting for me as usual. I stood there for maybe ten minutes before knocking on his door, and his mom told me that he'd already left and she didn't know why he hadn't waited for me. I could tell Mrs. Jackson felt sorry for me and was trying to make me feel better by saying that Ryan probably thought I'd gone ahead, but I knew he just decided to go without me that day.

I didn't see him all morning and I got to lunch late. I stood in line with the rest of the kids and when I turned to find Ryan and our table, I saw that it was already full. I almost just went and sat down somewhere else, and I really wish that I had, but I told myself I was being stupid. Ryan was my best friend and we'd always eaten lunch together, so I walked over to his (our?) table. The table fell quiet when I got there, only Jake smiled at me and started looking around to grab an extra chair. The rest of the table were all looking at Ryan with small smiles on their faces. Ryan looked slightly flushed, but when I placed my tray on the table, he looked me straight in the eye. "Maybe you should go and sit somewhere else today, Rebecca." Yeah, he actually used my full name, like he didn't know me at all. "And from now on," he had continued.

I remember going bright red and feeling humiliated with tears welling in my eyes. I remember how the cafeteria suddenly seemed really quiet and realized that most people had probably heard what he said to me. Now that Ryan was so popular, I guess what he did was newsworthy. I remember Jake's head snapping to Ryan in shock.

I just nodded as my mouth started trembling. I quickly walked across the cafeteria and sat at an empty table in the corner. I could feel people looking at me, but I refused to look up. I knew if I did, the tears would start to fall. A tray was put down across from me and I glanced up to see that Jake had come to sit with me, shaking his head in annoyance like he couldn't believe what had happened. We just sat there in silence, but I'll always remember how Jake stood by me that day and didn't let me sit there on my own, being whispered about and gawked at. I'm pretty certain that day is one of the main reasons I now hate being the center of attention.

I managed to stay there for about twenty minutes before excusing myself to the bathroom. I locked myself in a stall and broke down in tears. I didn't understand it. Ryan was my best friend, and when you're that age, your best friend means everything to you, and now he didn't want to know me and had humiliated me in front of everyone.

The next day when I got to lunch, I sat at the same empty table, and this time, almost immediately a girl called Sam who was in a few of my classes sat with me. She didn't mention anything about the day before, although she must have known about it, she just started talking about her favorite ice cream and I knew everything was going to be all right. Jake sat with me that whole week too, but I told him I was fine and he could go back to sitting with his friends. I knew he was mad at Ryan for the way he'd treated me, but he eventually went back to their table and resumed his place in their group.

I was miserable pretty much the rest of that week. When I got an A on my Math test, he was the first person I wanted to tell, and when we needed partners in gym class, I didn't know who to ask. But I only let myself dwell on it for a week. If he wanted to be like that, he could be. I didn't need anyone who thought that they were too good or too popular for me. As far as I was concerned, Ryan didn't exist anymore.

I don't know if he had a change of heart or even if his mom made him do it, but he did come over to my house about two weeks after the lunch disaster, but I wouldn't see him. I ignored my mom and wouldn't leave my room. Even when he tried talking to me through the door, I just ignored him. If he didn't need me, then I didn't need him either. He left after twenty minutes or so and that was that. I avoided him at all costs, not even looking in his direction if I could help it. We didn't speak at all for the rest of middle school.

Then we got to high school, and I remember the exact moment I realized he wasn't going to ignore me anymore. The moment I realized that he was going to go out of his way to annoy, embarrass, tease, humiliate, and antagonize me.

It was the first week of high school and I was sitting with Sam in the cafeteria. So far everything had been okay.

Sam had been really nervous about starting high school, but classes seemed to be doable, and we had made a few friends that we had starting sitting with at lunch. I'd not been paying attention and managed to knock my drink all over myself. I stood up annoyed and reached down and pulled on my shirt, dabbing at it with some napkins, trying to get the moisture out and to stop the stain. I'd suddenly felt myself being watched, and I had looked up to find a large table of guys were looking over with their eyes trained on me.

At the time I didn't know who they were, but it was a mix of ages, clearly some were upperclassmen, but Jake and Ryan were sitting there so I figured it was one of the sports teams. I immediately dropped my shirt, suddenly aware that I may have inadvertently flashed my stomach at them and sat back down looking away. Suddenly their whole table burst out laughing loudly, and when I glanced up, some were still looking at me but also at Ryan. Ryan had clearly made a joke at my expense, which they all found hilarious.

Later that week during lunch, I'd been listening to something one of the girls was saying when a throat was cleared behind me. We all turned to see a tall, blonde guy with bright green eyes standing behind us. He was looking directly at me. "I'm Billy Jameson," he told me. "Just thought you should know, Becca," he said before he turned and sauntered away. I had looked after him in astonishment, unsure what to make of this and wondering how he knew my name. When he re-joined the table who had been watching me earlier in the week, I'd gotten an uneasy feeling, especially with Ryan sitting over there staring at me blankly.

Over the next couple of weeks, Billy Jameson went out of his way to say hi to me when he saw me and chat with me at my locker. Turns out he was a junior who played on the basketball team. He was pretty hot, kind of popular (in a periphery sort of way) and pretty entertaining, but to be honest, I just found all the attention a bit overwhelming and a bit unwanted. I don't know why, but I just felt suspicious. After a few weeks of idle chit chat, he asked me out on a date. I'd been hesitant, unsure if I even wanted to (or if my dad would let me) start dating, but he'd turned on his charm and I agreed.

We went for burgers and then a movie. I figured we would head home after, but he told me a few of his friends were having a cookout on the beach and that we should stop by. I had been ready to head home, for some reason I was incredibly tired that day, but I'd agreed and gone to the beach. I expected it to be just a few of his friends, but as we walked toward the fire, there had to be at least twenty people sitting around. When Billy reached out and grabbed my hand, I started to feel uncomfortable. I mean, this was the first time a boy had held my hand and he just happened to do it when we were about to meet a bunch of his friends?

We stopped by the fire and he greeted his friends while I looked around nervously. My heart had sunk when I saw Ryan was there. He was sitting with Mason Blackwell and John Roberts, talking to a couple of girls who I recognized as being freshmen but didn't know their names. They were drinking beers and judging by how loud they were talking, they were pretty buzzed. It was as if Ryan sensed me watch-

panic crossed Billy's face.

"I'm going to leave," I said calmly to Billy. "And I'm never going to speak to you again."

I turned to his friend who had mentioned about the bet. "Maybe you'll get your money back when he picks his next unlucky victim." I cast one more look of disgust at Ryan and turned and walked away. I walked ten blocks just to get away from them before I started looking for a bus stop.

The next week at school Billy tried to play it down, but I calmly repeated I wouldn't be speaking to him again. When word got around school about what had happened, a few other girls who had been on dates with some of the older guys from the team realized that they were probably having bets placed on them too and promptly stopped dating them.

Ryan came and found me at my locker on Monday morning and apologized for the way he had spoken about me. He swore to me that he didn't know about the bet and he would never have let them go through with it. I stood and listened to him, watching his eyes dart away from my face nervously and his feet fidget on the floor. Then I closed my locker and walked past him without a word. We didn't have any interaction for months.

Luckily for me, Billy Jameson transferred schools later in the year. Jake tried to talk to me about Ryan a couple of times, explaining that he had just been drunk and talking shit, but I didn't want to hear it. Then when I was talking to Jake one day, Ryan came over and cracked some lame joke at my expense, acting as though we were old friends and I didn't hate his guts. He clearly enjoyed pissing me off.

It's carried on that way ever since. It's like he decided that ignoring me wasn't enough fun for him anymore. Now he wanted to embarrass me and tease me at any chance he got, and he did that throughout the rest of my freshmen year right up until now. I was hoping when I came back for senior year that he'd have grown up and left me alone, but on the first day back he was there pestering me. And that's pretty much our relationship now. I try to ignore him, he tries to annoy me. I cannot stand him or his friends and wish he'd forget I exist.

I snap myself out of thoughts of Ryan and walk into my house throwing my bag down on the floor, heading into the kitchen. My mom's in there with Mrs. Jackson, Ryan's mom.

"Hi, Becca, how are you?" Mrs. Jackson asks, smiling warmly at me.

I smile back at her and wonder for the millionth time how somebody as sweet and kind as Mrs. Jackson spawned the douche bag that is Ryan Jackson.

"Good, thanks."

"You're back late." My mom eyes me suspiciously. She's well aware of my tendency to pick up a detention or two.

I shrug. "Just went for a coffee with Sam after school."

"I've brought your parents over an invite for Bill's 50th birthday party just before Christmas. Of course, you're invited too." Mrs. Jackson explains.

I roll my eyes and my mom shoots me a warning look. Immediately after Ryan and I had our big falling out back in seventh grade, our mom's kept trying to put us together for things, hoping we'd sort it out. They soon realized that neither of us had any intention of speaking to each other again and dropped it. Clearly Mrs. Jackson has forgotten this. There is no way that I'm attending that party.

Mrs. Jackson misinterprets my look. "Oh, don't worry honey. It won't just be us oldies there. I've told Ryan he can invite some friends from school, so there'll be plenty of people you know there."

I smirk. *Great. Ryan's friends who I can't stand.* Surely Mrs. Jackson knows that we don't mix in the same crowd these days? She must be delusional.

"Don't forget you've got Jay on Monday," my mom reminds me.

"Yes, I know." She keeps reminding me like I'm stupid and I'll forget.

Jay is my little cousin. He's only five and his mom, my aunt, is kind of going through a lot at the moment. She divorced her husband, Jay's dad, last year and hasn't taken it very well. I think she's going through some sort of mid-life crisis; dressing seriously inappropriately and going on dates with some very dodgy men. My mom's worried about the effect all this is having on Jay and him not seeing his dad very much now that he lives out of state. My mom ends up watching him a lot, and lucky me gets to watch him once a week too or else she'll confiscate my car. I don't know what the big deal is. The kid's fine. In fact, he's a total brat and is well aware that he has all the adults in his life wrapped around his little finger.

"I'm going to do my homework," I tell them, leaving the kitchen and heading up to my room. I get to my desk and pull out my books but soon get bored and spend the next couple of hour's texting Charlie and day dreaming about seeing him tomorrow.

Charlie Jordan is basically all I've thought about since I met him at a party about two weeks before senior year began. I'd spent most of the summer visiting family in Europe, so I hadn't really been around. Sam invited me to a party that her boyfriend Chris, who goes to a different school than us, was having. I almost didn't go. I was still a bit jet lagged and couldn't really be bothered, but Sam had insisted, so I turned up.

The party had been okay, mainly full of people I didn't know, and I was feeling tired and crabby when I wandered into a separate room and found ten or so people sitting around listening to a guy playing his guitar. I listened for a few minutes, and then he looked up and our eyes had met. Well, that was it. I'd never felt an attraction like it. He was gorgeous, but not in your stereotypical way. He had dark blonde hair which was just a bit too long, big brown eyes and he was wearing a ratty old t-shirt and ripped jeans. When he smiled over at me, my heart had started beating faster in my chest. I couldn't look away from him, and suddenly I didn't want to go home anymore. In fact, I wanted the night to go on and on.

I tried to play it cool, of course, and act uninterested, pretending I wasn't watching him from the corner of my eye, but when he came over to talk to me an hour or so later, I don't think I hid my interest in him all that well. In fact, I was like putty in his hands. Turns out he was a friend of

Chris' from grade school and had just moved back to the area. When he asked me out on a date, I agreed instantly and that was that as far as I was concerned. He's pretty much all I've thought about in the two months since we met, and I promptly handed over my virginity to him a few weeks after our first date with absolutely no concerns. You'd think I hadn't guarded it for the first seventeen years of my life the way I quickly gave it up to him, but Charlie made me feel in a way I'd never felt before, and I wanted to be his completely. It's pretty safe to say that I am definitely in the throes of young love.

Like *totally* lost in it.

CHAPTER 2

I PULL INTO THE SCHOOL PARKING LOT THE NEXT morning still yawning. I've never gotten to school at this ungodly hour before. *Damn Henderson for my morning detention.* I pull down the sun visor and check my reflection in the mirror. My long brown hair is still damp from the shower which has made me late, but even I can't go four days without washing my hair; you genuinely would have been able to fry bacon in my hair this morning. My green eyes look tired, but there's no time for makeup. Thank goodness for clear skin.

I climb out of my car and grab the papers on my passenger seat and hurry up to the entrance. I'm almost at the steps when I look up and see Ryan Jackson and half the football team hanging around on the steps.

Shit.

If I'd seen them earlier, I would have used a different entrance. *Why the hell are they here so early?* They must use this time to creep on everyone coming into school and bully anyone that pisses them off. A quick scan of them tells me that Jake is absent. No one would say anything to me if he were here.

Great. Just great.

They go silent as I approach, and I walk up the steps, forcing myself to walk normally and not speed up because of them. I'm almost through when Kevin Wilson, a slimy, creepy senior jumps down from the railing and throws his arm around me, turning me back to the group.

"Well, if it isn't little Miss McKenzie. Not often we see you here this early."

I glance down at his right hand. *Who on earth does he think he's touching?*

"Yeah, well, I'm actually late so…" I shrug out of his hold and turn to walk away. He grabs me before I can get away and pulls me in closer to his side. His massive right hand is dangerously close to my right breast.

I look up at him. "Seriously, I'm late."

"Oh, come on, Becca, just chill with us for a minute."

"Hey, let her go, Wilson," Ryan pipes up.

"Oh, come on, Jackson. Why is it only you that gets to mess with Becca? I bet I'd know how to lighten her up," he says grinning arrogantly while his massive paw drops down and actually rubs my right breast. Deliberately.

"Fuck off," I say in shock. *I cannot believe he just did that!* I push him away in disgust. "Don't touch me."

He just laughs and holds his hands up. "Hey, relax, I won't touch you." He pauses while I just glare at him with anger. "But what about if I touch your stuff?" He lifts his right hand in the air and smacks it down against the book and papers in my hands. I watch as they all fall to the ground around me.

I'm mortified. Not only have I just been groped, but now I'm being publicly humiliated too. I kneel down to collect my stuff and too late do I realize that the loose fitting V-neck shirt I'm wearing is gaping forward as I lean over, and I'm giving them all a great shot of my chest. I lift the shirt to my chest, stopping it from dropping down, and Kevin starts to laugh and I know he saw straight down my top.

"Hey, Becca." I look up, which is a mistake because he's standing directly in front of me and his crotch is level with my face as he points his finger to his groin. "While you're down there, early morning blow job?" he asks, laughing down at me, and then he actually thrusts his groin in my direction.

I try to swallow down the lump that forms in my throat and see him stagger backward after someone gives him a violent push. I'm guessing it must be Ryan because the next minute he's kneeling down next to me and helping me to collect my stuff.

"I don't need your fucking help, Ryan," I spit at him. He pauses immediately, and I grab my stuff from him and finish picking up the last few things.

Okay, so I know I make out like I'm a strong, independent, don't-give-a-crap woman, but this is horrible. I mean, these guys are really intimidating and now they're all just watching me crawl around on the floor, publically humiliated. The worst part is that I'm upset, and I'm angry with myself for letting them get to me.

I stand up and turn back to Kevin, who is still grinning at me like he just did the funniest thing in the world. I glance around quickly, but no one else is laughing. In fact, most of the guys look pretty wary and are glancing over at Ryan. I refuse to look at Ryan; this is his fault. If he didn't treat me like crap, then no one else would think they could either.

I shoot Kevin a murderous look and turn to walk around him.

Actually, forget that.

I turn back to Kevin, who is smiling at me smugly, clearly very pleased with himself. I take a step closer and then kick my right knee up with all my strength straight into his groin.

He drops to the ground like a stone. He's in so much pain he's not even able to speak. He just lays there moaning in pain while holding what I'm sure is his tiny penis. There are shocked gasps from the guys watching.

I look down at him. "Touch me or my stuff again and I'll castrate you."

I turn on my heel and walk into school to the sound of his friends laughing loudly behind me.

CHAPTER 3

I T'S FINALLY FRIDAY NIGHT, THERE'S NO SCHOOL FOR two days, and I'm standing at the back of the room in a house that I've never been to before, staring at the bottle of tequila in my hand. I must admit the first few sips burnt the back of my throat, but now I like it, now it actually tastes good. I'm not much of a drinker but Charlie handed me this bottle when I turned up at the party, and I must admit it's doing wonders for my confidence. Usually, I'd be standing here on my own feeling self-conscious that Charlie is nowhere to be found. I came with Sam, but her parents are so strict she barely gets a chance to see Chris on her own, and I don't want to bug them. But instead of feeling awkward and alone, I'm casually surveying the scene and taking in what I see.

The door opens and Ryan Jackson walks in with Jake.

What the hell? Are you serious? The reason I avoid all McAllister parties is because I don't want to see people I know from school, and here I am at a Madison party and in walks my arch nemesis and his best friend. Okay, so I know I get along with Jake, but still, I'm adding to the effect.

I watch them as they make their way through the room. A girl with red hair lets out a squeal when she sees them and makes a beeline for Ryan, hugging him tightly when she gets close.

Geez, get a grip.

Ryan looks up and our eyes meet. Surprise crosses his face, but he quickly recovers. I must be drunk because I don't turn away instantly and watch as he nudges Jake and nods in my direction. A grin spreads across Jake's face and they both start walking toward me.

Shit. Too late do I realize that now I'm actually going to have to talk to them. So, of course, I do the only sensible thing I can think of and turn my back to them like I haven't seen them at all.

"Becca."

Maybe if I don't acknowledge them, they'll go away.

"Becca?"

Again, I just stand there.

"For fuck's sake, Becca. Turn around. We know you saw us."

Okay, so I'm going to have to turn around or look like even more of an idiot. I can still save this. "Oh. Hello, I didn't see you there."

Ryan's face breaks out into a huge grin. "Right." I choose not to dignify this with an answer and look pointedly away. "Such an attitude, McKenzie!" he continues.

Jake takes over (which is always best), "We don't usually

see you at these parties."

"Yes, well I choose not to go to McAllister parties because I'm not sure I like the caliber of people I see there." I'm hoping I sound aloof; the fact that I'm swaying slightly is hopefully not giving away my drunken state.

"So we just ruined your night by showing up, did we?"

I sigh deeply. "Why are you even here?"

Ryan shrugs. "We came to see Zara."

"And who exactly is Zara?"

His grin grows even bigger. "This is her house. It's her party."

Oh, crap. I knew I should have paid better attention when I arrived. The look on Ryan's face tells me he knows that I have no idea who Zara is. He'll probably use this information against me later and get me kicked out.

Jake looks between us and makes the wise decision to change the subject. "So, I heard you floored Kevin this morning. It's all the guys were talking about. I wish I'd been there."

"It was amazing, bro. You should have seen his face," Ryan jumps in.

Hang on a second. I'm not having this. "Fuck you, Ryan. Kevin Wilson wouldn't even know who I am, let alone think he can treat me like that if it weren't for you." *Wow. Alcohol really does make you say things you never would sober.*

Jake whistles awkwardly and a muscle in Ryan's jaw visibly tenses. "Well, he's got eyes, Becca, so I'm pretty sure he'd know who you are."

"That's not what I meant and you know it."

"What did you mean?"

"If you didn't take every chance you get to make me look like an idiot, then he wouldn't have thought he could pull that shit."

Ryan is glaring at me. "You don't actually think I wanted him to do that to you?"

"Since I don't have a clue how your pathetic mind works, how could I possibly know what you would think?" I demand. He's about to respond when I notice something out of the corner of my eye and I cut off Ryan's response. "Anyway, looks like your fan club has turned up, so you probably don't want to get caught talking to me. You know? Since I'm not good enough to be seen with you."

Ryan screws his face up at me, confused, and I nod in the direction of the door. John, Mason, and Luke have just walked in the door accompanied by Bianca, Katie, and Jessica; they're all part of his group at school. Surprise crosses Ryan's face and...is that annoyance?

He looks at Jake, who just shrugs. "They asked where we were tonight." Ryan looks irritated. He must have wanted to focus solely on Zara tonight without distraction.

Seriously, talk about first world problems.

The group spots Ryan and Jake and starts making their way over, and that's my cue to exit stage left.

A couple of hours later and I've found Charlie, and we're in the laundry room.

Making out.

Big time.

As in if I were at a party and saw me right now, I would definitely comment to Sam about how slutty I was being and how much a private room was required. I mean, literally I'm up on the counter top, he's standing between my legs which I've snaked around him, my hands are in his hair and his hands are starting to move lower and lower. I know I should stop, and I'll probably be mortified tomorrow, but what the hell. I'm in the moment, I've got a hot as hell guy in between my legs and I've drunk so much I'm not thinking about the consequences.

I can faintly hear someone call my name, but I ignore it. Then I feel someone grip my arm and pull.

Hard.

I'm literally pulled off the counter top and nearly smack my face on the floor, but strong arms catch me in time. I look up and Ryan's standing there.

"What are you doing?" I demand.

"Jesus, Becca! I could have been anyone walking in. If you wanna do that shit, then take it to a bedroom."

"It's none of your business."

"You'll get a reputation."

I try to scowl at him, but it's kind of hard when I'm seeing two of him. "What? Like yours?"

"It's different and you know it," he practically growls at me. He's right, I know it's shitty, but it's the truth. If anyone from school saw this encounter, Charlie would walk away the stud and I'd be the one called a slut and getting whispered about behind my back. In fact, Ryan's probably already figuring out the best way to use this information against me.

"Bro, get off my girlfriend," Charlie says, like he's only just tuned into the conversation. Ryan's eyes snap to me in surprise. *Ha! Yes, Ryan, I have a boyfriend. A hot, sexy boyfriend, so screw you. Not everyone treats me like something they've stepped in.*

Charlie reaches out and tugs me over to him. The sudden movement makes me dizzy and I crash into his side.

Ryan narrows his eyes. "How much have you had to drink?"

I ignore him.

"Seriously, Becca, you're wasted, you should go home. I can give you a ride if you need one."

I'm distracted by Charlie leaning into my body and whispering in my ear. "You know, we probably should go and find a bedroom." I can't help a smile crossing my face, and I let him lead me away, turning away from Ryan.

"Becs?" This stops me in my tracks. No one calls me Becs anymore. In fact, the only person who ever did was Ryan back when we were little. I look back at him.

"Are you sure you're okay?" I can't read his facial expression.

I nod, then follow Charlie up the stairs.

I'm lying on the front lawn of Zara's house, staring up at the sky. *Wow, there are a lot of stars out tonight.* I try to stand, but everything seems to start spinning, so I give up and sit back down.

"Becca?"

I look up to where the noise is coming from and see Ryan standing in front of me, staring down at me. I look away, too drunk to even bother responding.

"What are you doing out here on your own?"

"Go away, Ryan."

"Where's your boyfriend?"

Ah yes, Charlie. Right after we'd finished upstairs, he got a phone call from his band who had managed to score a last minute gig in the next town if Charlie could make it. He immediately agreed and asked me if I could find my own way home. To be honest, I'd actually been expecting to go with him and had been a bit surprised when he'd made it clear I wasn't invited. I'd just nodded and then was suddenly left on my own. I'd made a half-hearted attempt to find Sam but had soon realized the time; it was past her curfew and she was probably already at home. I even vaguely remember her trying to say goodbye when I'd been wrapped around Charlie. So I decided to do the sensible thing and go sit in the garden and try not to fall asleep.

"Becca? Are you even listening to me?" Ryan asks, sounding frustrated.

"Go away, Ryan," I manage to mumble. It's actually pretty hard to concentrate when you've drunk as much tequila as I have tonight.

"Are you on your own?"

"Yes!"

He holds his arm out toward me. "Come on, I'll take you home."

I glance at his arm and look away. "I'm fine."

"Come on."

"Go away! I don't want you anywhere near me!" I snap venomously. I really cannot be bothered with him right now. I have zero time for him at the best of times.

I see anger flash in his eyes, but he doesn't move. "How else are you gonna get home?"

Good question. I hadn't really thought about it. "Jake?"

"Jake's pretty busy right now," he replies smirking. *Ew.* I don't want to think about what Jake's *busy* doing.

"I'll get a cab," I state decisively.

"You've got cash?"

Right, money. I haven't got much cash on me and I don't even know where I am to call for a cab.

"I'll call my parents."

Ryan actually laughs out loud at this. "If your dad see's you like this he'll ground you for a month."

He has a point. My dad can be pretty strict, especially where underage drinking is concerned. I sometimes forget that Ryan knows my parents. Still, I'm not going with him. No way.

He sighs at me in annoyance. "Come on," he says impatiently. "I can't leave you here."

I shake my head and can feel my eyes starting to close. They soon fly wide open because before I know it, Ryan has knelt down and hoisted me up onto his shoulder in a sort of fireman's carry.

"Okay, okay," I say, struggling to get out of his hold. "Just put me down."

He complies and I scowl at him. *Was that really necessary?* We reach his car and he opens the door for me, practically shoving me into the seat. He reaches into the back seat and pulls out a bottle of water. "Drink this," he demands, shoving it into my hands. I sigh but do as I'm told. Settling into his seat, he starts the engine and quickly pulls away from the curb.

We drive along in silence, mainly because I don't like him and have no desire to get into a conversation with him, but it also occurs to me that I haven't had a proper conversation with Ryan in years. I don't have a clue what to say. That, and the fact that I'm concentrating hard on keeping my head still so that the spinning will stop.

"How long have you been seeing that guy for?" he eventually asks.

I shrug. It's been nine weeks and four days, but I'm not about to admit it.

"I just thought you were smarter than that is all. Running off to a bedroom with some random guy that dumps you at a party when you're in this state."

Random guy? He's my boyfriend! Well if he thinks that's dumb, I probably shouldn't mention that all the bedrooms were full so we ended up doing it in a large closet next to the bathroom. "Um, he didn't dump me. He thought I had a ride," I snap.

"Well, he clearly didn't bother to check."

"Oh, so what? And anyway who cares if I hooked up at

a party? God, you're a hypocrite. How many times have you done that?"

He doesn't answer and instead shakes his head. "You should have gone home when I told you to. You've drunk way too much."

"I'm fine."

"You're so stubborn. You can't admit I might actually have been right when I told you to leave."

"I'm not stubborn," I mutter.

He actually snorts with laughter. "Oh yeah, right. We're best friends, and then we have one disagreement and you haven't spoken to me in years. Tonight may be the longest conversation we've had since we were twelve."

I glance over at him surprised. This is the first time either of us has acknowledged the fact that we used to be friends in a long time. Not that we could have since I avoid him at all costs. Besides, he knows what he did. Ditched me because I wasn't cool enough, then let Billy Jameson bet on taking my virginity. If I think about it, it still annoys me to this day.

"What were you even doing there, anyway?" I ask him, eager to change the subject. "Get through all the girls at our school so now you're working on the ones from Madison?"

He rolls his eyes at me. "God you're annoying."

"Oh no, wait. They don't even have to be students, do they?"

The muscle in his jaw tenses. "Gee, don't hold back, Becca. Say what you really think." That is a low blow and I know it. Back when we were sophomores a rumor went around that Ryan hooked up with one of the newly qualified teachers that had just started at school. I have no idea if it's actually true, but I know she left after just one semester and I overheard my parents talking about a pretty sizeable donation Mr. Jackson had made to the school. I'm well aware that it's a no-go subject, but I don't care. I wanted to piss him off. He deserves it for referring to a past I'd rather forget.

"Stop the car," I say suddenly.

He ignores me.

"Seriously, stop the car."

He sighs loudly. "Becca, would you shut up? I'm taking you home. We'll be there in five minutes."

"No, it's not that," he glances over at me. "I think I'm going to be sick."

He screeches the car to a halt at the side of the road, and I only just manage to stumble out of the car before I throw up.

Everywhere.

CHAPTER 4

I'M STANDING OUTSIDE THE JACKSON'S FRONT door on Sunday morning and praying that no one is home. Or at least if someone is here, let it be Mr. or Mrs. Jackson. Basically, I don't want Ryan to answer the door. I'm carrying a huge casserole dish—yes that's right, a casserole dish—which my mother has insisted has to be returned to them at this very minute and cannot possibly wait until she sees Ryan's mom tomorrow.

I'm sure she's just punishing me; she'd never make me come over here otherwise. She knows Ryan and I don't get along. In fact, I'm certain that's what she's doing. I know I made a racket coming in Friday night and I don't think she bought for a second that the reason for me throwing up all day yesterday was food poisoning. Basically, she knows I was wasted but can't prove it so this is her way of punishing me. I really can't handle this today. Who knew it was possible to have a two-day hangover?

I try the doorbell one last time and start to turn to walk

away when it swings open. Ryan is standing there. Shirtless. It looks like he just got out of the pool 'cause he's wearing board shorts that are hanging dangerously low and there's little drops of water dripping down his chest.

Because I'm still feeling lousy, my reactions aren't the same as normal, and it takes me a good few seconds to tear my eyes away from his torso. He has serious abs going on and the V! He has *the* V! *Wow. Ryan got ripped!*

I look up and he's smirking at me, clearly not missing the fact I've just been ogling him.

"Hi," I mumble.

"Hey," he replies, raising an eyebrow at me. We're both aware how rare an occurrence this is. I haven't been to his house in at least five years.

"So my mom wanted me to bring this over," I tell him, holding up the dish in my hand. "Apparently it's absolutely essential your mom gets it back today and she couldn't bring it herself."

He nods. "Sure." Then he turns and walks into the house, leaving the door open behind him. *What? Wait! Now I have to actually enter the house? Why can't he just take it from me?*

I sulkily make my way inside and follow him to the kitchen. I place the casserole dish on the counter and turn to see him watching me cockily. Thankfully he's thrown a t-shirt on. Oh God, this is the real reason I didn't want to see him; I owe him an apology. He knows it, and I know it.

"So, um, thanks for driving me home on Friday night. I'd have been pretty screwed without you."

He nods his head, not speaking. *Right, he's really going to milk this.*

"And um, look, I don't remember everything I said to you in the car, or at the party, but I'm sure it wasn't all nice, so I'm sorry. It was really rude of me, especially since you were doing me a favor." I glance over at him and he's still not speaking, just watching me, a small smile playing on his lips. *He's enjoying this!*

"Look, if it's any consolation, I still feel awful today and I was throwing up all day yesterday."

"Yeah, it kinda looks like you haven't showered since Friday."

I glare at him even though he's right. I know I look terrible. "Look, I'm sorry, okay?"

He grins at me and shrugs. "Don't worry about it. We all do dumb shit when we're drunk."

Oh, right. That was actually easier than I thought it would be.

There's one more question I have to ask him and I really, really wish I didn't. "So, I remember you finding me with Charlie in that room," I say awkwardly staring at the ground. "Did anyone else from school see us?"

I've been hardcore worrying about that since I woke up yesterday morning. Even though we were dressed, I'm pretty sure we looked like we were about two minutes away from doing a live sex show, and I'm mortified at the thought of someone seeing me. It's bad enough Ryan did, but if any of the girls from school that were there did, I'm pretty sure they'll waste no time spreading that particular piece of gossip and make it their mission to humiliate me.

I look up at Ryan and he's shaking his head. "No, just me." I can't read the expression on his face.

I clear my throat. "Did you take any pictures?" I ask. Various pictures and videos of half-naked girls in different states of undress with guys have done the rounds at our school before. Hell, I bet it's even the guys they're hooking up with passing it around. I might be being paranoid, but I've had visions of a video of us practically dry humping, which let's face it, *is* what we were doing, doing the rounds on Snapchat, Instagram, Facebook, you name it.

Ryan's face darkens and his jaw visibly tenses with anger. "No, I didn't take any fucking pictures! God, you really don't think much of me, do you?"

I sigh with relief; I really was worried about that. It's not as if I'm exactly ashamed, but I do not need the whole school laughing and gossiping about me. "Sorry," I tell him. "Again. I was just worried, you know? I always remember Kylie Santos."

He nods slightly at this, but he still looks pissed at me.

Kylie Santos was a girl from my elementary school. When we got to high school, she got involved with an older guy who basically told her he was single, used her for sex and then ditched her. His psycho on-off girlfriend, Fran Cunningham, found out when she came across a couple of topless pictures of Kylie on his phone that Kylie didn't even know he'd taken. Then Fran and her minions plastered them all down the main hallway at school, using some special glue which made it harder for the teachers to take down. Later that day they'd also sent a video to most of the school of Kylie giving him a blow job. It had been shocking and humiliating and I remember being so upset for Kylie. She was a nice girl and didn't deserve that. Sam and I had come across her by the principal's office and she'd been absolutely heartbroken. I've never felt so bad for someone in my life and that was when she told us who had done it.

When Sam and I were walking home minutes later, we'd walked past Fran and her group and her spineless boyfriend, Harry Campbell, who had told Kylie so many lies. We weren't going to say anything, Fran Cunningham was a renowned bitch who most people bowed down to, but we'd heard her calling someone a slut just as we walked past and I snapped. I marched up to her, in the middle of a large group of popular kids and told her exactly what I thought of her and her pathetic boyfriend. She reacted as you'd imagine and had started screaming in my face and had even lunged for me. At that point, Ryan of all people (he must have been standing nearby), stepped in front of her to block her from getting to me and Jake dragged me away. I'd spent the entire evening panicking about what she was going to do to me the next day, worried she was going to try and attack me again but for some reason she did nothing except give me dirty looks until she graduated later that year. Kylie never came back to school but I've always remembered it and I've had visions since Friday night of similar pictures of me with Charlie adorning the school walls.

"Anyway, thanks for all your help on Friday," I tell Ryan and turn to leave.

He sighs loudly. "Hey, do you want a drink? My mom made lemonade this morning."

Mrs. Jackson is one of those supermoms who makes everything fresh and from scratch. I know she used to make really good lemonade. I'm about to refuse, but he's already pouring two glasses. I'm pretty certain he's pissed at me over the pictures comment and I don't want to annoy him further. He actually did help me out big time on Friday. I shrug and take a seat at the breakfast bar. I look around the room, trying to figure out something to say.

"So, I'm sorry if I ruined your chance with Zara the other night, with you giving me a ride."

"Zara?" he asks.

"Didn't you hook up with her?"

He smiles. "No, idiot. That was Jake. That's the reason I was there because Jake didn't want to show up on his own."

Oh.

"Right, sorry. I just thought…" I mumble and vaguely remember a rumor at school about Jessica Murphy being into him and realize I probably did get it wrong.

"You don't know me as well as you think you do."

"Never said I did," I shoot back, looking over at him. He's watching me again. I don't think I know him at all, not anymore. Well, I did think he was an arrogant player who used girls when he felt like it. Just because for once in his life he was nice to me rather than trying to annoy me doesn't mean I should revise my whole opinion on him.

"And at least now you know what that guy's like. I mean, ditching you when you're in that state all alone at a party."

"You mean Charlie?" I ask. "Oh, that was just a misunderstanding, he called me yesterday. He thought Sam was still there and I was gonna get a ride with her."

Ryan just looks at me raising an eyebrow.

"So, yeah, we're fine. Totally good. Just a misunderstanding, but thanks for helping me out."

He's looking at me like he's about to say something, probably about Charlie, and I narrow my eyes. He has no right to have an opinion of Charlie or anything else to do with my life.

"This Charlie thing is serious, then?" That is none of his business. I'm saved from answering when his phone starts to ring next to me on the table and I pass it over to him.

He shakes his head. "Leave it."

I shrug and glance around the room. This is kind of awkward. It's not like we have anything to say to each other and I should probably go.

"When did you meet him?"

"Over the summer."

"You were in Europe for the whole summer."

I look back at him in surprise. It's not a secret I spent the summer in Europe, but I didn't think it would hit his radar. "It was when I got back. Just before school started," I concede. He raises an eyebrow like he's expecting more of an explanation. "He's friends with Chris, Sam's boyfriend," I explain. "Sam is this girl that goes to our school, she has dark blonde hair and pale skin, she drives a—"

"Yes, I know who Sam is, Becca!" he snaps, cutting me off while I smirk at him. "We've only been in the same homeroom since we were twelve," I grin at his annoyance. I know full well that he knows who Sam is, but it's fun to annoy him. He rolls his eyes at me. "You are so shitty," he tells me but can't help smirking back at me. Suddenly his expression turns serious, but I'm distracted by his phone ringing; it's his mom again. He dismisses it with a wave of his hand. "Listen, about what happened at school on Friday, with Kevin Wilson..."

"Ryan, don't—" I start.

"No, Becca. Seriously, I would never want you to think I'd be cool with anyone grabbing you like that," he tells me, staring at me intently. I search his face to see where the joke is or when he'll start laughing at me, but he looks serious as hell.

I shrug. "Forget it. It's fine."

"No, it's not fine, Becca."

"He came to find me on Friday afternoon, tried to apologize," I tell him.

"Oh yeah?" Ryan asks, not looking the least bit surprised. "What did you say?"

"Told him to get lost."

Ryan grins. "Of course you did." I can't help but grin back at him.

His phone starts ringing again. When I glance down, it's his mom again. She must really want to speak to him. "Answer it," I say pushing it towards him.

He rolls his eyes but picks up the phone.

"Hi, Mom," he says, but his expression changes as he tunes into what she's saying. Shock crosses his face and...is that panic?

"Yeah, yeah. I'll be right there," he says and quickly hangs up.

"Is everything okay?" I ask as he stands hurriedly and starts looking around. He stops in the middle of what he's doing, turning to me and suddenly looking lost.

"No. My granny… She's…she's had a stroke. Shit."

My mouth falls open and a wave of sympathy for his whole family overwhelms me. I spent countless hours with his granny when I was little and even after Ryan and I fell out, she'd still come over to my house with Ryan's mom from time to time. I really hope she's okay.

He stands there for a minute looking completely helpless but then quickly recovers and grabs his wallet and phone. He shoves some keys at me.

"I gotta go to the hospital. Can you lock up?" he says rushing out the house and leaving me alone in their kitchen, hoping that everything will be okay. I'm unable to get the look of panic and worry that crossed his face when he was on the phone out of my mind for the rest of the day.

CHAPTER 5

'M IN ENGLISH CLASS ON FRIDAY AFTERNOON, yawning and waiting for the bell to ring, when I look up and see Ryan walk in. I do a double take. I wasn't expecting to see him today. I'd known the news about his granny wasn't good when Jake found me mid-week to tell me that she was in a coma and the whole family had been at the hospital since Sunday. I wasn't quite sure why he was telling me, probably because I was with Ryan when he first found out, but he went quiet when the rest of his friends appeared like it was a secret and he didn't want them to know. Then my mom told me at breakfast this morning that she had died last night. Ryan's mom had called her earlier, and from what I could tell, the whole family was devastated. I knew they were all very close.

I watch as he makes his way to his desk. His eyes are downcast and he avoids the greetings that meet his arrival. His shoulders are slumped and he looks exhausted.

Poor guy.

The bell rings as Henderson calls the class to order, and I turn my attention back to class and the papers that Henderson is handing out. Today we're reading poetry, I look down at the poem and my eyes widen in dismay. *Are you kidding me? Death Become Us by Louise Sinatti'.* Geez, not today.

Henderson starts reading out the lines and I can't help but feel for Ryan. He really doesn't need this right now.

When the darkness in the night creeps in
Whilst sat amongst thy loved ones
When the last breath on this earth is taken
When the light goes out in thy eyes
When you are taken to that empty place
That place where no one else awaits
When you must face the wrath of God
And see what future is for you
When you leave behind your loved ones
And go to that next place
Or is there even another place
Or just a dark and empty space
Where the dark night consumes you
In your final resting place
Oh God.

I swallow hard after reading the lines. I mean the poem is complete garbage, but if I'd just lost my grandmother, I sure as hell wouldn't want to be reading about dark and empty spaces.

"So what is the meaning behind this then?" Henderson asks. "What is she getting at?" He looks around and gets no response.

"Come on, class. I want an answer."

Still no one speaks.

He looks around. "Mr. Jackson, what do you think? You usually have plenty to say."

I freeze. *Oh no.* Seriously? Asking Ryan about death? Today of all days?

Ryan doesn't respond.

"Come on, Mr. Jackson. Please, enlighten us here."

I turn to look at Ryan, who hasn't even looked up from his desk. There is silence.

"Ryan?" Mr. Henderson asks again.

Most of the class is looking over at him now and I can see his face going red. His hands are clenching into fists while he clearly tries to control his emotions.

"Ryan, what do you think the poem means when she talks about the dark night consuming?"

Ryan's almost bright red now and I can see his chin start to wobble. I recognize that face from when we were children. It's the face that he always pulled just before he started to cry. He looks up in panic and his eyes find mine.

"AAARGHHHHHH!" I scream, jumping up and pointing. "There's a mouse!"

Instantly the class goes into overdrive, girls jumping out of their seats, the guys laughing and everyone staring at the spot where I've pointed. It takes Henderson a full ten minutes to calm everyone down after which he invites me back after school to "discuss my melodramatic nature."

I sit down, knowing I've got another detention on the

way and knowing my mom will go nuts when she finds out, but I don't care. Henderson's stopped questioning Ryan about death.

I walk out of school heaving a sigh of relief. It's almost a full two hours later than I usually leave. Henderson kept me for ages, lecturing me on how I need to pull my act together. Then I swung by the art room to pick up some paints I left there and Miss Smith insisted on an in-depth discussion on where my project was going.

The parking lot is almost empty as I stroll toward my car texting Charlie about our plans for later. I'm so distracted that I'm practically at my car before I notice Ryan leaning against it. I stop a couple of feet away and he stands and faces me.

"Hey," I say surprised.

"Hi."

"Did you just finish football practice?" I ask, confused.

He shakes his head in response. "Nah, didn't have any today."

"Oh." He's been waiting here for two hours for me to get out of school?

He takes a deep breath. "Look, I just wanted to say thank you for before, in English. I was about to lose it and I know you jumped up like that to get everyone to stop looking at me."

I consider denying it, playing it down but honestly

what's the point when he already knows. "Don't worry about it." I pause. "Ryan, I'm so sorry about Granny Susie. She was a really great person."

He smiles sadly. "Yeah, she was."

"She made the best brownies out of anyone ever."

He laughs softly at this. "They were pretty awesome."

We stand there awkwardly; I have no idea what to say. He looks around the empty parking lot but makes no move to go. "What are you doing tonight?" he asks suddenly.

"Me? I'm going to a movie with Charlie."

He nods and looks at the ground.

"What are you doing?" I continue. "Staying home and spending time with your parents? Your mom must be devastated."

"No, they went up to San Fran this morning to tell Lisa in person. They won't be back tonight." I nod. That makes sense. Lisa is Ryan's older sister who lives out of town. She just had a baby and I'm sure Kathy would have wanted to make sure she was okay in person.

"So Jake?"

Ryan shakes his head. "He went out of town last night to look at colleges with his folks. It's been planned for a while."

Oh. This I wasn't expecting. "So I guess it's down to Mason and Kevin and those guys, huh?" He shakes his head, smiling ruefully. "No, don't think I can handle those guys right now. Bianca's having a party, but I haven't told them about Granny Susie, and I'm just not in the mood."

Oh, crap. I open my mouth and then close it again. *Oh, come on!* This is the first time I will have seen Charlie since last Friday.

"Okay, so I should go. Thanks again." He says and turns, walking toward his car. His shoulders are slumped and his head is downcast. He looks so sad.

Oh, fuck it.

"Hey, Ryan, wait."

He turns round.

"Wanna come back to my house and watch movies all night?"

He looks surprised, but a slight smile appears on his lips. "What about Charlie?"

I shrug. "I can see him tomorrow."

He frowns slightly, like he's trying to make up his mind. "Oh, come on, I'll even buy you a pizza."

Apparently this decides it and he smiles at me. "Okay. Thanks."

Several hours later I'm curled up on the sofa having watched the entire trilogy of *The Godfather* films. I start yawning, it's almost midnight and I've eaten enough pizza and ice cream to last me until the end of the year. Ryan reaches out and pulls my dad's old copy of *Goodfella's* off the shelf. Apparently he's developed a penchant for gangster movies since we last hung out.

He turns to me and sees me yawning. "Are you tired? I can go?"

I shrug and shake my head. "It's fine, put it on."

He smiles and gets up to stick it in the DVD player. He's definitely better than when he first got here, apart from when my mom came in and gave him a hug and I thought he was going to wobble a bit, he's been okay. Quiet, but okay. To be honest, I think my mom was pretty surprised when she walked in and saw us on the couch together. She shot my dad a look, but I know she's pleased with me. When I went to fetch the ice cream from the freezer, she kissed me on the forehead and whispered, "Well done, sweetie."

Ryan sits back down on the sofa and glances over at me. "What?"

"Do you have any more chips?"

Geez, the guy eats like a horse, but I get up anyway. What can I say? I'm a good hostess.

I wake up with a start, disorientated and not knowing where I am. I look around and realize I've fallen asleep in front of the TV. It's still on although the DVD finished a long time ago. The clock on the wall tells me that it's just after four in the morning. I look down and see that I've got the blanket that usually sits on the back of the sofa covering me. Ryan must have covered me when I fell asleep.

I glance over and he's out cold, wheezing softly and leaning slightly toward me in his sleep. I look at him for a minute, which I know sounds creepy, but this is the first time in years I've been able to study him up close. His dark hair flops over to the side and being this close I can see it has flecks of lighter brown in it that I haven't noticed before. He's got light freckles covering the bridge of his nose, his jawline is strong and his nose is just slightly crooked making him look less like a pretty boy. His eyelashes match his hair and even though his eyes are closed, I know they're the same deep turquoise blue as the Caribbean ocean.

Damn. Ryan grew up seriously hot.

I slowly lift myself off the couch. I should probably wake him so he can go back to his own bed because God knows he'll have a neck ache in the morning after sleeping like that all night, but he looks so peaceful and he's had such a shit week that I can't bring myself to do it. I place the blanket I had covering me gently on top of him, moving quietly so that I don't wake him. I exit the room, turning the lamp off as I go.

◆

I wake up late the next day, yawning and stretching in bed. I'm tired, but at least I did my good deed for the week and, to be honest, it was nowhere near as bad as I thought it would be. Grief, it would seem, makes Ryan much less of a dick.

I smell bacon coming from the kitchen and stumble out of bed, making my way downstairs.

"Morning, sweetie," my mom smiles over at the stove. I turn to my dad, who is at the island reading his paper, and nearly fall over when I see Ryan there next to him.

"You're still here," I say flatly.

Ryan's gaze flicks over me quickly before he looks away,

and I suddenly don't feel as comfortable in the sleep shorts and tank top that I wear to bed. I'm not dumb enough to think he was checking me out or anything, but my body is way more exposed than he or any of the boys at school will have ever seen it. The tank top doesn't quite reach the top of my shorts, flashing a couple of inches of my stomach and the shorts are short, serious leg is on display. But it's annoying me that I've been made to feel like this. For God's sake, this is my house and I'm being made to feel uncomfortable?

"Rebecca Louise McKenzie!" my mother snaps at me. I look at her and the thunderous look she gives me tells me I'm out of line.

Ryan clears his throat. "Your mom makes an awesome breakfast. I'm done, though, so I can go?"

My dad looks at me in annoyance. "No way, Ryan, the game's about to start. It'll be good to have someone to watch it with for a change."

I glare at him. *The absolute traitor!* I always knew he wanted a son. I glance at Ryan and he at least has the good grace to look sheepish. He shifts in his seat and I suddenly remember why he's here in the first place. His granny just died, his house is empty and his best friend is out of town. God, I am being a bitch. I force myself to smile at him

"Don't leave on my account. I'm going out, anyway." I smile sweetly at my mother and spin around to exit the kitchen.

CHAPTER 6

I'M AT MY KITCHEN TABLE STARING DOWN AT MY phone. I have just received a very irate phone call from my mother clearly stating that if I do not get my butt over to the Jackson household in the next ten minutes to pay my respects, then she will take my car from me for the next six months. Apparently she was expecting me over two hours ago when school ended.

Dammit!

I was hoping she would forget about me. I know I'm being stubborn, but I promised myself years ago that I would never go to Ryan's house again, well not unless I can help it, and I want to stick to that. It's not like he'll want me there either. I can't not have my car for six months, so I heave a big sigh, feeling incredibly woe is me, and head over to the Jackson's house. I let myself in since no one answers the door and head into their large front room. I immediately feel myself being watched and turn slightly to see five pairs of eyes trained on me. Ryan's sitting over by the window.

It turns out he did tell a couple of people after all. Jessica, Katie, John and Mason are all staring straight at me and it's not exactly welcoming. I turn away and go find my parents.

After giving Mr. and Mrs. Jackson my sympathies, I'm in their kitchen picking at food and wondering when would be a reasonable time to leave when someone calls my name. I turn to see Lisa Jackson walking toward me and smiling widely.

She wraps me up in a hug, which I happily return. I've always loved Lisa.

"It's so good to see you!"

"You too," I return and genuinely mean it. Lisa used to drive Ryan and me around whenever we wanted her to and would always give us money for candy and junk food. As far as I was concerned, she was the perfect big sister.

"You look amazing!"

I scrunch my face up at her. What's she talking about? I'm wearing my jeans and a baggy V-neck t-shirt that I've had on all day. I was actually starting to feel stupid for not wearing something black like everyone else, but then I remember Lisa hasn't seen me for a couple of years so she probably still remembers the twelve-year-old me.

"Why are you in here all alone?"

"Oh you know, just stuffing my face."

She narrows her eyes at me. "So you and Ryan still don't talk?" I pull a face and she laughs. "Ah, well, it's up to you. You don't need to tell me how much of a brat he can be. Thanks for chilling with him the other day, though, when mom and dad were with me. I don't think he wanted to be alone."

I nod and blush slightly. I didn't realize that was common knowledge.

"There's some other kids from your school here, though. Gotta be better than being on your own?"

"We don't exactly run in the same crowd these days. And I can't stand the girl he's seeing," I explain.

"He has a girlfriend? Who?"

"Um, Jessica? The blonde one? At least I think she wants to be."

Lisa starts laughing. "That is not his girlfriend. And if she were, I'd be having serious words."

I grin back. "Yeah, I guess your brother's not exactly the committing type."

"Oh, he is. He's just not got the right girl yet." She cocks her head to the side like she's studying me. "I hear you've got a boyfriend, though? What's he like?"

I immediately blush and she starts to laugh, but I can't help the giddy smile that always comes to my face when I think about Charlie. I still can't believe he's mine. "He's great. Really, really great."

She smiles at me and glances over my shoulder. "Hey, Jake."

Jake approaches us and I turn to smile at him. I didn't realize he was here, but then again, of course, he would be. He doesn't return my smile. In fact, he looks positively pissed at me.

"Right. I better go feed the baby before she starts screaming the place down. Make sure you come and find me before you go, Becca." I nod as she walks away.

"Seriously, Becca? You're gonna sit in here all night?" Jake glares at me.

My jaw drops open. *What is his problem? I came over, didn't I?* "What?"

"This is Ryan's house, this is his grandma's wake, and you're not even gonna say hello?"

Oh. When he puts it like that, it does sound rude. "Right. Yeah, sorry."

He turns and stalks away, and I wander over to where they're all sitting. They all look up at me like I'm some crazy imposter. *Great, this will be fun.*

"Hey," Ryan says.

"Hi." There's an awkward pause. "I hope today went as well as it could have," I manage to mumble.

"It was fine. Thanks for coming." I nod, looking around. "Your parents made you come, didn't they?"

My attention snaps back to him. "No," I say, but I haven't responded quickly enough, and I know he doesn't believe me.

Ryan glances around the room and looks over at Jake. "This blows, let's go downstairs."

He stands and everyone follows him. I'm about to turn away when Jake pushes me from behind and sends me a look, making it clear I'm supposed to follow them.

We head down to the basement, which is decked out like a den. This used to be Lisa's domain when we were kids, but clearly Ryan's inherited it now. I look around taking in the changes while we all wait for Ryan to speak. "What do you guys want to do?" he asks.

"Dunno, watch a movie?" John asks.

"We could play spin the bottle?" Jessica suggests.

I look over at her in disgust. "This is a funeral." I pause. "And we're not twelve."

Ryan smirks as she blushes. "I was just trying to cheer Ryan up," she defends herself.

I cross my arms. "And you're the one to do it?"

"What no round two, Becca?" Mason asks grinning over at me.

My eyes flash over to him and narrow. Before I stopped ignoring this crowd entirely, I went to Jake's thirteenth birthday party and got stuck playing a game of spin the bottle. Mason spun and it landed on me; he promptly launched himself my way. That was my first kiss. We'd never spoken before that and I don't think we've ever spoken more than two words to each other since. He's grinning at me smugly but quickly stops when he glances behind me. Jake's probably just sent him the same death glare he's been giving to me.

"We'll play a few games on the Xbox," Jake decides, shooting me a look that clearly tells me to shut up and stop arguing.

"There's too many of us," I state.

"We can team up. You're on my team, Becca," he decides before I have a chance to back out.

Two hours later and I'm pretty good at this video game—

whatever it's called. I'm getting into it and can't believe the time when I check my watch. The moods lightened up and everyone is actually being civil, even cracking a few jokes, to my surprise, and I'm surprisingly quite enjoying myself. I'm about to shoot down a wall to free myself when my phone starts to ring. I don't hear it at first, but Jessica, who is sitting this game out, picks it up off the table and waves it at me.

"It's Charlie," she says, a big smile on her face.

I'm immediately distracted from the game and reach out to grab my phone, leaving me open to get shot much to Jake's annoyance. I scowl at his reaction as I answer the call. *Overreaction much?*

"Hey, sexy." I can't help but smile at his greeting to me and stand up to move away from the sofa for some privacy. I talk to him for a couple of minutes before hanging up and heading back to the group.

"So, I've gotta go."

Jake turns and glares at me. I mean seriously, if looks could kill. "What! We're in the middle of a game."

"You can finish it."

Jake just gives me a thunderous look, cocking his head toward Ryan.

Oh right. "Um, sorry again, Ryan. See you at school," I say.

Jake shakes his head in disgust. What's his problem? Ryan doesn't care. He hasn't even looked up from the TV. Jake's clearly in a bad mood and has decided to take it out on me. I wave half-heartedly at them before leaving the room, trying not to rush, eager as I am to see Charlie.

emma doherty

I trek up the stairs and into Charlie's waiting car. It's
only later that night when I'm finally climbing into bed and
thinking over the day's events when I remember my conversation with Lisa. How did she know about Charlie? I yawn
widely and decide it must have been my mom that told her.

CHAPTER 7

I TRY NOT TO WINCE AS CHARLIE HITS A BUM NOTE on his guitar and it echoes through the garage. I'm watching Charlie's band practice, and I'm trying to stay engaged but, to be honest, they do not sound the best. I mean, I've only ever seen them live once because they've not had many gigs, but they were definitely better than this. The drummer Jimmy, who is also Charlie's cousin, keeps looking over at me and I get the distinct impression he doesn't like me, and I'm starting to feel uncomfortable.

The song comes to an end and Charlie calls the practice, looking over at me. Two of the guys, Jack, and Dean leave right away waving goodbye to me, but Jimmy hangs back and ends up sitting on the sofa next to me. Charlie goes over to the fridge to pull us out some drinks, but it's empty.

"I'm gonna go grab some sodas from inside," he tells us and exits the garage before I have a chance to go with him. I look over at Jimmy, who's flipping through pictures on his phone. Silence stretches between us and I can't help but feel like I want him to like me, knowing how close he and Charlie are.

"That was a good practice," I lie.

He grins at me. "We blew."

I start to laugh unable to argue with that.

"You go to MacAllister, right, Becca?" he asks.

I nod. "Yeah. S'alright. You like it at Madison?" I ask, cringing at how eager I sound.

"Sure."

"It's good to have Charlie back in town?" I persist. God this is so not me, desperate to make someone like me.

He looks over at me and opens his mouth to say something but then stops himself.

"Look, I know you don't like me," I blurt out.

He looks surprised. "I don't not like you, Becca, it's just..." he trails off as Charlie wanders back in and hands us our drinks.

Charlie looks between us and our blank faces. "What have you said?" Charlie demands of Jimmy, his gaze passing to me. I shake my head blankly. I've no idea what's going on here. Charlie seems to relax and drops down onto the sofa between us, throwing his arm around me and pulling me into his side.

I smile up at him. "Sam wants to know if we want to go to the movies with her and Chris on Saturday," I tell him.

He pulls a face. "I wish I could Becca, but I've gotta go out of town this weekend. My parents are making me visit our grandparents. Right, Jim?" he says waving his hand toward Jimmy.

"Dude, you are fucking unreal!" Jimmy snaps irritably, standing up and grabbing his bag.

"What's your problem?" Charlie shoots back, standing to face him.

Jimmy looks at him in disgust and turns and walks out the garage. Charlie sits back down next to me and I look at him nervously. "What was that about?"

Charlie rolls his eyes dismissively. "Jimmy's a pussy. Forget him. He's just pissed at life."

"I don't think he likes me."

Charlie reaches out and entwines his hands through mine, tugging me closer to him. He ducks down so that his eyes are level with mine. "Of course, he likes you, Becca. What's not to like?"

I shrug self-consciously. I know I'm not making this up.

"He's probably just jealous that you're not his," he says. I allow a small smile, even though I know it's not that. "Have I told you how pretty you look today?" he continues. His mouth turns into a crooked smile and suddenly it's all I can focus on. I forget about Jimmy and whatever that argument was about. All I can focus on is Charlie's mouth and the desperate need I suddenly have to kiss him.

I remember the night I lost my virginity to him. It started off like this. This need I had to kiss him constantly, the not wanting to have any distance between us, me pressing up against him so I could be as close as possible.

We were in his room and had been watching a movie. We'd only watched about twenty minutes of it before the movie was forgotten completely and we started the mother of all make out sessions.

Now, my involvement with guys up until that point had been pretty tame and fairly casual. Billy Jameson had put me off dating anyone for a long time, and my involvement with guys was pretty limited to a few make out sessions at the odd (non-MacAllister) party I attended with Sam or when I worked as a summer camp counselor. I had kissed a few guys, but the most physical it had ever gotten was a bit of over the clothes groping.

It was different with Charlie, though. I felt this draw to him that I had never felt before and I was almost scared that he was going to wake up and realize he was too good for me and back off. During this particular make out session, he pushed me down on the bed and climbed on top of me, propping himself up on his elbows and hovering over me. I was so lost in him and in such a Charlie induced daze I didn't immediately realize that his fingers had unbuttoned the top of my jeans. I froze when I realized it and he immediately stopped and looked at me with a question.

I had guarded my virginity pretty carefully up to that point. I had definitely been in situations before where I could have taken it to the next level, but I had always chosen to keep it vanilla and not go there. I'd never *wanted* to go there. I still wasn't sure I wanted to go there with Charlie. We'd only been dating for four weeks and I always pictured myself making a guy wait for it. But there was no denying the attraction I felt for him and I could see how much he wanted to move our relationship forward and if I'm totally honest, I didn't want to disappoint him. So I took a deep breath, flashed a nervous smile and gave him a small nod. That was all the encouragement he needed.

It was all over fairly quickly, to be honest, and although it hurt more than I expected, it wasn't as bad as some of the horror stories I'd heard from my friends. I remember sitting in my car afterward and thinking that I was no longer a virgin and how strange that was. That was definitely not how I pictured losing my virginity, off the back of some random run-of-the-mill make out session, but even though it was unexpected, I couldn't say that I regretted it. Although part of me did wish he'd made a bit of an effort, had set the scene and maybe at least had some candles dotted around the room, but then I remembered how he'd smiled at me afterward and I was just happy that he was happy.

The next time I had seen Charlie, he had wanted to do it again almost right away. I remember being surprised and thinking, "*What? But I already did it once,*" but then I guess it's true what they say. Once you start having sex, that's it. You keep having sex. It did get better and I loved being that close to him and have absolutely no regrets about sleeping with him.

He reaches out and runs his finger across my jaw, pulling my attention back to him. "Now, that we're alone, Becca, how are we gonna pass the time?" he teases me and suddenly tugs me forward so that I'm sitting on his knee. I adjust myself so that my legs are straddling him and suddenly, just like that, I forget everything else and I'm back to being lost in Charlie, and there is nowhere else I'd rather be.

CHAPTER 8

"IT'S SENIOR YEAR, BECCA. YOU HAVE TO GO TO homecoming!"

I smirk at Jake sitting across from me. "Why? So they can name me homecoming queen?"

He starts to laugh. "I'd pay to see that!"

I grin back at him. We both had a free last period and bumped into each other by his locker so we've been sitting outside on the benches waiting for the rest of school to let out. It's been fun. Jake and I used to hang all the time and though we always chat and catch up when we see each other, it's usually only in passing since he's always with Ryan and I always do my best to avoid him. It's pretty rare that we get to hang out one on one these days, but it's been just like old times.

"Who are you gonna go with?"

He shrugs. "Dunno."

I cock an eyebrow. "Zara?"

He shrugs. "Maybe. Maybe not."

"Well if you're gonna take a girl from this school, I can probably guess her name in like five guesses." He raises an eyebrow and I smirk at him. "Seriously, you guys all date like the same ten girls. Dude, it's pretty incestuous! And it's like a rule that they have to be a cheerleader."

Jake starts to laugh. "Shut up, Becca."

"I'm being serious."

"I dated Sally Hopkins for six months last year." I roll my eyes, conceding that one. Sally's not a cheerleader, but she is on student council so it's just as bad. "And Ryan's dated tons of people who aren't cheerleaders."

I start to laugh. "That's because Ryan's dated most of the school. And that's another reason I wouldn't go to the dance; like I want to see Ryan crowned King and him thinking he's even more important than he already does!"

"You're too harsh on him, Becca."

"Oh come on, Ryan gets whatever he wants, whenever he wants and whoever he wants. And you know it."

"Not whoever he wants."

I roll my eyes. "We both know that for some strange reason Ryan can get any girl in this school. And has dated most of them."

"He dates around to distract himself."

"From what? His perfect life?"

Jake's gaze levels me and he doesn't say anything for a couple of minutes. "You really are clueless, Becca." I roll my eyes. I don't really want to get into a discussion about Ryan with Jake. When we first fell out, Jake used to try to talk to me all the time about him, but he stopped doing that when he saw how annoyed it made me. I really hope he's not about to start up again now. And besides, Ryan's life *is* perfect. He's a star athlete, ridiculously popular, has a great family and doesn't have to worry about money. If Ryan's only problem is me thinking he's a douche, then he's got it pretty good. "You're like the most oblivious person I've ever met," Jake continues.

I scowl at him. "I resent that," I tell him. "I'm incredibly perceptive." Jake cocks an eyebrow at me and I start to laugh. Okay, so that's a lie. I'm not incredibly perceptive but why should I pay attention to things that don't affect me? I have enough to figure out with this whole first boyfriend thing without paying attention to other people's lives.

Jake sighs. "Look, you really should come to homecoming. We'll show our faces for like two minutes and then go down to the beach or hit up a party or something."

"We?"

"Sure." He grins. "You can be my date. And you're not a cheerleader," he finishes smugly.

I can't help smirking at him. There's not a chance I'm going to homecoming and it's definitely not Charlie's scene, but it's nice that Jake wanted to go with me, his friend, rather than trying to use it as a chance to hook up with some girl he's probably already been with a million times. He used to invite me to anything and everything, but I always said no. Then he stopped asking and I have to admit that sometimes, I missed him asking. That's another thing I blame Ryan for—getting in between my friendship with Jake. Granted, it's me avoiding doing anything social with Jake because Ryan will be there, but still. I blame him.

"Who's not a cheerleader?" My head turns and I see Mason slide into the seat next to me. I look around and see students spilling out of the school building. The bell must have rung and we didn't notice. "What up, McKenzie?" he greets me. I stare back at Mason, surprised he's acknowledging me and he offers me an easy grin, like it's the most natural thing in the world for us to be sitting next to each other chatting. This is weird. Mason and I don't talk.

"Becca," Jake answers Mason's question. "She's gonna be my date for homecoming."

I roll my eyes at his words and Mason starts to laugh. "Serious? Can I be there when you tell Jackson?" They share a look and I screw my face up confused. *Why would Ryan care if I went to a lame school dance with Jake?* Then I remember that he doesn't like me and probably wouldn't want me hanging out with his best friend.

"He's joking," I clarify to Mason. "I am definitely not going to homecoming."

"Becca, come on!" Jake carries on. "We'll go in a big group, rent a limo. It'll be fun. Ryan's going stag so the three of us can go together. Like old times."

I cock an eyebrow at him. Like old times? Not a chance. I know I've spoken to Ryan a bit more recently, what with his grandma and everything, but that does not mean we're suddenly friends again. "That ship has sailed." Jake sighs in annoyance. "Homecoming's lame, anyway."

"Yeah. It'll be totally lame," Mason agrees. "Your boy will get crowned, we'll leave, then we'll get wasted. Same as always."

"My boy?" I ask confused. I look over at Jake, who's looking at me intently. "Who's my boy?"

Mason's eyes find Jake, who shakes his head just ever so slightly at Mason. "Oh, I just meant your neighbor. Like Ryan's your neighbor and will probably be king."

I raise my eyebrows but don't say anything, because my phone beeps in front of me and I reach out to read the message.

Charlie: I've been thinking about you all day.

"What are you smiling at? Who is that?"

I look up at Jake distracted and realize I have the widest grin on my face. That's what Charlie does to me. He makes me happy. "No one."

"Your new boyfriend?"

I'm surprised. "How do you know about Charlie?" I don't remember telling Jake about Charlie and I didn't mention it was him I was leaving Ryan's for after his grandma's wake. A feeling of dread comes over me when I realize Ryan probably told him he caught us dry humping at Zara's party.

Jake looks at me for a second. "So, are you like really into him, or what?"

I shrug my shoulders.

"No, I'm being serious. Do you really like him?"

I roll my eyes and am about to respond with some sarcastic comment when I glance behind Jake and see Ryan over his shoulder making his way over to us from the main steps. His eyes lock with mine for a second and it springs me into motion, gathering up my books that lay in front of me. I really can't be bothered to deal with any of Ryan's insults right now, especially if he's been telling Jake stuff about Charlie and me.

"Right, well, see you guys later then."

Jake looks confused at my sudden departure and turns around to follow my gaze. He turns back at me with a look of annoyance on his face. "Stay," he says. "Come get food with us."

I shake my head and stand, turning to go.

"Wait!" I turn back to Jake, sighing in annoyance just as Ryan reaches the table.

"What?"

"You should come back to my house with me. My mom keeps asking about you."

This makes me falter. Jake's mom is amazing. She's this fun-loving, excitable, free spirited hippy that always has time for everyone. It's got to be going on a year since I last went to his house and saw her.

My phone beeps again.

Charlie: I miss you.

My heart swells with emotion at those words. I miss him too. Badly. It's been nearly five days since I saw him at his practice and I haven't stopped thinking about him since.

"Becca!"

I glance up at Jake. "What?"

He rolls his eyes at me. "Come back to my house? Lizzy would love to see you too. She asks about you all the time." I look back at Jake, who is wearing a triumphant smirk. He knows that'll get me. Lizzy is his little sister. She's almost ten years younger than us and absolutely adorable. When she was a toddler, she followed me around everywhere. Come to think of it, it must be even longer than a year since I've seen her. "Just come for an hour."

I let out a small sigh. I would love to see Jake's mom and Lizzy, and I don't have anything better to do, but I don't want to go if Ryan and Mason are going too. Call me stupid, but I'm just not comfortable around them. "Who else is going?" I ask, flicking my eyes toward Mason and Ryan.

"I'm out," Mason tells me. "Gotta head home."

I look at Ryan, who doesn't say a word; he just has this smug look on his face. He knows I don't want him to go, but he's not about to say he won't. I look over at Jake.

"Oh, come on. Remember the crush Lizzy had on Ryan when we were kids? It's only grown," Jake tells me. "She'll kill me if I don't let him come too."

I can't help but grin at that. Lizzy might have followed me around everywhere when she was little but she positively hero worshiped Ryan. Typical. Even eight-year-olds have crushes on Ryan. No wonder he has the ego he does.

My phone beeps again.

Charlie: You look really pretty today.

My head snaps up and I spin around, my eyes scanning the crowds trying to see if he's nearby.

"Becca!" I turn to face Jake again. Irritation is creeping into his voice. "Are you gonna come?"

I start to nod in agreement when my phone beeps a fourth time.

Charlie: By your car.

My head whips around to the student parking lot and I spot him. He's leaning against my car with his gaze locked on me. Butterflies erupt in my stomach at the mere sight of him. He's here. At my school. He's come here to surprise me. I instinctively take a step toward him then remember Jake.

"Sorry," I tell him. "I've got to go. Another time, though." Then I turn and walk toward Charlie without a backward glance and a huge smile on my face.

"Hey," he greets me.

"Hey."

"Good surprise?"

I nod my head eagerly. Best ending to a school day ever. "Great surprise."

He reaches forward and pulls me by the waist closer to him and drops a quick kiss on my lips. My heart starts beating wildly in my chest. This is what he does to me.

He glances over my shoulder. "Who are those guys?"

I look behind me. Jake, Mason, and Ryan are all looking over at us. God knows why they're so interested. When Jake and Mason see me looking, they both turn away but Ryan doesn't. He stares straight back at me.

"The blonde guy is Jake, a friend of mine from way back. The other two are his friends. I don't talk to them."

Charlie looks at me and cocks an eyebrow. "Wanna introduce me?"

I shake my head at him. "No. I wanna get out of here." Flashing a smile, I say, "My parents work late on Tuesdays."

This captures his attention and a slow smirk spreads

emma doherty

across his face. He drops his arm around my shoulders and leads me to the driver's seat before climbing in next to me. We make it back to my house in record time.

CHAPTER 9

I GO UP ONTO MY TIPTOES AT THE END OF THE hallway and try to spot Sam in the crowd. She's been out of school sick for the last couple of days, and I know she's back today, but I had to skip lunch to finish an assignment and I haven't seen her all day. I see the back of her head at her locker and make my way over to her.

"Sammy Sam," I sing as I approach her using my nickname for her. She turns around and smiles at me, and I'm about to start blabbering on about my day when I notice who she's talking to.

Ryan Jackson.

I immediately shut my mouth and glance past him. *Seriously? He's popping up everywhere lately.*

"Hey, Becca," he says.

I nod in his direction but don't bother replying. I need to talk to Sam about Charlie and I can hardly do that when he's standing there.

"I was just giving Sam some notes from Spanish that

she missed when she was sick," he tells me.

"Yeah? She needs to catch up, not get further behind by following your notes," I reply smartly.

"Becca!" Sam says, a warning in her voice.

Ryan just rolls his eyes at me but doesn't make any move to leave. We kind of stand there for a few seconds. Nobody says anything.

"Can we help you?" I eventually ask him.

"Just thought I'd enjoy some of your riveting company, McKenzie."

I roll my eyes. "Wow. The most popular guy at school wants to talk to *me*? I'm *so* honored," I say sarcastically.

He grins and winks at me. "Glad you've finally noticed. Don't forget star of the football team and just generally the hottest guy in this place. Or so I've been told."

I pull a face and turn to Sam. "I need to talk to you."

She glances over at Ryan, who rolls his eyes in my direction. "Bye, Sam," he says, moving away.

"Bye, Ryan. Thanks for the notes," she calls after him as he heads over to where Jessica Murphy and Bianca Gallagher are waiting to talk to him. She turns back to me. "That was kinda rude," she tells me, "and he's definitely not stupid and you know it." She has a point. Ryan's actually quite clever. He more than holds his own in most of his classes from what I can tell. Annoyingly, even I have to admit he's not your classic dumb jock.

"Forget Ryan, I need to talk to you," I tell her. She nods in agreement and I follow her into the girl's bathroom where she promptly stops in front of the mirror and starts trying to French braid her hair. She's gotten really into braiding her hair recently but is totally useless at doing it. It's funny to watch.

"What do you think of this?" I ask her holding out my phone. It shows a picture of a watch.

She whistles under her breath. "Nice, really nice." She takes it from me and starts to scroll through the pictures. "It's really expensive, though."

"I know, but it's nice, right?"

"Sure," she agrees, smiling.

"But is it too much?"

"For what?"

"For Charlie. It's his birthday in a couple of weeks."

She blinks at me in surprise. "This is for Charlie?" she asks. I nod. "I thought this was for your dad's birthday. And, like, your mom would pay for most of it?"

"You think it's too much then?" I ask, suddenly embarrassed. I know we've only been dating for three months, but I want to get him something nice, something he'll really appreciate.

"No, no." She pauses. "Well, maybe a bit."

I sigh in frustration. I know the watch is over the top but I've never had to buy a boyfriend a present before, and I'm totally clueless. I might like to pretend I'm all laid back and chilled out, but who am I kidding? I'm crazy about Charlie and want to get him a present that reflects that.

Sam starts again with her braid. "How 'bout we head to the mall now? We could look for something together, maybe something a bit more low-key."

I nod in agreement. "Yeah, okay."

Sam smiles at me. "I've never seen you like this before. You really like him, don't you?"

I shrug and look away, knowing I'm probably blushing like a five-year-old. There's no point denying it; Sam can see straight through me, anyway.

"But weren't you worried he was getting distant?" she asks.

I shrug dismissively. Last weekend Sam went to a friend's with Chris and saw Charlie there. He'd told me he'd had band practice. At the time, I got really paranoid, but after stressing about it for days, he laughed when I finally told him and explained he'd finished early and had assumed I'd already be in bed so hadn't called me. Simple, really.

"Nah, we're fine."

The door to the bathroom swings open and Jessica Murphy walks in with Bianca Gallagher.

I turn back to Sam and watch her as she adds more pieces of her hair to the braid. I start to laugh as hair starts becoming loose. "You're really not doing that right," I tell her, taking a swig from my water bottle. She lets out a groan of frustration and drops the hair in her hands.

A throat is cleared next to me and I turn to see Jessica has moved to stand right beside me. Jessica Murphy is pretty much the undisputed queen of our school. She's Miss Popularity, head cheerleader, with blonde hair, blue eyes, and a Victoria's Secret model body. She looks like she's just stepped out of a magazine. We've attended the same school since we were twelve and I don't recall us ever having a conversation before.

"Becca, right?" she asks me.

I narrow my eyes at her. We may never have spoken more than two words to each other before, but I know for a fact she knows my name. I mean, we *were* all just at Ryan's house together. She's just trying to put me in my place in the social standing of this school. *How pathetic.*

"Ryan and I were just talking and I think we're gonna throw Jake a surprise birthday party," she starts conversationally.

I nod, not really understanding why she's telling me this. We both know I won't be going to the party, even if she were to invite me, which I seriously doubt she will.

"Ryan asked for my help. We're you know..." she says, leaving the end of the sentence open ended. Is she trying to tell me that her and Ryan are hooking up? God knows why she feels the need to bore me with this information. I try to stifle a yawn. To be honest, I'm amazed her and Ryan haven't hooked up sooner. They've kind of danced around each other for years, moving in the same circles, dating each other's friends but as far as I know, they've never gotten together. I get the impression it's more her into him than the other way around, but I don't doubt for a second that she'll get him, and the truth is they'd probably make a pretty good, all-American couple. The perfect prom king and queen.

"So you've been around him a lot more recently," she continues.

I nearly spit out the water I've just taken a swig of. "Excuse me?"

"You just seem friendlier. You were at his house the other day, you were talking to him just now in the hall and you're always by his locker."

I narrow my eyes again. *Is she for real?*

"Just now I was talking to Sam and he was there. And we're neighbors. Our parents are friends and they made me go over to his house to pay my respects because you know, his grandma died. And my locker is next to his, so I can't really help being there every now and again."

She nods, glancing sideways at Bianca, who is also looking at me. I'm starting to feel slightly ambushed. "I'm just interested, Becca, no need to get defensive. I heard you guys used to be pretty friendly and I know you still speak to Jake."

"We're not friendly at all. And so what if I speak to Jake?"

She smiles sweetly. "Nothing's wrong, Becca. Relax. I just thought I'd let you know that Ryan is into me, just so you know."

My jaw falls open. Is she actually warning me off him? Have I entered a parallel universe? And it's kind of pathetic if she has to tell people that he's into her. If it's true, shouldn't it be obvious?

"I have a boyfriend!" I tell her defensively. "Not that it's any of your business."

She turns to the mirror and pulls some makeup out of her bag and starts putting lip gloss on. Her eyes find mine in the mirror. "I know. Charlie, right? I hear you guys make a really cute couple." I can't begin to imagine how she'd know what sort of a couple Charlie and I are. "You know that color really suits you, Becca," she continues, smiling sweetly.

I glance down at my plain black t-shirt. *Is she being sarcastic?* I look over at Sam in bewilderment. She shrugs and starts heading toward the door and I follow her. "Bye, Becca," Jessica calls after me. "We should talk again sometime."

Sam and I exit the bathroom and start walking down the hallway.

"What just happened?" I ask Sam. "Did she just warn me away from Ryan Jackson?"

Sam shakes her head, equally confused. "I have no idea. That was weird."

"What's weird?" Jake asks, appearing next to us.

"Is Ryan hooking up with Jessica Murphy?"

"Nah, she wants to, though. Why?"

"Well, I dunno but I think she just warned me off him in the bathroom."

Jake actually howls with laughter. It takes him a minute to pull himself together and then turns to Sam. "She did. I think. In a roundabout kinda way," Sam confirms.

"Wait till I tell Jackson. That's hilarious!"

"Oh God, don't feed his ego anymore."

"He's not interested in her, Becca. Not at all."

"Like I care. They deserve each other, if you ask me. Just tell him to keep her away from me."

We turn, continue walking out the main entrance and down the steps out toward the parking lot. Jake veers off to the side, steering Sam and me toward his friends. Mason and John are talking to Ryan, who in the ten minutes since he was standing with Sam at her locker has managed to find some girl from the grade below and now has her sitting on his knee. Her friends are hovering around them, almost as if they want to talk to them but don't know what to say. The girl on Ryan's knee reaches up to wrap her arm around his shoulders.

Seriously? Ryan has some girl draped all over him, yet I'm *the one Jessica Murphy is snapping at?*

Ryan looks up as we approach and his gaze quickly sweeps to me. He moves the girl by the hips off his knee and to the side so that she's sitting next to him, rather than on him, much to her annoyance. He stands so that he's level with us as Jake smirks at him, raising his eyebrows as Ryan greets us.

"Uh, Ryan!" The junior girl snaps; he looks at her blankly. "I don't believe you!" She declares before turning and flouncing off.

"What was that about?" Ryan asks looking genuinely confused as John and Mason snicker at him. I can't help but laugh. Ryan turns to me. "Something funny, McKenzie?"

"Nah," I smirk. "Just watching you lose your game."

He crosses his arms and narrows his eyes then steps right into my personal space so that I have to tilt my head back to look him in the eye. "Oh, I've got plenty of game, McKenzie," he tells me, peering down at me. I grin back at the sheer cockiness of him. "I can show you anytime you like," he continues.

I roll my eyes. "Yeah, yeah," I say as I hear Mason snickering. A glance to the side shows Jake, John, and Mason grinning at his words, clearly entertained. The junior girls next to them have their mouths hanging open in disbelief. Clearly they didn't get the memo that Ryan's using me once again to make his friends laugh.

"Did you guys know Becca thinks I'm the most popular guy at school?" he asks his friends. "And the hottest. And the best on the football team."

"You said that!" I do not want them thinking I actually think any of those things are true.

"She secretly wants me," he continues. "Hey, all you have to do is admit it, McKenzie, and I'm sure we could work something out."

"Excuse me while I vomit," I tell him to further laughter from the guys. Ryan's grinning at me, his arms crossed almost as though he's challenging me— to what, I don't know.

"Ready?" I ask Sam, turning away from them.

She nods and I turn to walk past Ryan, but he steps to the side blocking my route. I scowl up at him, then change direction, but he steps in front of me again, not letting me pass.

"God, Ryan, move!" I demand and shove him out of the way as he laughs at me.

We're a few steps away from them when Jake calls out to me. "Hey, Becca, why don't you come back with us to Ryan's? We're gonna play Xbox again."

I turn round to face them, walking backward. "No," I reply instantly.

"Why not?"

"Just don't want to," I say bluntly.

Ryan smirks and John starts to laugh. "Don't you live,

like, next door to him or something?"

"No, just on the same street. Still too close, though."

The junior girls scowl over in my direction, annoyed that I'm still distracting the boy's attention. God, some girls are pathetic.

"Come on, McKenzie," Ryan says grinning. "I'll let you win this time. Then if you're a good girl, I'll even walk you back home after," he teases me, moving his eyebrows up and down suggestively.

My eyes narrow. *God, he's patronizing. Let me win? I was better than him!*

"And we all know what happens when a guy walks a girl home to her front door," Jake says grinning from ear to ear.

"I'm actually gonna throw up now," I say and turn back around. I can hear them chuckling behind me. "Go find some naïve cheerleader to use that shit on, Ryan," I call over my shoulder.

"Hey, Becca!" I roll my eyes in annoyance and turn back to Jake. "You change your mind about coming to homecoming with us yet?"

"Nope. Not gonna happen."

I turn my back to them and carry on walking and get to my car. Sam climbs in next to me and glances over at me. "Since when have you been hanging out with Ryan Jackson?"

"I haven't. My parents made me go to his grandma's wake and we played a few video games. Apparently he's no longer upset and is back to being an asshole, so I can go back to pretending he doesn't exist."

Sam laughs. "Like he'd ever let you forget he exists."

I shrug as I pull out of the lot.

"Maybe Jessica's right to be jealous after all." She grins. "He was definitely flirting with you."

I snort. Yup, actually snort.

"You think Ryan Jackson would stoop so low as to flirt with me? He was trying to make the guys laugh and using me to do it. Trust me."

She pulls a face like she doesn't believe me and I roll my eyes. "What's this about homecoming?"

"Jake wants me to go with them. Something about it being last chance and all that."

"You gonna go?"

I send her a look and she smirks back at me. She knows that was a stupid question. Neither of us could care less about homecoming.

"So anyway, has Charlie said anything to Chris about me?"

She sighs in annoyance. "Becca! Charlie is all you think about."

Well, duh.

CHAPTER 10

"**H**EY, SAM. HEY, BECCA."

I glance over to see Jake sitting at a huge booth to the side with a bunch of jocks from school.

We just walked into Sal's the local pizza joint, and I'm doing my best to not be annoyed at Chris and Charlie who are running twenty minutes late. I wouldn't usually care and just be happy to see Charlie, since he's always so busy these days, but I'm so hungry that my stomach feels like it's eating itself and now I have to wait for them to arrive before I can order.

"Hi," Sam replies.

Jake nods at a couple of empty spaces across from him. "Take a seat," he says.

I'm about to protest, but Sam just shrugs and slides into the booth. I follow after a couple of seconds, slumping in and end up across from Ryan.

"Becca? Becca?"

"What?" I ask looking up at Jake.

He starts to laugh. "What's up with you?"

I shrug and Sam starts to laugh. "She's starving and the guys are running late, so she has to wait to order till they get here," she explains.

The waitress comes over and clears away their empty plates. I actually consider grabbing one of Jake's crusts that he's left on the plate but think better of it. Another waitress comes over and puts a large pepperoni pizza in front of Ryan.

"Why are you just getting yours?" I ask quickly not taking my eyes away from the pizza. It smells amazing.

"I just got here. Why you want a piece?"

I glance up and he's looking at me in amusement. "No, it's fine."

"You can have a slice," he offers.

"No, I'm really not that hungry," I insist, just as my traitorous stomach growls loud enough for the whole restaurant to hear. Ryan's eyes light up and he raises his eyebrows at me. He slowly nudges his plate toward me.

"Go on, all you have to do is ask nicely."

My eyes snap to his and he's grinning at me, eyes sparkling mischievously. He's enjoying this. All I can smell is the glorious pizza as I try not to look at it.

"Yeah, go on Becca, say please," Jake teases me, clearly enjoying this too.

"Pepperoni is your favorite," Sam adds. *Traitor.* She's supposed to be on my side. My stomach growls again. Loudly.

I look at the pizza and then back at Ryan, who's watching me smugly. I know it sounds pathetic, but I'm so hungry. It's fine, I can be nice. I look at Ryan and open my mouth but then close it again. He raises an eyebrow at me. I sigh heavily and open my mouth again before closing it. He starts to laugh.

"You can't bring yourself to do it, can you?" he asks. He rolls his eyes and pushes the pizza towards me. "Go on take a slice and put us all out of our misery."

I'm about to protest, but my stomach rumbles again. This is so embarrassing. I quickly reach forward, grab a piece and wolf it down in no time.

"Thanks," I smile.

Ryan laughs. "That nearly killed you taking that from me, didn't it?"

I ignore his comment and sit back and listen to the conversations going on around me. Jessica and a couple of other cheerleaders enter and come over to the booth, Jessica squeezing in next to Ryan and glancing over at Sam and me in disdain. I try not to roll my eyes remembering our conversation in the bathroom at school.

"Forget to shower today, Becca?" she asks.

I glance down at my arms which are covered with the ink I spilled on them in art class, that I couldn't be bothered to scrub off.

"Oooh burn," I shoot back sarcastically as Ryan sniggers.

"Play nicely, Becca," Jake warns me.

I roll my eyes and glance around the restaurant trying

to see which booth is free so that Sam and I can move and have a place ready for when Chris and Charlie arrive. I spot an empty booth further down the restaurant and turn to tell her, but I'm distracted when I see her nodding her head, her mouth pressed together while she tries not to laugh at something Bianca Gallagher is saying.

"We did yoga together every day. He was just so beautiful, you know? So deep," Bianca is saying earnestly to the table, explaining about her latest hook-up. "We shared not just a physical connection but a spiritual connection."

A burst of laughter escapes from me and I quickly start coughing trying to cover it up while Sam nudges me in the side.

"Sorry," I mumble, looking down at the table. "Something got stuck in my throat." I glance up and Ryan is snickering at me, a small smile playing on his lips.

Bianca glares back at me. "Well, like I was saying before I was so rudely interrupted, Sven and I just understood each other. He was so kind and got me on a level that nobody else ever has before. He's incredibly spiritual," she says, and another burst of laughter escapes from me. I can't help it. Bianca Gallagher is a complete princess. She drives a Mercedes and is always decked out in designer clothes from head to toe, and she's making out like she belongs at Woodstock and has the ability to get all deep with a guy who is clearly feeding her a line. He used that spiritual bullshit to get her into bed.

"He's a really wonderful guy. We didn't just have sex. We made love."

I snort with laughter again and clamp my hand over my mouth to shut me up. This girl is crazy. Why is she telling everyone about her sex life anyway?

"Is there a problem?" Bianca demands of me.

I shake my head, pressing my lips together to try and avoid laughing again. But come on, it's pretty funny. Bianca has gone bright red and is looking at me like she wants to kill me. She opens her mouth to say something else, but Ryan cuts her off.

"Becca just remembers a guy called Sven who used to teach our mom's yoga when we were little. He used to really make us laugh," Ryan tells Bianca, barely containing his grin of amusement.

I glance at him and start to laugh. There is no guy that used to teach our moms yoga, but he's given me the perfect excuse to let my laughter out. Sam starts chuckling along too and Bianca narrows her eyes and turns on Sam. "What are you laughing about?"

"Oh, Sam knew him too," Ryan explains, his eyes twinkling mischievously and I grin at him.

Bianca sits back in a huff and crosses her arms across her chest, clearly annoyed that Ryan has stuck up for us and therefore she can't have a go at us. "So your moms are friends?" she questions.

Ryan nods and looks over at me. "Oh yeah, Becca and I go way back. Becca just doesn't like to be seen in public with me." I narrow my eyes at him. I consider that a bit rich since he was the one who dropped our friendship when he became too popular for me. "Sven would be so sad," he says with a completely straight face. When my eyes find his, it's impossible for us both not to start laughing all over again.

I shake my head and pull myself together, ignoring the glare of death I'm getting from both Bianca and Jessica and the curious looks I'm getting from the rest of his friends. I almost burst out laughing all over again when I feel Ryan kick me under the table. I refuse to look at him or else I'm pretty sure Bianca will throw something at my head.

I feel a hand on my shoulder and turn to see Charlie standing behind me with Chris beside him.

"Hey," I smile at him, but he's not looking at me. He's looking at the guys sitting down across the table from me, Ryan in particular, and he doesn't look pleased.

I pull myself together and shuffle to the end of the booth to get out, and he reaches out a hand to help me up. When I take his hand, he pulls me hard, yanking me into his body and crashes his mouth against mine.

Yup, that's right. He kisses me, hard, even using tongue. Right. In front. Of. Everyone.

I swear, his hand is on my ass and everything.

There's a second of silence and then the catcalls and wolf whistles start. I'm mortified and know I've gone bright red. Charlie is smiling smugly at me. I know my previous record at the party may differ, but I'm really not one for PDA. I can't believe he just did that!

I turn and grab my bag, the only one not laughing and whistling is Ryan, who's staring down at his food probably trying not to throw up after witnessing that major PDA. I don't blame the poor guy. I flip them all the finger and let

Charlie lead me to another booth with Sam and Chris following (and laughing) behind.

CHAPTER 11

CHARLIE GRABS MY HAND AND PULLS ME OUT OF his car, telling me to hurry up as he tugs me along behind him.

He's so cute.

After a lot of stress and despair (on my part), Sam finally convinced me to get Charlie tickets to see The Red Rhinos for his birthday. I'd never heard of them but Sam told me Chris had mentioned them and they were an up and coming British band that were touring the States. When I saw the look on Charlie's face when he opened his card with the tickets inside, I knew Sam had been right. He loved them.

We make our way up to the entrance of the small club and I'm suddenly nervous, thinking I might get carded but the bouncer barely looks at us and when we make our way in. The room is swamped. Like literally filled to capacity. You can barely move. I look around and I'm suddenly apprehensive. I love going to gigs and I love live music, but it's usually chilled and open mic nights. Not like this. This place is crazy. You can't take a step without bumping into someone. The crowd in here seems a lot older than us. Everyone's got a drink in their hand and seem to be shouting at the people in front of them. I automatically feel myself step closer to Charlie.

He wraps his arms around me and when I look up at him, his eyes are shining. He bends down and kisses me quickly on the mouth and my grin spreads. He's happy. He loves it and that's all that matters. This night is about him and as long as he's happy, then I don't care about anything else.

He leads me over to the bar and orders us a couple of drinks while my eyes scan the venue behind us. I check my phone; Sam and Chris are coming too and are supposed to meet us here, but I haven't seen them yet. I take the drink that Charlie offers me and attempt to not screw up my face when I taste the liquor in it. I still haven't forgotten how hellish I felt after that Madison party and I do not want a repeat performance of that.

"Charlie?"

My head turns and I see a tall blonde standing a little further down the bar looking our way. Charlie steps out in front of me blocking my way. She comes over and hugs him in greeting, and I see her eyes sweep to me in interest and I wait for him to introduce me, but he doesn't. I step closer to them, trying to listen to their conversation, but they're leaning into each other and talking quietly. That coupled with how loud it is in here means that I can't hear a word of what they're saying. Someone knocks into me from behind and

I drop my purse on the floor. By the time I've managed to pick it up in and amongst all the different legs, the blonde has disappeared.

"Who was that?"

Charlie glances down at me. He replies but I can't hear him over the sound of the warm up act on the stage. I shake my head indicating that I can't hear and see him glance down the bar again. My eyes follow him and the blonde is standing down there with a couple of other girls, and they're all looking over at us.

Suddenly Charlie grips my hand and starts pulling me through the crowd, shoving people out of our way and tugging me to move faster. He doesn't stop until we've reached the other side of the bar where it's marginally quieter and then when he does it's so sudden that I bang into the back of him. I look up at him in confusion.

"What's wrong? We were supposed to wait over there for Sam and Chris."

He smirks down at me and looks around him quickly.

Now I'm confused. Who was that girl? Why was he so eager to get away from the bar? And why is he looking at me like that? "Charlie, who was that girl?"

"Just some girl from my old school."

"Your old school? So why didn't you introduce me?"

"Because she's a nobody. Just some bitchy gossip."

I raise an eyebrow at him. "You were worried about what she'd tell me?"

A slow smirk crosses his face and his eyes flash with amusement. "Becca, she knew me when I was just a pimply little kid, and if she told you all my secrets you might not let me do to you what I want to."

"What? What do you want to do?" I'm confused and keep getting distracted by the people brushing past me. I glance behind me, trying to spot Sam in the crowd, but before I know what's happening Charlie grabs my wrist and is pulling me into a hallway that looks like it leads to the bathrooms. Before we reach them, he pulls me down a hallway that leads off from the one we're in and takes a sharp left and then a right so that we're facing a dead end with just a fire exit at the end. Just when I think we're about to go outside, he pushes me up into the corner and when I turn around, he's stepped in front of me, blocking my view with his body only inches from mine.

My heart starts hammering in my chest, and when I look into his eyes, they're already boring into mine, a glint of mischief in them. His hand drops down and brushes my bare thigh, just under the hem of the dress I wore especially for him. I hardly ever wear dresses, it's not usually my style, but I wanted to look good for him, so I pulled on a midnight blue shift dress that skims the top of my thighs and matched it with black high-heeled boots. My breath hitches as his hand brushes the hair out of my face and my eyes dart behind him, looking at the dark hallway behind us.

He drops his head so that it's level with mine, a small grin on his face, and his lips brush mine. I jerk my head away from him and shake my head slightly. "What if someone walks past?"

He grins at me and glances quickly behind him. There's

no one there, we are pretty sheltered here and unless you wanted to use the fire escape, then it's pretty unlikely that anyone would come down here. He turns back to me and the look he gives me flips my stomach and I feel myself leaning into him despite my reservations.

"Thanks for the birthday present," he whispers before covering my mouth with his, and then just like always, nothing else but Charlie matters. I'm totally consumed by him and forget about everything else. Just like always.

◆

I wish I was still in that corner by the fire exit. We made out for a good ten minutes and I was ready to forget about the gig and get out of there, but then we heard over the speakers that The Red Rhinos were starting and Charlie pulled us back out into the main room. Although I tried to stop him and was trying to tug his arm back, he pulled us right into the middle of the crowd, getting practically to the front of the stage. He positioned me so that my back was up against his chest and although that was okay at first, making me feel semi-comfortable, the crowd around us soon started jumping to the rock songs the band is blasting out. I try to join in, but I don't recognize the music and even in my heeled boots I still feel really small compared to those surrounding us. Pretty soon the whole area had turned into a mosh pit and when I look around, Charlie had been swept closer toward the stage.

My panic begins rising. I hate big crowds. Absolutely

hate them. I hate being the center of attention in the middle of a crowd and I hate being surrounded by people in a confined space. I'm definitely claustrophobic, there's no doubt about it. I shouldn't have let Charlie pull me into the middle of all these people, but I'd wanted to please him and not make a fuss. Now I don't know what to do.

I take a step to the side and get pushed back again; someone's beer sloshes against my back and I feel a hand swipe at my legs. I have no idea if the hand swipe was intentional or not but it just raises my anxiety levels even higher and I start trying to inch my way out of the crowd.

"Excuse me," I say, trying to weave my way out of the crowd but I can't get anywhere. I look around and realize that I'm surrounded by guys. Drunk guys who are jumping up and down into each other as they sing along at the top of their voices. Someone pushes into me and I go flying into the guy beside me who pushes me away; I feel like a human pinball machine getting ricocheted in between them. This is a total nightmare and I can feel the panic start to peak within me, and I feel like the crowd is closing in on me.

Suddenly someone grabs my arms and pulls me hard out of the group. I'm pulled through the crowd until we break through to the end and reach the front of the club. That's when I realize the guy who grabbed me is Luke Masters, a guy from school. He turns around to look at me, giving me a reassuring smile as he pulls me to the door that leads to the exit. As soon as we break free into the cool air, I breathe a sigh of relief, and Luke leads me over to some tables that are set up outside where people are standing and smoking. He sits me down on a chair and instructs me to stay there, and then he disappears for a couple of minutes before returning with a bottle of water for me. I guzzle the water greedily and eventually my breathing starts to return to normal. That was horrible, absolutely horrible.

"You okay?"

I nod and offer Luke a small smile. "Yeah, thanks. I just..." I trail off. I don't know what that was, I just know that I had to get out.

"It's cool. My sister gets panic attacks. I know how scary it can be."

I guess that's what it was. A panic attack. I've only ever had one before and it was in a similar situation when I got separated from my mom on a busy street in LA when I was younger, but I've not had one since then.

I smile gratefully at Luke. He's a really nice guy. He transferred to our school sophomore year and is in a ton of my classes, and we always got along really well. In fact, at one point I was pretty sure he was going to ask me out on a date. He definitely hinted at it, then he joined the football team and all but stopped talking to me. Ryan probably told him I was a social leper that should be ignored at all costs. Looking at him now he seems genuinely concerned and I'm reminded of what a nice guy he is. "Thanks, Luke."

"You sure you're okay? You looked pretty scared in there at one point. Want me to call someone for you?"

"No, it's fine."

"You sure? I could call Jackson for you? I'm sure he'd come right away."

Jackson? Ryan Jackson? The only way he'd come would be to laugh at my freak out. I shake my head. "It's fine. I'm with my boyfriend, but we got split up."

Luke nods and grins at me. "Maybe best to stay near the back next time?"

I grin back. "Hell yes." I reach into my purse and check my phone, expecting a message from Charlie wondering where I am, but there's nothing. He's clearly enjoying the band too much to notice I'm not there. There's just a couple of messages from Sam asking where I am and I quickly fire off a text telling her my location. Luke keeps me company until she finds me with Chris in tow.

Sam and I spend the rest of the evening outside leaving the boys to enjoy the band inside. She feels the same as me; it's way too busy and sweaty in there. We laugh at ourselves for thinking that we were cool enough to attend a rock gig and instead order wings and fries and wait for the boys who come out a couple of hours later, their faces shining with excitement and I realize tonight wasn't such a washout after all. Charlie clearly loved the band, so that's all that matters.

CHAPTER 12

I PLOP DOWN IN MY SEAT OPPOSITE SAM FOR LUNCH. We've sat at the same table for the full three years we've been at this school and it's always the same crowd. No, we're not the most popular and some of us could even be described as geeky, but I love my lunch crowd. It's my favorite time of the day.

I glance down the table and see Erica already in full-on story mode. Erica cracks me up. She has the most active love life out of anyone I've ever met and somehow weird stuff always seems to happen to her. She lifts her hand in greeting at me but doesn't even slow down the pace of her story. Seriously, she should be on stage. She takes a breath, pausing for dramatic effect, then literally freezes, her mouth gaping open slightly.

What's happening? Everyone else has gone silent too. I turn around to see what's happened, finding Ryan standing next to me. He's wearing a tight white t-shirt, which shows off his tan, and when he lifts his backpack onto the table, you can actually see his muscles clenching. His hair's all stuck up like he's been running his hands through it and his eyes are glistening with amusement.

Okay, even I'll admit he looks good today.

The cocky smile on his face tells me that he's well aware it's his presence that has caused the open mouths and silence. It's pathetic but that's the kind of power Ryan holds at this school. People pay attention to him and he doesn't exactly swing by our table often.

"Ryan!"

I turn around and see Jessica Murphy at their usual table. She waves at him to hurry him up, one hand on her hip, clearly wondering what he's doing over here. I turn back around. "You're wanted."

He shrugs, dismissing my comment. A smug grin appears on his face. Jake comes bounding over, grinning from ear to ear and throws his arm around Ryan's shoulder. "Did you tell her yet?"

"Tell me what?" I'm starting to feel confused and a bit self-conscious. Why is everyone staring at him? It's embarrassing. It's only Ryan.

Ryan smirks, knowing he's got my attention. "We skipped the first couple of periods this morning and swung by the mall."

I roll my eyes. Why do I need to know this?

Ryan's smirk turns into a genuine smile at my reaction. "Anyway, there's a new store there. We went in and found something you might like." He unzips his backpack slowly, fully aware he's got an audience and pulls out a multipack of candy.

"HOLY SHIT!" I shout, and three tables nearby turn around to see what the commotion is. I grab at the bag. "Where did you find this?"

Ryan and Jake burst out laughing at my reaction, and I'm grinning like an idiot.

Okay, let me explain. My great-grandparents on my mother's side were English. When I was little and they were still alive, we used to visit them and I would always come back with bags and bags of this candy. They're called Refreshers, and it's literally the best candy in the world. I got Ryan hooked on it too when we were kids. I was so obsessed with it I wrote to a bunch of different stores telling them it was the most delicious candy in the world and they should all stock it, but I never heard anything back, which made me furious. They don't sell it anywhere around here and I haven't had any in years.

I look up and he's pulling more multipacks out of his bag. There are bags and bags of it. I'm literally bouncing in my seat with excitement. Ryan and Jake finally stop laughing.

"Wait, there's more."

Jake pulls his own backpack off his back and pulls out some cans of soda.

"APPLE TANGO?" I'm back to screeching. *I love this stuff!* This sets them off laughing all over again. The girls at my table are just looking at us in shock, along with quite a few other tables which are staring curiously at us. Ryan and Jake aren't exactly laughing quietly.

"Oh my God, oh my God, oh my God!" I don't remember the last time I was this excited about something. "Where is this place?"

Ryan smiles at me in amusement. "It's in the mall on the bottom floor. It's this English candy store; they've got tons of stuff."

"Thank you guys so much. This is the best thing ever."

Jake grins and slaps Ryan on the back. "Hey, it was all Jackson. He remembered that you were obsessed with this stuff when we were kids. He practically bought all their stock, I just helped carry it."

"Oh God, let me give you some money." I reach down and start rummaging in my bag for some cash. I pull out some bills and hold them out to him.

He holds his hands up in protest, shaking his head. "Don't worry about it. It was worth it to see your face." He grins at me one last time and not his usually cocky smirk, but a genuine smile like it's just the two of us in the room. He picks up his empty backpack and turns, sauntering over to his own table and the curious stares he finds there. Jake follows still chuckling to himself.

I turn back to the girls absolutely beaming. Everyone is staring. Sam is raising her eyebrows questioningly at me and Erica's jaw is practically on the floor.

"What?" I say, looking around.

Erica's eyes widen at my apparently stupid question. She pulls herself together. "Ryan Jackson, the guy who rules this school, bought you half a candy store just because he remembered you liked that stuff when you were a kid?"

Rules this school? She is so dramatic.

I roll my eyes, dismissing her. "He's just being nice," I say. "Seriously, guys, you've got to try this. This is the best candy in the world." I rip open a bag and start dishing it out. I can't stop smiling. In fact, I don't stop smiling all day.

CHAPTER 13

SATURDAY AFTERNOON COMES AROUND AND I just got off the phone to Charlie. We were supposed to hang together this afternoon but my mom dropped Jay on me with no warning and Charlie isn't into the idea of babysitting with me. Can't say I blame him. Now I'm stuck with the devil child until my parents get home.

I turn around to see what the brat's doing but he's left the kitchen. I wander into the TV room, expecting him to be watching a movie, but he's not there either.

"Jay," I call. There's no response. "Jay!" I call again, louder this time. There's still no response. I start walking quickly through the house looking in all the different rooms calling his name. With each empty room, I can feel my panic starting to build. He's nowhere to be found. *Shit!* Where is he? I run back downstairs and notice that the front door is slightly ajar.

Oh God.

My heart starts racing; he must have left the house.

I rush outside shouting his name. I run to the end of my driveway, looking up and down the street but still can't see him. Oh God, this is bad. This is really, *really* bad. What if he's left this street and is on the busy main road? Or what if he's been snatched? Or hurt? He's so small. Tears spring to my eyes. This is bad.

"Jay!" I scream as loudly as I can, running up and down the street hoping I'll see him hiding behind a car or something.

"Becca!" I hear someone call my name and turn to see Ryan at the bottom of his driveway. I rush toward him panicking.

"I can't find my cousin. He's only five and I don't know where he is." I'm wringing my hands anxiously. I don't know what to do.

Ryan reaches out to touch my arm trying to calm me down. "Becca, relax," he says just as Jay strolls out of Ryan's house and heads down the driveway toward us.

"Oh my God!" Relief floods my body and I reach out to grab Jay, pulling him into a tight hug. Then I get mad and hold him away from me.

"What the hell were you thinking? You don't just run off like that, Jay!" I scold shaking him hard.

"Becca, stop." Ryan pulls Jay away from me. I stand up, my whole body is shaking; a mixture of adrenaline, relief and anger.

"Don't ever do that to me again!" I shout, pacing up and down. One glance at Jay tells me he doesn't care at all that I'm mad. He just pulls a face at me. "I didn't know where you were!" I shout again. "Never do that again." Jay just rolls his eyes at me. Actually rolls his eyes. At me. Like *I'm* being unreasonable.

"I wanted to see, Ryan," he says.

Wait, what? This is news to me. How does he know Ryan? I turn to look at Ryan accusingly. He holds his hands up like he's innocent. "He just turned up," he explains.

"AND YOU DIDN'T THINK TO LET ME KNOW?" I explode.

"We were just coming to," he says. "He just wanted to use the bathroom first."

I put my hands on my hips and sigh. "How do you even know each other, anyway?"

"Duh, Becca! We've known each other forever," Jay says like I'm stupid.

I turn to Ryan for an explanation. He shrugs. "Your parents bring him over with them sometimes and we kick it."

This is news to me. Jay grins up at Ryan. Clearly he's a member of Ryan's fan club.

"Ryan's way cooler than you, Becca," Jay tells me. "Ryan's a player!" he declares proudly.

I raise my eyebrows at Ryan. "You've told my five-year-old cousin that you're a player?"

Ryan blushes. "No, of course not."

"Jake and Mason said so," Jay continues coming to Ryan's rescue. "He gets all the girls."

I roll my eyes. "Come on, we're going," I say reaching for Jay's hand.

"I want to stay here!" Jay shouts in protest. I ignore

him and grab his hand, pulling him down the driveway. He yanks his hand free and runs back up the driveway.

"Seriously, Jay, move! You are already in trouble for just disappearing," I shout at him.

"I don't want to go with you."

"Tough!"

"No! You don't want to look after me anyway."

I freeze at this. I hadn't realized he could hear me on the phone with Charlie. I suddenly feel ashamed of myself and refuse to look over at Ryan.

"I wanna stay with Ryan," he shouts again, his voice getting even louder. *Ughhh!* What am I supposed to do?

I look at Ryan, who just shrugs at me. "He can stay, if you want," he tells me.

"You'd really watch him for a bit?" I ask, surprised. I did not have Ryan down for the babysitting type.

"Sure. We can just play some ball or something."

I don't know what to do. Part of me is angry with Jay and thinks he shouldn't be rewarded for running off, but then if I drag him home, I'll have to deal with him.

"But you'll have to stay too," Ryan continues. "I can't watch him all by myself."

Well, that decides it then. I shake my head and go to grab Jay again, but he just runs away from me. I sigh, exasperated. I really do not have any control over him.

"Just stay," Ryan says to me. "I'll play a bit of ball with him, tire him out, then he'll be more chilled. We can order pizza later." I glance up at this and Ryan's grinning at me. "I know you can't resist pizza," he teases.

I smile at this. I do love pizza. But I don't want to hang out with Ryan. I mean, we're not friends and I seem to be seeing him more and more recently, and I don't like it. I know I'm being stubborn, but I decided years ago that he wasn't worth my time, and I plan on sticking to it.

Ryan rolls his eyes at my indecision. "Don't worry, I won't think we're suddenly best friends again or anything."

I laugh out loud at this since it's so close to what I was actually thinking.

"Please, please, please, Becca!" Jay calls from further up the driveway.

I shrug and nod. Ryan smiles and opens his mouth to say something but is interrupted by the sound of honking horns. We turn to look and see two cars full of Ryan's friends pull up at the bottom of the driveway. I hear Ryan mutter something under his breath and I instantly feel my whole demeanor change and become more tense.

"I forgot they were coming over," he explains. "I can ask them to leave if it makes you uncomfortable?"

I glance up at him in surprise. He'd actually ask his friends to leave just because I don't like them?

"No, they're your friends, it's fine," I reply as I watch Jay run up to the car and jump straight onto Mason's back and high five the rest of the guys. Turns out Jay knows these guys better than I do, and I briefly wonder how long my parents have been bringing him over here.

Jake comes over grinning and throws his arm around my shoulder, hugging me into him.

"Hey, Becca, what are you doing here?"

"Long story," I mutter as Jessica Murphy comes over and wraps her arms around Ryan's waist and glances over at me with disdain. A couple of the other cheerleaders also make their way over looking at me curiously.

I turn to Ryan. "Right. Well, thanks for your help with Jay but we'd better go." Ryan just looks back at me, shaking his head slightly. "Come on, Jay," I call.

"You said we could stay," he shouts from Mason's back. Everyone is silent watching us.

"You could still stay?" Ryan asks me, and I'm surprised that he's saying it so publically. Usually, he'd never be caught dead talking to me, much less socializing with me. He reaches up and detaches Jessica's arms from around his waist and takes a step closer to me. I shake my head. My face feels warm from having everyone looking at me. I wish I didn't always blush.

"Just come on," I snap at Jay as Mason sets him down on the ground.

Jay doesn't move, just crosses his arms at me defiantly. I sigh in frustration. Great this is all I need, my five-year-old cousin to embarrass me in front of this crowd.

"It's fine, Becca. He can stay," Ryan tells me.

Jay whoops in delight and runs into the house. This breaks the tension and everyone else starts making their way inside.

"You mean it?" I ask. He nods. "Thanks. My parents will be back by six so just bring him back to the house. Then you can get on with your night. You guys clearly have plans."

Ryan nods. "You're just gonna sit at home on your

109

own?"

I shrug. "I can go see Charlie now since you've got Jay." I know my mom is going to be pissed with me, she'll definitely see this as me shirking me responsibilities. I know I don't like most of the crowd that have turned up, but she's known Ryan since he was born and I know she likes him and it's only for a couple of hours until they get back. To me, it's worth dealing with her wrath and leaving Jay with Ryan. The truth is my want to see Charlie outweighs my worry about annoying my mom. For me, Charlie trumps everything.

Ryan nods abruptly at me and I turn and walk away. I don't know why, but I feel like I've been caught doing something wrong, being seen with Ryan in public outside of school. I shrug it off. I get to the bottom of his driveway and glance back up, expecting everyone to be inside now, but Ryan's still standing there watching me leave.

I look away quickly and walk home.

CHAPTER 14

S CHOOL'S OVER FOR THE DAY AND I'M SHOVING my books into my locker before meeting up with Paige and Sara, two girls in my history class who I eat lunch with. We've been assigned to work together on a history project on the German Holocaust, and we're supposed to go through the work and figure out the best way to do it. I slam my locker shut and nearly jump out of my skin when I see Mason Blackwell leaning against the locker next to mine looking at me. I didn't know he was there and he grins at my reaction.

"Scare you?"

I shrug and my eyes dart past him to his friend John, who's also on the football team, standing next to him. Both of them are pretty tight with Jake and Ryan, but I don't think I've ever spoken more than a couple of words to them before I saw them at Ryan's house for his grandma's wake. Mason and John went to my middle school and were some of the new friends Ryan ditched me for. I shift uncomfortably, unsure why they're both looking at me. Surely they're not here to speak to me? Usually, I'd only cross paths with them if they were with Jake, or even if they're with Ryan when he's trying to irritate me, but there's no sign of either of them right now. In fact, the more I think about it, I realize I've seen a lot more of them recently, especially Mason. He's always saying hi to me and dropping into step with me when he sees me in the halls. He acts like we're friends or something, like he knows me. Reluctantly, I'm having to concede that he seems quite cool.

"So what happened to you on Saturday?" Mason asks.

"Saturday?"

"Yeah, when we turned up at Jackson's you were there, but then you disappeared."

Oh right. I feel my face warm slightly. How embarrassing that they actually think I was at Ryan's house out of choice. And that he'd want me there.

"I had plans. I was only there looking for Jay."

"That's a shame. You should have stayed. Jackson was in a shitty mood all afternoon after you left. What did you say to him, anyway?"

"Nothing," I say defensively. "He's probably just annoyed that he got stuck with Jay when he was trying to get laid or something."

A lazy grin crosses Mason's face. "Nah, Ryan doesn't care about getting laid, at least not by anyone who was at his house on Saturday. And he loves Jay, we all do."

"You guys all know my cousin?" I ask surprised. How did I not know this? Honestly, no one tells me anything.

John nods. "Yeah, we've seen him over at Ryan's a bunch of times. He's a good kid."

I screw my face up at that. "He's kind of annoying."

John laughs. "He's got a lot of energy."

I snort. "That's one way of putting it." I pick up my bag off the floor and turn to walk away.

"Do you know where Jackson is?" Ah, so they are looking for Ryan. That makes sense then. I turn back to face them; they both have these weird smirks on their faces. I shake my head. Why would I know where Ryan is? He's their friend, not mine. "No."

"If you do see him, tell him we're looking for him," John tells me.

"I won't see him. We don't talk. Just look for the biggest group of girls, he's probably creeping on them." They both grin back at my words and I turn and walk out the doors knowing I'm late meeting up with Paige and Sara.

———————◆———————

I'm seated on the benches outside of school with Paige and Sara. We've been here for nearly half an hour but haven't really got much done. They're totally distracted and I keep having to repeat myself.

"Paige, does that sound okay to you?" I ask glancing up from the paper I'm scribbling the information I need on. She's not even looking at me. I sigh in annoyance. I pushed back a date with Charlie for this and they're not even listening to me. Her eyes are fixed behind me and I turn to see what they're so focused on.

Yup, that'll do it. What looks like most of the football team are on the grass behind us throwing around a ball. I roll my eyes when I notice half of them don't have their shirts on. Trust them to play skins vs. shirts…another excuse to show off their bodies. Paige and Sally are not the only girls looking their way. When I glance around, I see more members of the female student population than were here when I sat down.

I turn back to the girls. "Seriously?"

They both send me sheepish looks and finally start to focus on what I'm saying and pitch in with ideas on how we're going to get this done.

"Oh my God. They're looking over here," Sara whispers.

Paige's eyes widen and she quickly glances over my shoulder. "Oh my God, they are!" She stills completely and I have to force myself not to sigh in annoyance. I'm pretty sure they're not looking this way or if they are, it's probably for a perfectly sensible reason. "Oh shit, they're heading this way. They're coming over here!"

Now I *do* roll my eyes. Why on earth would the school football team be coming over here? I'm pretty sure they've got better things to do than talk to three girls they think they're socially above. They're delusional. I thought they would be too sensible to get dragged into the whole popularity cliché at this school but nope, apparently not.

A second later I look up and Sally and Paige have gone completely still, eyes wide. Then a huge shadow crosses the table and I look up, and they're right, what looks like the whole football team is surrounding us. Like completely sur-rounding the table. When I glance around at them, they're all smirking in my direction, and I immediately start to feel uneasy. The last time I was this close to the team, Kevin Wilson was groping me, but a quick look around shows that he's not in the group, which is a small relief.

"Hey, Becca," Jake says grinning down at me. I'm sure my face isn't exactly welcoming. He knows I hate this crowd. I have no idea why he's brought them over here.

I glance at his bare torso. "I'm not talking to you, Edmondson, until you cover yourself up."

He grins. "Finding it hard to control yourself, huh?" he teases before pulling his shirt out of his back pocket, wiping it across his sweaty forehead, then throwing it in my face.

Ewww! Gross. I quickly yank it away from me while his friends chuckle. "You shit," I tell him, but I can't help smiling back at him. I can never stay annoyed at Jake for long.

"So, McKenzie, we need to talk to you," John says sitting down next to Paige, who quickly moves away from him like she thinks he's going to burn her something. I raise my eyebrows at him. Talking to me twice in the space of one afternoon? Pigs will start flying across the school next.

"What?" I ask suspiciously.

"Jackson's bombing English."

I narrow my eyes incredulously. Ryan may not be vale-dictorian material but he's not dumb, and as far as I know he's never had any problems in English. I glance around to see him but surprisingly he's not with them. Jake notices me looking for him. "He's talking with Coach."

"He's bombing English?"

"Yeah."

"What's that got to do with me?"

"Well, if he fails English he can't play on the team. And we need him if we're gonna win state," Jake tells me. I shake my head, still not knowing what this has to do with me. I genuinely couldn't care less if they win state or not, and Jake knows this.

"So we were thinking," John continues, "that since you have English together, you could tutor him."

I laugh out loud at this. No. Absolutely not. No way. "No," I tell them.

"Oh come on, McKenzie," Mason pipes up. "We need you. The whole school needs you."

I glance around and the whole team are staring at me with what I'm sure they think are puppy dog eyes. This is ridiculous. I don't even tutor. I shift uncomfortably in my seat. I hate having this many pairs of eyes on me. "I can't."

"He really needs your help." This from Luke. I roll my eyes in his direction. I mean, don't get me wrong, I'm grateful he helped me out at The Red Rhinos gig, but that doesn't mean he can gang up on me now that he's back with his friends.

"If he needs a tutor, go to student support. You know, where they have actual tutors."

"But you guys are in the same class."

"So are a ton of other kids."

"It'd be easier if you do it."

How on earth would it be easier? I have no idea.

"Look, I'm sure Ryan will have no trouble finding a tutor." There are plenty of girls in this school who would gladly volunteer to have the chance to spend some alone time with Ryan. Maybe it'll do him some good to spend some time with a tutor, someone with brains, rather than the girls he's usually surrounded by.

"Yeah, but you live so close to him. It'd be easier," Mason pipes up.

"There are these things now, called cars."

Mason grins back at me. "You're such a smartass, McKenzie."

"Listen, Becca," Jake says. "He'd never ask you himself, but you should do it. It'd be better if it's someone he knows."

I sigh in annoyance. Sure Ryan knows me...knows how to drive me crazy! It's literally the worst idea I've ever heard. I have no desire whatsoever to tutor Ryan. "Ask Sam," I say suddenly. I grin at my answer. This is perfect. "Sam's in our class too and she can actually stand Ryan."

Jake rolls his eyes, like I'm not getting it. I don't see what his problem is. This is the perfect solution. Sam's way more patient than me and actually better at English too.

"What's going on?" I turn and see that Ryan's joined the group, looking warily at his friends. No one says anything, they just smirk back at him. He looks at me quizzically.

I shrug. "Are you flunking English?"

"What? No!"

I turn to Jake with a raised eyebrow. "Well, maybe not flunking," Jake concedes, "but you were saying you were having trouble with that latest assignment, right?"

Ryan looks confused. "Um, yeah, I guess."

"Well, we were just getting McKenzie to tutor you and help you with it."

Understanding sets in on Ryan's face and he cocks an eyebrow at Jake before shaking his head in amusement. He turns back to me and scratches the back of his head, watching me with an amused smile. I feel like there's a joke that I don't understand. I'm hoping I'm not the punchline.

"Don't worry," I tell him. "I said no. You should ask Sam, she'll do it." I glance down at my phone as it starts ringing on the table next to me. It's my aunt. I'm just deciding whether to ignore it, knowing it will probably be her asking me to watch Jay, when it stops ringing. I look back up at Jake and I'm surprised that they're all still looking at me. "What?" I ask. My phone starts ringing again and this time, I go to answer it, but when I say hello, the line's dead.

"You know it's rude to answer your boyfriend's calls when we're talking to you," Jake tells me irritably.

I roll my eyes. I don't know why he's being moody with me. He's usually so laid back. "It was my aunt," I tell him. "If it were Charlie, I would have answered right away."

Jake shakes his head in annoyance at me. "Just agree to help Jackson with his assignment."

I shake my head. "Sam will be better than me. Or you could help, couldn't you, Paige?" I ask Paige, who is just staring at the boys in awe. She takes English with Henderson too, just a different period. She turns bright red when they all turn in her direction and looks at me in panic. I smirk and stand up.

"Becca, it'll be easier if it's you," Jake tells me firmly. "You live on the same street."

I sigh in annoyance. "Ryan, tell them," I demand. "You and me alone together? We'd kill each other."

I hear muted laughter ring out and Mason playfully shoves Ryan in the shoulder. "What do you think, Jackson? Think you can handle some one on one time with McKenzie? Just the two of you?"

Ryan starts to laugh and shoulders Mason back. "Idiot," he mutters, but he's smiling. I roll my eyes, feeling like there's a conversation going on which I don't really get. And truthfully? I don't particularly care about whatever lame joke they're playing on me.

"I'm out," I tell them. I look over at Paige and Sara. "You guys need a ride?"

They scramble to their feet, throwing their books and folders together. I move to walk toward the parking lot, stopping at the end of the group and turning around, waiting for Paige and Sara. When they've got their stuff together, I take a step backward but unfortunately it's just as a group of freshmen come running down the main pathway from school. They knock into me, making me lose my balance, sending my books flying and forcing me sideways. I'm just about to hit the ground when Ryan, who is standing closest to me, reaches out and firmly wraps his arm around my waist and pulls me into him, steadying my body against his and stopping me from falling.

We both seem to freeze, and I know I've gone bright red. This is the closest I've ever been to another boy from school. My whole body is being held against his and I can feel eyes on me. Ryan's gone really still too, his cheeks look slightly flushed and he seems to have stopped breathing, which is weird since I'm the one who's just been knocked over, not him.

"Um, thanks," I mutter, detangling myself from his hold on me and taking a step away, ridiculously embarrassed to be the center of attention due to my own clumsiness. John passes me my books, which he's picked up for me, and I take another step to the side, eager to get away from them all and this ridiculous feeling of being scrutinized. I quickly turn and walk away with Sara and Paige trailing behind me as the whole group bursts out into uncontrollable laughter behind us. I freeze and cringe in embarrassment. I don't know what that was about, but it's definitely some joke at my expense they seem to find hilarious. I'm surprised Jake's letting them openly mock me, though. I turn around, but instead of seeing them all laughing at me as I expected, they're all grinning and laughing at Ryan, who is playfully shoving them all away from him and shaking his head at whatever they're saying to him and telling them to shut up. He turns and sees me looking back at him, and he almost looks shy when he catches my eye before he grabs Jake in a headlock and starts to wrestle with him.

I shake my head and continue on to my car. Weird. That whole exchange, from when the team came over to when Ryan pulled me into him, was just weird.

CHAPTER 15

"**A**RE YOU HUNGRY?" CHARLIE WHISPERS IN my ear.

I smile at his close proximity and shake my head. Content, that's the word for the way I feel right now.

I haven't been able to see Charlie for a week. Not since the evening Jay threw his disappearing act. He's been so busy with the band and school that we haven't had the chance to meet up. But now it's Saturday lunchtime and I'm laying on a blanket in the local park under a massive oak tree with him next to me, and I'm so relaxed and happy to be with him.

He picks up his phone and puts on some music, leaving it by my head, and then he dips his head and starts dropping feather light kisses on my shoulder, leading up to my neck. I squirm under his touch but don't protest, arching my neck to give him better access. By the time he reaches my mouth, I'm almost ready to forget that we're in a public place and pull him onto me. He drops one last kiss on my mouth and smiles down at me.

"You're so pretty, Becca."

I laugh and shake my head. I know I'm not ugly or anything and I've caught the odd guy checking me out, but I'm nothing compared to Charlie. He's the beautiful one with his long dirty blonde hair that falls into his eyes no matter what he does, his warm brown eyes and gorgeous tanned skin. I still feel like everyone must wonder what he's doing with me when they see us together. I just hope he doesn't open his eyes and realize he's way out of my league.

He starts trailing his index finger slowly up and down my arm, concentrating on my skin like it demands his full attention. When he slowly turns and looks me in the eye, I feel it everywhere, and I'm ready to get up and demand that we find some privacy.

My phone starts to ring next to me, but I completely ignore it. I'm so in this moment with Charlie that I can't imagine anything in the world that is more important. When it rings for a second and then a third time, I reluctantly roll over and see it's my mom. I answer it with a sigh.

I listen as she tells me that Jay's big soccer game is starting soon and his dad isn't coming into town for it like he promised and his mom left him with her this morning and she doesn't know if she will make it either. Apparently Jay's trying to put on a brave face but is pretty upset. My heart sinks for him. I know he drives me crazy, but he's a little boy whose soccer team has made the final in some junior cup, and he just wanted his screwed up parents there to watch him like all the other kids parents will be. She's asking me to come, and although when she first asked me I'd told her I didn't want to, this changes things and I immediately agree. I hang up and stand, straightening out my clothes.

Charlie looks at me in concern, clearly wondering what the conversation was about. "What's up?" he asks.

"We have to go," I say bending to pick up my bag.

"Why?"

"My cousin's parents have bailed on his soccer game and he's pretty upset."

"What does that have to do with you?"

"Well, he needs people there to cheer him on. So he can forget about them. Come on, it starts in twenty minutes. It's at Highgate Fields," I say, waiting for him to get up.

"You want me to come with you?" he asks in surprise.

I screw my face up, isn't that what I just said? "Yes. Come on, Charlie, he's five years old and just wants people to cheer for him. We'll only be an hour or so. They don't play for very long."

"But your parents will be there?"

"Yes. So?"

I watch as his eyes start shifting around and realize that he's never met my parents before, and judging from his re-action, he doesn't want to meet them today.

"Actually, Becca, I forgot..." he trails off, not able to come up with a valid excuse.

I cross my arms and look down at him. "What's the problem?"

"It's not really my scene, Becca. You know, parents and all that. Why don't we just stay here? We were having fun, right?"

My jaw falls open. *Seriously?* "We don't have to sit with my parents, we're just going to support Jay."

"Why don't you give me a call after?" he asks.

"Why bother?" I snap in response. "You know, Charlie, I never ask you to do anything and you can't even spend an hour at a soccer game cheering on my abandoned little cousin."

He doesn't reply and I shake my head and walk away to my car. When I reach it, I slam the door closed so hard I'm lucky my hand wasn't in the way or I'd be down a finger. Usually, I'd never argue with Charlie. I never want to rock the boat with him. We typically have nothing to argue about, but I don't think I was being unreasonable. I shake my head in annoyance then remember Jay and step on the gas to get to the game.

***

"GO, JAY!" I call from the sidelines as Jay comes running past me. He turns and grins at me, waving his hand.

I'm with my parents on the side of the field and after my dad gave me a rundown of the rules, I have a vague understanding of what's going on. It's pretty close at the moment with both teams not looking particularly likely to score.

I hear loud cheering and shouting from down the field and turn to see Ryan, Jake and a couple of others shouting and cheering for Jay. Jay's face lights up when he sees them, but he just about manages to resist the urge to run over and say hi to them.

"What's Ryan doing here?" I ask my mom in surprise.

She shrugs. "He's been down a few times to see Jay play."

"Really?" I ask incredulously. Why didn't I know this?

"Yes." She smiles at my surprise. "I mentioned to Kathy about Jay being upset this morning and she must have told him because he doesn't usually bring so many friends with him."

I don't have anything to say to that, so I just glance in their direction again and see Jake and Mason laughing at some joke while Ryan stays focused on the game.

"You know, Becca, he really is a nice boy."

"Yeah, that is nice," I reply. And it really is. I don't know why no one's ever told me before, but then I guess why would they? It's not like I've ever shown any interest in Jay or Ryan before.

"I know you guys have had your problems, Becca," she continues. I shoot her a look and she holds up her hand in a gesture of surrender. "Look, I don't know what it was that stopped you guys from being so close, but all I'll say is that people change and you could do a lot worse for a friend than Ryan."

I'm about to shoot back a sarcastic comment about how one good deed doesn't erase other things, but I stop myself. This is a nice thing to do. I can give him that.

I turn my attention back to the game when I suddenly hear my dad shout and see that Jay has the ball and is dribbling it down the field toward the goal. He passes it to a teammate who then passes it back to him, and Jay takes aim and shoots…and scores!

I actually jump up and down with excitement, cheering along with everybody else. Jay is ecstatic and his teammates all run over to him jumping onto him, celebrating. I can't help but smile. This may be a local team in an under six category, but the team and the crowd watching, me included, are acting like Jay's just scored the winning goal in the World Cup final.

The teams go back to the center and only have time to kick the ball once more before the referee blows the whistle for time. Jay's team all cheer in delight at winning the game. Jay comes running over to me and launches himself at me, wrapping his arms around my neck and hugging me tightly.

"We won, Becca!" he shouts loudly, grinning from ear to ear, and I'm so surprised and touched that it's me that he's come over to first that I just hug him back tightly before swinging him round in the air. He laughs happily and when I put him down, he high fives both my parents before running over to Ryan and launching himself at him too. A wide smile crosses my face at seeing him so happy, and I know I did the right thing ditching Charlie to be here.

I look over at my mom and she wraps her arm around me, kissing me lightly on the side of my head. I know she feels responsible for him, and for the first time, I don't feel annoyed with him or dismissive of him and his situation. He deserves the same childhood that I had, loving and happy, and if his screwed up parents won't give that to him, then we'll have to. I decide then and there to make more of an effort with Jay.

I glance back over to Jay and laugh when I see Jake and Mason each have hold of an arm and a leg and are swinging him around while the rest of his team watches, waiting for their turn. Ryan looks over at me and I smile and wave at him. He smiles back and I move to make my way over to him. I take a step forward and smack straight into a leather jacket clad Charlie.

He looks down at me, a small smile playing on his lips. "I saw his goal," he tells me. "The little dude did good."

I just gape at him in surprise. He came?

Charlie smirks at me and gently lifts up my chin to close my mouth before I catch flies. He drops his face to mine and kisses me quickly on the lips. His mouth moves sideways to my ear. "I'm sorry I was an ass," he whispers, and I pull my face back to look up at him.

He reaches into his pocket and pulls out a big bar of chocolate. "I even brought him chocolate to celebrate," he shrugs, "or commiserate."

A grin slowly stretches across my face and I reach out and hug him to me. "Thank you," I say into his chest.

He untangles himself from me and looks behind me to where my parents are standing, trying to act like they're not watching us.

He smiles over at them, steps forward and reaches out his hand to shake their hands. "Hi there, I'm Charlie," he introduces himself, shaking my dad's hand and then moving over to my mom. I'm grinning from ear to ear.

He came. He didn't want to, but it was important to me so he came anyway and is now making small talk with my parents because he knows it will make me happy. I turn round to call Jay, who comes dashing over still smiling and happily accepts the chocolate from Charlie. I glance down the field and Ryan, Jake, and their friends are heading to the parking lot, not bothering to come over. I briefly think this is pretty rude, especially of Jake, but then remember that they've come to support Jay, which was really nice of them, and honestly, I'd rather talk to Charlie.

I'm happy. Jay's won his game and it feels like Charlie and I have taken a step forward in our relationship. Today has been a good day after all.

CHAPTER 16

LOOK DOWN AT THE PHONE IN MY HAND AND TRY hard not to burst into tears. Charlie just hung up on me. The rational part of me knows I wasn't being out of line by asking him where he's been and who he's been with. I've barely seen him in the last two weeks since Jay's soccer game and he's been really hard to get a hold of. I felt like we'd made an extra commitment to each other that day with him meeting my parents and all, but since then I've just had the occasional text and it's not unreasonable of me to ask him what's going on. However, the other part of me, the part that adores him and cannot stop thinking about him, wishes I'd kept my big mouth shut and not messed things up, because now he's angry at me and I don't know where I stand.

God, I want to scream the whole school down I'm so frustrated. I always thought those girls were crazy. The ones who just agreed with everything their boyfriends said, no matter what the situation. I laughed at Erica when she'd let herself be ignored and then just go running back like nothing had ever happened. But now I'm in a relationship and I'm all in love and infatuated and the truth is, if you like someone, you like someone. There's nothing you can do about it.

I storm down the empty hallway after school and slam my locker open loudly. I'm so angry at myself I could actually slap myself. I stayed back after school to work on my art project but rather than focus on that, I instead thought about Charlie the whole time and then decided to call him when I was already in a bad mood. I didn't even let him get a word in for the first five minutes, not until I realized he wasn't speaking, and then when he did speak he sounded so cold and annoyed and I honestly couldn't blame him. I don't know what I was thinking. He pointed out that he doesn't know what I do when I'm at school, but he trusts me and would never doubt me. He finished the conversation by telling me he needed some space from me for a couple of days, and now I'm scared I've really fucked up and he won't want me anymore.

I throw my books into my locker, taking my anger out on them, and I bite down on my lip to stop the tears of frustration that are threatening to spill over.

"Are you okay?"

I jump and spin to my left to see Ryan standing there. He's wearing sweats and a t-shirt. On his head is a backward baseball cap and he's carrying a sports bag over his shoulder. He must have just finished practice. I glance to the side, surprised that he's unusually on his own. When my gaze stretches behind him down the hallway, I see Jake and a couple of their teammates further down looking over at us, almost as if he was with them but has broken off to come and talk to me. When the group sees me looking over, they turn and exit the hallway.

I turn my attention back to my locker. "I'm fine."

"You're upset about something."

"It's nothing," I tell him, hunting through my locker. *Where's my damn algebra textbook!*

"Tell me. Maybe I can help?"

"There's nothing wrong."

"Come on, tell me, Becs." There it is again, that old nickname. I turn my head to look at him. He's studying me intently.

"Don't call me that."

"Why?"

"Because it's not my name."

"Yes it is," he says with a smile.

"No. My name is Rebecca. Or Becca. Not Becs. It's too..." I pause. "It's too familiar," I tell him with a sigh.

"Hey, Ryan," two girls greet him, smiling flirtatiously as they walk past us. My eyes follow them, glad for the distraction, but when I turn back to Ryan, he hasn't even glanced in their direction. His eyes are still focused on mine.

I raise my eyebrows at him. "You don't want to follow them and see if there's a spare classroom you can take advantage of?"

He smirks at me and glances away briefly before looking back into my eyes. "I'd rather talk to you," he says quietly.

And I get it.

Just for a moment, I get why Ryan seems to have such an effect on the girls around here. Why Jessica Murphy is crazy about him even though she could have almost anyone else. How he seems to have girls lining up just to talk to him, how everything just comes so easily to him. When he focuses all his attention on you and those clear blue eyes pin you still, I can see what the big deal is. I mean, all he did was tell me he wanted to talk to me. God knows what it's like for a girl when he's actually trying to hook up with them.

"Tell me, Becs," he repeats. "Is it Charlie?"

He's asking me to trust him, to share with him whatever's bothering me and for a second, I think I will. Maybe it would help to get a guy's opinion to see where Charlie's coming from and for him to tell me how I can fix this, but the truth is, I don't want him to know my private business. I don't trust him not to use it against me at some point in the future. Not necessarily to spread it around for gossip, but just to hold over me in case he ever needs something from me. I know we've been on better terms recently and my opinion on him is definitely starting to change, but he's still the guy who screwed me over when I was twelve years old. And that's something I can't forget.

I shake my head at him and his mouth presses into a thin line. I know he doesn't believe me. He knows it's probably Charlie that's upset me, that's gotten this reaction out of me, but he also knows I've chosen not to confide in him. Chosen not to let him in.

I mumble something about leaving and turn to walk off, but he reaches out and grabs my wrist, gently tugging me back around to face him and pulling me closer to him. I pull my hand away from his grip, probably more aggressively than is needed, and pretend not to notice the look of hurt that briefly crosses his face.

"It's Jakes birthday soon," he blurts out before I can make an excuse to leave again. "His mom wants to throw a party and for it to be a surprise. She wanted me to invite his friends."

"I know," I tell him. His eyebrows furrow in confusion. "Jessica Murphy told me. She's helping you arrange it, right?"

He shakes his head. "No, I'm just inviting people for his mom. She's doing the whole thing. I think a barbecue in the evening, and then they'll take off and leave us the house to party in."

"She told me she was organizing it with you. Right before she warned me to stay away from you."

"She did what?" he demands. He looks genuinely angry.

I shrug. "Well, she didn't say those exact words, but I'm pretty sure that's what she was hinting."

"Becca, we're not together. I promise you."

I sigh. "You don't have to explain yourself to me, Ryan. Just keep her away from me, okay? I don't need your psycho hook-ups hassling me."

He opens his mouth to say something, then closes it again. "So, will you come to Jake's party?" he eventually asks.

I sigh and shake my head. I don't know why he's bothering to ask me. We both know I won't go; it's the last place I'd want to be. I love Jake but can't stand most of his friends.

He groans in frustration. "Come on, Becca. For Jake?

emma doherty

It's not like I'm asking you to come to *my* party or anything. You actually like Jake, you two are good friends." He sounds bitter and almost…jealous? I quickly dismiss the thought. Even Ryan wouldn't be bothered that his best friend talks to someone he doesn't. Surely he's not that pathetic.

"Just think about it, okay?" he asks me. "For Jake? He'll want you to be there."

I sigh and nod my head, knowing full well I won't go. I turn to leave again and this time, he doesn't try to stop me.

CHAPTER 17

RYAN WON'T HAVE ANY TROUBLE GETTING PEOPLE to Jake's party. He's a great guy and we all know it. Jake transferred to our school in the middle of second grade and his easy humor and constant grin meant he was instantly liked by everyone. His good looks didn't hurt either, even at that young age. Of course being the naturally pessimistic person that I am, I was unsure of him. That changed one day in gym class when he was the captain of one of the teams. I had been annoyed knowing that he and another boy would just pick all the best boys and us girls would be left until last. Ryan, of course, didn't care, knowing he would get picked first anyway, especially now that it was Jake picking. Jake had stood at the front of our class and then picked me first. I was totally surprised but couldn't hide my delight. Ryan ended up getting picked first for the other team and didn't stop sulking all week when mine and Jake's team won. That was it—I was sold on Jake too.

He's always been a good friend to me, always loyal. He's

just a good guy. It's that simple.

About three weeks before the end of sophomore year, I walked into the cafeteria at lunchtime and instantly felt a weird atmosphere. Not a hostile atmosphere. But something was definitely up. Students were talking amongst themselves in low tones and there wasn't the usual rowdy noise and laughter that filled the room during lunchtime.

"What's going on?" I asked sinking into my seat next to Sam and across from Erica.

"You didn't hear? Jake passed out during gym class," Erica told me.

"Jake Edmondson? Is he okay? Is he with the school nurse?"

"No, as in passed out, fainted onto the floor. They couldn't wake him up," Erica continued, her face displaying the seriousness of the situation.

I turned to look at Sam in confusion. "What do you mean they couldn't wake him up?"

She shrugged, worry clear in her eyes. "They had to call an ambulance. He hadn't woken up by the time they'd gotten here."

I swear my stomach dropped through the floor. *Not Jake. Not Jake. Please, don't let anything be wrong with Jake,* I remember thinking over and over. This explained the hushed tones in the cafeteria. Jake was popular but not in the usual way. He wasn't unobtainable and cliquey, he was friendly and happy go lucky. He had time for everyone and the fact that he was in the hospital, possibly seriously ill, would worry a lot of people.

"But he's fine now? He woke up in the ambulance, right?"

"No one knows," Erica replied. "I don't even think his best friends know. The school banned anyone from going over there because we'd just get in the way of his doctors and family."

"Right, yeah. I didn't think of that."

I turned in my chair to look at Jake's usual table, but it was mostly empty. I glanced to the door just as Ryan walked in with a couple of friends, and his face told me just how serious the situation was. It was ashen and his eyes looked red, like he'd been crying. Oh shit. This was serious.

"Shit," I whispered. "Shit, shit, shit."

Suddenly, Sam reached down and grabbed her purse and pulled her jacket over her shoulders. She turned to look at me. "I have the keys to my brother's car from this morning and I have my permit. I say we just go over there and find out."

I looked at her, trying to focus on her words. It was so unlike Sam to suggest doing something against the rules, driving a car without someone with a license in it and heading over to the hospital when we'd been banned from going.

"Becca," she continued, snapping her fingers in my face. "This is Jake, he's one of your oldest friends and he could be really ill right now. We can go over there and find out what's going on."

I jumped up. "Right. Let's go."

She pulled me back. "We should ask if Ryan wants to come. He's his best friend."

I was about to protest. I didn't see why Ryan couldn't sort himself out, but one look in his direction showed just how worried he was. I nodded my agreement and followed Sam over to their table which had steadily filled up with worried faces.

Sam stopped across from him. "Ryan? We're gonna drive over to the hospital to see how Jake is. Do you want to come?"

A look of surprise crossed his face, almost as though that thought had never occurred to him. He turned to his right and Mason had shaken his head. "They said we'd be in the way and upset his parents."

Ryan turned to me helplessly, almost as if asking me what to do. I sighed and shrugged. "We could be there in like twenty minutes and leave as soon as we know how he is." That seemed to be all the confirmation Ryan needed. He jumped up and followed us out of the cafeteria, walking so fast we had to run to catch up with him.

Well, that was it; it was like a tsunami effect. Suddenly everyone was jumping up and heading to the parking lot. We all arrived at the hospital around the same time and none of us were told to leave.

Turns out Jake had bacterial meningitis and that nine hours I sat in the waiting room were the most terrifying of my life, waiting to know if he would make it or not. Somehow I ended up sitting next to Ryan, and for once I didn't immediately distance himself from him. When I briefly got up to use the bathroom, I came back to see that someone had taken my seat so I sat in an empty seat across the room.

Ryan immediately moved and came to sit next to me. It was like he didn't want to be apart from me. We barely spoke, but I think it was the memory of the young friendship he, Jake and I had shared that made him want to be close to me. He knew I loved Jake just as much as he did. A lot of the students left after a couple of hours, but I couldn't leave without knowing he was okay, and when my mom arrived with Mrs. Jackson bringing food and offering their sympathies to Jake's parents, I refused to leave. Finally, when they told us he'd gotten through the worst of it, I let her take me home.

The next couple of weeks were pretty shitty for Jake. It was a really slow recovery and he was totally exhausted. I visited him every couple of days and he seemed to be returning more and more to his normal self. Then summer was here and I was off to Sam's childhood summer camp to work as a junior counselor. I spent eight weeks away from home, calling and texting Jake to check in with him but really just getting on with my summer.

I got back from camp a week before school started and my dad took me to get my driver's license (I turned sixteen over the summer). I drove over to Jakes to see him and was delighted to see he had made what looked like a full recovery.

"You look good," I told him leaning against the doorframe that led to his family room. He turned around in surprise at my voice and grinned when he saw me. I returned the smile and walked in to meet him, leaning down to hug him tightly while he sat on the sofa. "Really, really good," I whispered. I still couldn't believe how close we had come to losing him.

He hugged me back, and then we sat and talked about our summers and he told me how much better he was feeling. I pulled my car keys out of my bag and dangled them in front of him like a prize.

"I got my license. Want to go for a ride? We could drive down to the beach?"

He nodded in agreement. "Only if Jackson can come, he'll be here any minute."

"Ryan Jackson?" I asked, annoyed that he was coming over. "Isn't he still at camp?" Ryan went to a football camp every summer to work on his game; Jake usually went too. As soon as I said it, I regretted it. I hated admitting I knew anything about Ryan's life, but it was impossible sometimes not to pick up on what my mom and his mom would say when they were over at my house.

Jake shook his head. "No. He didn't go."

"He didn't go?"

"No. He said he wanted to stay here with me this summer. He's been here every day."

My jaw fell open. Ryan Jackson could be that selfless? That good to his friend? Wow.

Jake chuckled at my reaction. "I know, nice, right?" When I didn't respond, he laughed again. "Don't worry, I won't tell him you don't think he's not a complete asshole."

I rolled my eyes and followed Jake outside, and sure enough, there was Ryan, strolling up the drive. He stopped short when he saw me and nodded a greeting in my direction, looking surprised and a bit flustered. He didn't look particularly thrilled when Jake announced we were going for a drive in my car, about as thrilled as I felt about taking him, but he didn't put up any arguments. I don't think either of us wanted Jake to pull the "I nearly died" card out and he obediently climbed into the backseat of my new car.

As I was checking my mirrors and pulling away from the curb, Jake turned to me. "So, Becca, you hook up with anyone at camp?"

"Like I'd tell you two," I replied but blushed bright red, which Jake didn't fail to spot.

"That means yes," he told me triumphantly, which I didn't argued with since it wasn't a lie. Jake turned to Ryan in the backseat who was looking stonily ahead, paying no attention to the conversation. "Tick tock, Jackson, tick tock," he said to him, smirking.

I shot him a dirty look. *Tick tock?* I didn't care how long he thought it was taking me to get to the beach, I was not crashing my new car by rushing.

CHAPTER 18

SOMETIMES I THINK MY MOM IS THE BEST PERSON in the world. I mean, she's fearless. When she was eighteen years old, she backpacked around the world on her own. She explored the globe for eighteen months, going off the beaten track, working in orphanages in South East Asia, walking the Inka Trail in Peru, learning Spanish in Mexico and how to ride horses in Australia. She didn't care that she was alone; she took off and made friends for life along the way who she still keeps in contact with today. Then she came back to America and went to college.

Now, my mom is beautiful, like really beautiful. Even I can see it and when I look at pictures of her from when she was a teenager, she looked like a model, but she has literally never cared about what she looks like. My dad says the first time he spotted her was at a student rally, protesting against a homeless shelter in the local town that was about to be knocked down. She's incredibly passionate about things that she cares about. He took one look at her and knew he had to speak to her, but when he went over to introduce himself, she looked straight past him and went and started arguing with a nearby cop or something.

By all accounts, my dad was a pretty big deal in college. He was on a football scholarship and was tipped for the big time before he busted his knee. According to my uncle, he was a bit of a player, always with a different girl, but the day he saw my mom that all changed. He was desperate to meet her, to speak to her. Finally, he bumped into her at some party or another and watched her turn down several members of his football team with humor and good nature. He was completely besotted when he finally gathered up the courage to talk to her. She grinned at him, invited him to a debate she was going to the next day and that was it. He was locked down and they've been together ever since.

She graduated in the top ten of her class, went to law school, turned down a fancy job at a top law firm and instead works for legal aid, assisting those that she feels really need her help. Her and my dad are still crazy about each other. She told me it was tough for them after his football career ended, but he works as a sports journalist now and I think he's pretty happy. The only crappy thing is that my mom's suffered two miscarriages. One before me and one after. But she even turned that into a positive and set up a support group for mothers that have had similar experiences, and she still runs it to this day.

So, yeah, sometimes I think she's the best person in the world.

Today is not one of those days.

"You cannot keep threatening to take my car from me every time you want me to do something!" I tell her vehemently.

She smiles calmly back at me. "Yes, I can. I paid for it, I can take it away."

I let out a huff of annoyance. "I cannot pick Jay up twice a week from school, mom! I have plans and he has his own parents."

Annoyance crosses her face. "You know how Aunt Ruth has been recently. I'm just asking you to help out more, Becca. I'm slammed at work and need your help."

"This is so unfair," I bark back at her, conveniently forgetting how I'd vowed to make more effort with Jay. Don't get me wrong, I make more effort to talk to him and play with him when I see him now, but why does my schedule have to change around him?

"Becca, I am genuinely worried about your aunt. You could show a little thought for someone other than yourself for once and help me out," she snaps back at me. I bite my lip to stop from retaliating. I think she's being completely unreasonable, but she hardly ever snaps and shouts at me, so she must be really worried about Aunt Ruth. I don't know why, she can take care of herself, she's just letting off some steam.

I set my mouth into a firm line and cross my arms.

She sighs and offers me a small smile. "I'm sorry, Becca, I'm just a little stressed."

I nod but don't smile back at her.

"How about I take you shopping this weekend?" she

offers. Now I know she feels bad for snapping.. "We could make a day of it, grab some lunch? I know we haven't spent much time together recently and Jay's around a lot more now."

"You actually think I'm jealous of you spending time with Jay? Give me some credit, mother!" For some reason, I can feel tears tickling the back of my eyes.

She frowns.

"Just tell me whatever you want me to do it and I'll do it, all right?" My voice cracks slightly and I get up to leave the room before she starts interrogating me.

Too late.

"Sit, Becca. What's going on with you?"

"Nothing."

"Becca, I know you. Something's wrong." I look away from her, sit back down at the table and stare down at my phone. Surprise, surprise still no message from Charlie. I've really messed up this time. "You know, I'm a really good listener, Becca. You can talk to me about anything," she continues.

I shrug and she sits down across from me, watching me carefully, waiting for me to speak.

"I've not seen Charlie around for a while," she finally says.

My eyes shoot up and I see the sympathetic smile she's giving me. "You know Becca, sometimes things don't work out the way we want them to."

I sigh. "I messed up."

"If he can't see how special you are and how lucky he is

to have you, then he's not worth it."

I scowl in her direction. Of course she's going to say that to me. She's my mom, she's bound to think that. "You know plenty of guys would love to date you, Becca."

"Mom, stop. You don't know anything."

"I can think of at least one boy from your school that I'm pretty certain would love to date you," she says smiling at me. I roll my eyes. How on earth would my mom know any of the guys at my school? Much less who they want to date. Besides, even if that were true and not just her obvious attempt to cheer me up, I don't want any of the losers from my school. Charlie's the only guy I've ever felt like this about.

The doorbell rings. When I make no move to answer it, my mom sighs and goes to open the door while I stare at my phone, debating if I should call Charlie.

My mom clears her throat behind me and I turn to see her standing in the doorway with Charlie behind her. My jaw falls open slightly, I'm so shocked to see him here. He's picked me up from my house countless times, but he's never been in, not whilst my parents have been home. He's always messaged to tell me to come outside or beeps his horn. My mom raises an eyebrow in my direction, then excuses herself from the room. Charlie looks at me and offers a small smile. I return it tentatively. *Please don't break up with me.* He wouldn't be smiling at me if he were going to break up with me, right?

He walks over and sits down beside me.

"I'm so sorry," I tell him immediately. "I shouldn't have picked a fight. I didn't mean it."

"You know, Becca, it's been a long time since I've had a girlfriend. I guess I just forgot about checking in all the time and seeing you all the time. You were right, I should have called more. I was busy, but that's all, I promise. There's no one else. Just you."

"So you're not mad at me?"

He smiles. "Just don't start fights again for no reason, okay?"

I actually feel weak with relief. I clamber onto his knee, wrap my arms around him and kiss him like my mom's not in the house. He pulls away after a minute and picks my arms up from around his neck, turning my hands over so that my palms are facing him. He slowly starts to stroke my left wrist, running his finger over the skin softly. It feels relaxing and intimate and wonderful.

"You know, your wrist has been looking a little empty," he tells me.

I pull my eyes away from my wrist and look up at him. He's smiling at me. He reaches into his pocket and pulls out a simple silver charm bracelet. I gasp in surprise.

He remembered!

A couple of months ago I lost the charm bracelet my mom got me for my sixteenth birthday. I spent days and days looking for it but eventually figured it must have fallen off at some point. My mom was furious but not as pissed as I was. I loved that bracelet. I wore it every day and was devastated I'd lost it.

Charlie reaches for my wrist and gently fastens the clasp. The bracelet has just one charm on it—a guitar. "The guitar is for me," he tells me. "So even if I'm off doing my thing, I'll always be with you."

I grin from ear to ear. I don't care how cheesy that is, it's the nicest thing anyone has ever done for me. It's like in the olden days when boys used to give their girlfriends their signet ring. This is what that feels like. It feels like a commitment. He reaches over and pulls my head down to meet his and gives me the sweetest, gentlest kiss imaginable.

I love him. I actually love him. It's on the tip of my tongue to tell him when he grins mischievously at me, glancing toward the door to make sure my mom's not hovering nearby. "You know my parents are out tonight," he whispers.

Relief floods me. He's forgiven me and everything's back to normal. I nod my head and let him pull me to my feet. I yell goodbye to my mom and I'm out the door and in Charlie's car thanking God that everything is back to normal and that he still wants me.

CHAPTER 19

SAM AND I ARE SITTING WITH ERICA AT A TABLE outside of school. Erica has just been dumped by her latest boyfriend and is suitably devastated. Well, it *is* her birthday so pretty crappy timing. Personally, I don't think it's that big a loss. I mean, the guy was shorter than her and permanently reeked of garlic, but being the good friend that I am, I went and picked up a box of donuts after school and brought them back for after she finished drama club. I'm on my third with half the box to go when I look up and see Jake, Ryan, John, Mason and another girl, Katie, standing by the table.

"Hey guys," Jake says and sits down. Ryan and Mason join him while John and Katie step closer standing just behind them. I frown but manage to stop myself from pulling a face. Apparently Ryan and I are on speaking terms again now, so I can't exactly moan if he sits at the same table as me. And he did buy me all that candy.

"Who bought those?" Ryan asks, nodding at the donuts.

"Becca," Sam replies. Apparently that's the answer they wanted because both Ryan and Jake immediately help themselves. My jaw drops open.

"Hey, they're for Erica!" I exclaim. I glance over at her, but she doesn't look the least bit bothered about sharing. She's just staring at them like they're some sort of mythical creatures. "It's her birthday," I explain.

"Happy Birthday, Erica," Ryan says, giving her his trademark cocky smile. She practically melts and I have to bite my lip to stop from grinning. I'd put money on Erica not knowing that Ryan knew who she was. He's probably just made her week.

"Thanks," she mumbles, turning slightly pink. Ah well, at least they've cheered her up. "Well done on getting Homecoming King," she tells him quickly.

I have to hold back a snort and glance over at Sam, who is smirking back at me. This is not the Erica we're used to, all shy and tongue-tied. Ryan did get homecoming king at the dance last week, just like I predicted. Ryan smiles back at her, looking like he's trying hard to not start laughing. "Thanks, Erica." He turns to me and raises an eyebrow. I start to laugh. He's so full of it.

"Yeah, Ryan. Well done," I tell him sweetly. He grins back at me and flips me the finger. I shake my head in amusement and pick up the box of donuts and hold it toward the rest of their group. "Want one?" I ask.

The boys help themselves, but Katie shakes her head. "No thanks, if I ate that stuff I'd be the size of a whale." She laughs. "I don't know how you do it."

Okay, that sounded dangerously like a compliment. Ever since I saw her at Ryan's after his grandma's funeral, she's gone out of her way to say hi to me. It's a bit weird.

"So, did I hear you guys went to a Red Rhinos gig a couple of weeks ago?" Jake asks. Sam nods at him in response. "Were they good? My cousin sent me some of their stuff. She's a huge fan."

"Yeah, they were cool," Sam answers.

Jake looks to me for my answer. "They were awesome," I agree. And if Charlie's excitement afterward was anything to go by, they really were.

"You liked them?" Ryan asks me suddenly. He's looking at me directly.

I nod and he raises an eyebrow at me.

"It was just too busy," Sam tells him. "Like crazy busy. You couldn't move it was so packed."

"And you had a good time?" Ryan persists, looking at me.

I nod again, this time, looking down at the table.

"You hate crowds," Ryan says, and I look up to see he's looking me straight in the eye, and I feel the blood rush to my face. I hate it when he does this. When he acts like he knows me. Especially in front of other people. I don't know why he can't just act like we don't know each other, which is the way it is. The way it's been for years.

"It wasn't that bad."

Ryan shakes his head at me, annoyance crossing his face. "He shouldn't have left you on your own."

Luke told him. It's pretty obvious. Luke told him that

I freaked in a crowd and that Charlie was nowhere to be found. I did wonder after that night if he would mention it to his friends but when no one ever said anything, I figured he hadn't bothered and I was grateful, but clearly I was wrong. Apparently Ryan knows all about my panic attack but just hasn't mentioned it until now. I feel my face get hotter and it's not just because he's called me out, but because he's right. Charlie shouldn't have left me. I've told myself that it's okay, that he was off having fun and it was his gift from me, but the truth is I was having a panic attack and if Luke hadn't been there, I don't know what I would have done.

I shift uncomfortably in my seat. If Ryan thinks he knows me so well, then he should also know that I don't like being the center of attention, especially in front of his friends, the popular kids at school who pass on gossip like it's a sport. Ryan goes to open his mouth again and I feel my anger rise. "Leave it," I say quietly. "It has nothing to do with you."

Ryan looks at me for another minute and I see Jake lean into him slightly, nudging him with his arm, then he finally glances away. His jaw is tense and I can tell he's annoyed, but he doesn't say anything else and I let out a breath I didn't know I was holding. Jake takes over the conversation and cracks some joke and Mason joins in. They all burst out into laughter, breaking the tension at the table, and I listen to their idle chatter and feel my face cool to its normal temperature.

"So, are you guys coming to the big game tomorrow night?" Jake asks suddenly.

"What game?"

This is met by a chorus of moans and eye rolls.

"Jesus, Becca. Do you walk around with your eyes closed? It's the biggest game of the year. We're playing Madison," Jake says.

Sam chuckles next to me and when I look at her blankly, she shrugs. "Everyone has been talking about it," she explains.

I guess that makes sense. Madison is our local rival, so I guess it'll be a big game.

"Oh right. It's not really my scene," I say.

"Oh come on, Becca, where's your school spirit?" asks Katie. She starts to laugh before I can. "God, I really do sound like a cheerleader."

"Come on, it's Jackson's big night. He's gonna break the school's passing record and there's gonna be scouts there," Jake explains. "You should all come," he continues, looking over at Sam and Erica. Erica nods enthusiastically; apparently she's lost the ability to speak.

"Yeah and we're having a party at my house after, which you should all come to. My parents are away," Mason pipes up.

"Yeah, yeah definitely," Erica says nodding and practically bouncing in her seat with excitement. I'm pretty sure she's waited her entire high school career to be personally invited to a team victory party. The memory of her ex is clearly long gone. I'm surprised Mason has invited us, to be honest. Maybe he's not as bad as I thought he was. Sam is nodding agreeably too.

"You're gonna go?" I ask Sam.

"Sure, sounds fun," she responds. I raise my eyebrows in surprise.

Mason and Jake break into an in-depth discussion about how they can't possibly lose this year, and I can't help but smile at the way Erica is hanging off their every word like they're gods or something. I glance over at Ryan, and he's already looking at me.

"Will you come to the game Becca?" he asks quietly. "Please?"

I open my mouth to immediately say no, annoyed at him for calling me out about Charlie and getting involved in my business, but something stops me. I think it's the way he's looking at me, ignoring everyone else like it's just the two of us.

I nod slightly and catch him flash a small smile before I quickly look away.

❖

I genuinely did have every intention of going to his game. Even my parents were going to sit with Mr. and Mrs. Jackson. Turns out it was a pretty big night for Ryan after all, and I figured it wouldn't kill me to attend at least one football game while in high school. Then Charlie's plans with his family changed at the last minute and he managed to score tickets to a gig of one of his favorite bands and we were out long after the game finished.

I did, of course, hear all about it from Erica the next

week at school. Apparently Ryan had been amazing (her words), throwing a bunch of touchdowns and impressing everyone that was there. The highlight though was that at the party afterward. He introduced her to a guy named Matthew Smithy, who according to Erica is definitely in the top twenty-five percent of popular kids at our school (albeit the lower end), and she promptly made out with him all night, completely forgetting how heartbroken she's been.

The night, it would seem, was a success for all concerned. Ryan got his record, Erica mixed with the social elite and I got to spend an entire evening with Charlie, just the two of us.

CHAPTER 20

DAMN IT!

I'm in the girls locker rooms and I'm pissed off. Miss Greene, the girls gym teacher, won't accept the note from my mom, dismissing me from gym class this morning—and it's a double period. Okay, so I wrote the note (I've had my mom's signature down since I was thirteen), but apparently only a doctor's note will suffice now.

I look around grumpily, wishing I'd ditched. And to make matters worse, Miss Greene has just announced that since it's crappy weather outside, we're joining the boys in the gym. *Fantastic.* Apparently I'm one of the few that feel this way, as Jessica and a couple of the other cheerleaders squeal in excitement, tying knots in their t-shirts so that they can flash even more skin and rolling up their already tiny shorts. Pathetic.

I lag behind the rest of the class as we enter the large gym, hoping Greene won't notice. That doesn't work when she turns around and shouts for me to get a move on. I sigh heavily, hoping she's aware of the torture she's about to put me through. I mean, seriously, it's freezing and I have way better things I could be doing. I swear we're only joining the boys because she's banging Mr. White, the boy's gym coach.

Mr. White stands at the front of the gym and blows his whistle. "Since there's so many of us today and we have a bit of time, we're going to have," he actually pauses for dramatic effect, "a dodgeball tournament."

I hear a few excited yes's from around the hall. *Are you kidding me? Dodgeball?* Like I want to end up covered in tons of bruises.

"We're gonna do mixed teams to make it fair; teams of two, boy, girl. Find your partners."

I'm just contemplating how I can get away with pretending I've sprained my ankle when an arm drapes loosely around my shoulder. I look up and see Jake grinning down at me. I didn't realize he was in here.

He smiles. "How 'bout it? Partners?"

I sigh. I suppose if I have to pair up with someone, Jake is the best choice. "Okay, fine."

He steers me toward the back of the gym where he's been standing and I realize Ryan's in this class too. *Seriously? I barely speak to him in five years and now he's everywhere.*

Jessica Murphy is next to him looking very pleased with herself. Now I realize why she was so happy about joining the boys in gym class. I'd heard around school that she'd finally hooked up with Ryan at the party after the game on Friday and she was very happy about it. Then when I was in Spanish yesterday morning she'd been telling her friends (loudly enough for the whole class to hear) that Ryan was just the best kisser ever and she was pretty sure they'd be an official item by Christmas. Luckily I'd skipped breakfast that morning or I might have vomited all over my desk. She's now practically attached to him and grinning like she should get a medal or something.

The whistle blows again and I turn to listen to Mr. White.

"So we're gonna play this like a proper tournament. We'll have a group stage and then the winners from there will play each other until we get to the final. Whichever team hits an opposing player three times wins that match. You'll have to work together, okay?"

People around me nod in agreement and I'm barely able to stifle a yawn. I fully intend to get myself out right away, and then I can sit and watch/daydream about Charlie until the end of class.

I turn to Jake to tell him my plan, but he's already watching me with a small smile playing on his mouth. I narrow my eyes, but before I can say anything, he turns to Ryan.

"Hey, Jackson, I'll never win with McKenzie, she's too short. Swap with me?"

Wait a second, what? Since when is five foot six that short? AND YOU ASKED ME!

"Hey! Wait!"

Jake doesn't even acknowledge me but saunters over to stand next to Jessica, who's facial expression I'm pretty certain reflects my own. Ryan scowls in my direction but swaps places anyway since he doesn't have much of a choice.

"Ry-Ry and I wanted to be on the same team!" Jessica says to Jake.

I actually snort with laughter. *Ry-Ry? That's what she calls him?* I turn to him and can't help the huge smirk that covers my face. This is too funny. He just sends me a thunderous look in return.

Jessica sends me a look which would terrify the hardest of criminals. "We're together now," she says pointedly.

Why she's bothering to tell me, I don't know, but one glance at Ryan tells me he wasn't entirely aware that they were together. He looks incredibly awkward.

I smile sweetly back at Jessica. "Lucky you. Maybe you should ask your friends for tips because he's already been around all of them, hasn't he?"

There are a few snickers and muted laughs from around us and I realize that some of the football team are also in this class and were listening to our conversation.

Jessica narrows her eyes at me and crosses her arms, glaring at me. I glance at Jake, and he's shaking his head at me in annoyance. "That was harsh, Becca," he says. I shrug. Ryan can take it and he's definitely dished it out enough to me over the years. Besides, it's true.

"So what happened to you on Friday, anyway?" Jake asks, changing the subject.

"Friday?"

He looks at me like I'm stupid. "The game? You were supposed to come."

Oh, right. "Um, yeah. Charlie got tickets to this gig so we went there."

Jake pulls a face, like my reasoning is unacceptable. Geez, it was only a game.

"Well, you missed a great game. Ryan did awesome," Jessica states loyally.

I roll my eyes and turn to Ryan, who is staring straight ahead, jaw clenched. "Well done on the record. Erica said you did great. And so did my parents," I say graciously.

"Shut the hell up, Becca!" he snaps back angrily.

My eyes widen in surprise. *Okaaay, he's clearly in a bad mood.* The next hour or so is going to be too much fun.

It turns out Ryan is pretty good at dodgeball. I know I shouldn't be surprised really considering he's a football player and all, but he's definitely in a foul mood and making our opponents pay. He's throwing the balls so hard at the opposition that I swear half the class with be covered in bruises tomorrow. To begin with, I actually do try to get involved, moving out of the way and trying to catch the ball if it comes my way, but it would seem that Ryan has decided that I'm not necessary in this game and catches all the balls before I can get to them before firing them back over the line to get the other team out. I soon lose interest and start glancing at the clock, hoping time will fast forward so we can get this dumb game over with. Ryan does so well at covering me and not letting me get near a ball that I'm the only girl who makes it out of the group stages without even a single life lost.

We're about to start playing the quarter-finals when he seems to remember that there are two of us in the team. He holds a ball out to me. "You want to have a throw?"

"I think you've got this," I say sarcastically, stifling a yawn.

This just seems to infuriate him even more and he quickly throws the ball at me so hard I don't have time to react and it bounces off my left hand.

"Ow!" I cry out.

There are snickers from the watching crowd.

"Ryan, you're not supposed to get your own teammate out," Mr. White says grinning. This gains further laughs from the watching kids. Now that the group stages are over, there's only one match at a time so that everyone else can watch.

The game starts up again and I start to realize that maybe Mr. White was a bit crafty in arranging the teams, as now we're coming up against some of Ryan's teammates and it doesn't seem as easy as it was earlier.

I'm still just kind of hanging around the back of the court when a ball comes flying past my head. Ryan sees it and when it comes time for us to regroup for a couple of minutes, he tells me to go stand in the corner of the court.

"Why?"

"Because they can come at you from too many different angles when you're in the middle and I might not be able to cover you."

"So? Maybe I should just let them get me and then we can sit out and watch for the rest of class."

He looks at me in disbelief. "You're joking, right?" This comes out louder than I think either of us expected. *Geez, he's competitive.*

"It's only a game, Ryan."

"Yes, well, Becca, I like to win. So we are going to win this tournament," he bites out through gritted teeth.

I just stare at him blankly.

"BECCA!"

"Why are you shouting?" I ask feeling slightly bewildered. What is his problem? Shouldn't he be on top of the world? Still high from his football game and college offers?

"Cause you're being annoying. Just do what I say and we'll win."

"Hey, Jackson, do you want to finish this lover's tiff later? We're up next and want to play sometime today," Jake calls from the sideline which causes snickers from his and Ryan's friends.

We both turn to glare at him, although it would seem that Ryan doesn't glare for as long as me because before I know it, he's slipped his arm round my waist and has picked me up and dumped me in the corner where he's been telling me to stand. I'm so surprised I can't think of anything to say. I shove him away from me and hear further laughter from the crowd and know I've gone bright red.

Asshole.

We sail through the next couple of games, although I might as well not be there, then we're up against Jake and Jessica in the final and I couldn't care less.

"What's wrong, Becca? Don't wanna play?" Jake taunts

me from his side of the court. I flip him the finger and get a stern warning from Miss Greene and a chuckle from the rest of the watching class.

They send a couple of balls our way which we manage to dodge and Ryan manages to throw one back and hits Jessica on the leg. After a few more throws no one is out and it's time for us to collect the balls from around the court. Jessica and Jake hover together looking like they're coming up with a strategy, I glance briefly over at Ryan but he doesn't even look my way, he's just stood there radiating tension. I have no idea what's going on with him.

Miss Greene blows the whistle and Jake and Jessica run forward as one and both launch their balls at us hard. Ryan goes to catch one from Jake but misses and leaves me wide open, Jessica's ball slams into me. Hard. Well, into my left breast, to be exact.

"Shit!" I hiss and double over in pain, feeling like I've been punched. I hear muted laughter from the crowd as I clutch the spot where it hit, only just stopping myself from rubbing my boob because even *I* know that's a bad idea. I glare over at Ryan, "What the hell? I thought you were covering me?"

"I went for Jake's ball."

"And you couldn't do that from in front of me? I thought you were supposed to be a star footballer?" I hiss.

"How would you know?" he shoots back. "You've never been to any of my games."

I look at him in confusion. Why is he being such a brat? Everyone knows he's a star athlete, Surely he can cover two balls coming at him in a game of dodgeball? "Oh, I'm sorry if I haven't seen you prance around a field in tight pants, throwing a stupid ball about."

His fists clench at his sides and he looks like he wants to explode. "I swear to God, Becca. You need to shut up."

I send him a dirty look, still clutching my boob. "You're the one who wanted to make sure we saw this out. Well, next time do your job and cover me. That fucking hurt!" I spit at him.

"Oh. Want me to kiss it better?" Ryan says sarcastically, gesturing to where my hand covers my boob. This gains snickers from the crowd and I realize they're all listening in. I can't believe he just said that. Trust him to add to my humiliation.

"Okay, okay," Miss Greene calls, "simmer down you two. And watch your language, Miss McKenzie."

I turn to look at her and she's trying unsuccessfully to hide her smirk. I glance back to Ryan. "What is your problem?" I demand quietly, trying to keep my voice as low as possible. He has no right to talk to me like this, I've done nothing wrong.

"You are," he responds.

I shake my head at him in disgust and turn to face Jessica across the court whose eyes are glued to us. "Jessica, swap with me," I call out. "You can finish off on Ryan's team."

She moves toward us and I start to walk across the gym toward Jake, but Ryan grabs my wrist and pulls me back roughly, "No way," he hisses in my ear. "You're on my team."

"Yeah, well I'm over you treating me like crap," I whisper viciously back at him. "I'd rather be on Jake's team."

"Trust me, I know you'd rather be on Jake's team. I get it, you prefer him to me. In fact, I know you'd prefer anyone over me but you are on my team for this match and you are actually going to stick to something that you've agreed to for once!"

What the hell is he talking about? He looks absolutely livid, his face is flushed from anger and his nostrils are flared. His hand is still wrapped tightly around my wrist. Jessica reaches us, flashing a cautious smile at Ryan and a dirty look at me. I turn to walk away, but his grip on my wrist tightens.

"Jess, go back over there," he tells her. "Finish off with Jake."

She looks like she wants to argue but when she sees the look on his face, she reluctantly turns and returns to Jake, who's watching us warily.

"Get your hand off me," I practically spit at him, tugging my hand away from him just as Mr. White blows his whistle.

"What's going on?"

"I want to swap with Jessica."

He shakes his head in annoyance. "You can't swap now. You're in the final. The bell's about to ring and we need to finish."

"She's not swapping," Ryan says firmly. His tone brokers no arguments.

I sigh in annoyance. "Fine." I'm ready to storm off but realize it won't get me anywhere and turn to walk back to my corner. What the hell have I done wrong for him to be treating me like this?

"Okay, okay. Let's go again," Jake is calling.

I resume my position at the back, Ryan covering me. The whistle goes and I mutter "total dick," under my breath just loud enough for Ryan to hear. I just see his whole body stiffen at my words before I glance down and notice my shoelace is undone. I look back up just in time to see Ryan purposelessly step out of the way and the ball smacks into my face.

This hurts. This really, really hurts. I don't even swear this time, I think I'm too shocked. No one really says anything. No one laughs, they just kind of murmur in sympathy. I think they can tell it's worse than the previous hit. I look across and Jessica is grinning like she's just won the Super Bowl.

The bitch!

The face is supposed to be off limits, and who knew she had such a throw on her? I actually feel a bit dizzy and tears have come to my eyes. I bite down hard on the inside of my mouth to stop them from falling. Have you ever been hit in the nose? I can promise you it hurts. I hold my hand to my face to see if there's any blood.

"Shit, Becca, are you okay?" Jake asks, coming over and touching my arm.

Ryan's behind him. "Becca, I'm sorry. I didn't mean—"

"Shut up," I snap at Ryan as I shrug Jake off me. "I'm fine." I feel anything but fine. *Thanks, Ryan, once again you've made me look like a total idiot.*

"Becca?" Ryan says. I won't even look at him. He just

let me get smacked in the face. On purpose. In front of everyone.

This is too much. I hate him, I physically hate him. I don't care what his problem is. He shouldn't be taking it out on me.

"Just finish the game," I practically snarl.

He passes the ball over and we resume playing, but the excitement has gone from the game and everyone's watching me waiting to see what my reaction will be. Great. By the end of school, everyone will know how Jessica smacked me in the face and how Ryan let her.

The bell rings and there's still no winner. I drop the ball and walk to the locker rooms without looking back. I can feel eyes on me, like my watching classmates think I'm about to go crazy, and I feel humiliated, totally, totally humiliated. He's done it to me again. Ryan Jackson has made me look like an absolute fool. Again.

───────◆───────

It's later in the day and I'm by my locker, my head still banging from the headache I've had since gym class. I'm still furious, and the curious glances and whispers that I've been getting from other students make it clear that the news of Jessica smacking me in the face has spread like wildfire.

I look up and see Ryan heading down the hallway, flanked, as always, by a couple of cronies. I slam my locker shut and stalk off in the opposite direction, ignoring him when I hear him shout my name. I'm almost at my car by the time he's caught up with me and spun me around to face him.

"What?" I demand. I'm in no mood for this.

"Look, I'm sorry about the dodgeball thing earlier," he says.

"Really? What part?" I ask sarcastically. "The part where I'm now covered in bruises thanks to your psycho girlfriend? The part where you took your shitty mood out on me? Or the part where you made me look like a complete idiot yet again?"

"I'm sorry, but you weren't even trying."

"Because you ignored me for more than half the class and only then decided to try and involve me!"

"Well you wouldn't listen to me!" he shouts back.

"I don't give a shit, Ryan," I say and turn to walk away, but he grabs my arm and turns me around, not letting me leave.

"She's not my girlfriend."

"Yeah, well you might want to tell her that because I'm pretty sure she thinks that she is. Nice choice Ryan, you picked a real gem there."

"You think she was jealous?"

"What? No. Of course not. Why would she be jealous of me? She was pissed off with your little act back there. And she's not the only one."

"What act?"

"Picking me up! What the hell was that about?"

"You wouldn't move!" he shouts back.

"And what was the other thing? Oh yeah, kissing my

bruise better?"

He has the good grace to at least look away when I say this. "That was a joke."

"Yeah, at my expense, as usual. Just something else for you and your friends to laugh about."

"What is your problem with my friends? You don't even know them. John told me he's tried talking to you in class a couple of times after we were all at my house that time and he couldn't get two words out of you. And, for some reason, Katie really likes you, but you can barely smile at her."

"I don't need the popular parade taking pity on me."

"Taking pity on you?" he scoffs. "You've got such a chip on your shoulder, Becca, you know that? You decide something and then that's it, there's no changing it."

"Stop acting like you know me!" I shout.

"I do know you, Becca," he throws back.

"Is that why you decided to teach me a lesson today then? Pull me down a peg or two, because of that chip on my shoulder?" I ask.

"You are so damn stubborn. If I'd been anyone else you'd have listened to me out there and made an effort."

"Oh get over yourself, Ryan. You don't have that much influence over me."

He looks away, jaw clenched like he's trying to decide something. A minute passes and he turns back to me. "You didn't come to my game."

My jaw falls open. *This is what he's mad about? You have got to be kidding me.*

"Grow up, Ryan! Half the school went to your stupid

little game. You got your precious record, and then went to the party afterward and banged one of the hottest girls at school. Boohoo for you," I say spitefully. I don't care how bitchy I sound, how dare he humiliate me and let me get hurt just because there wasn't one more face in the crowd at his moment of glory.

He clenches his fists like he's trying to control himself; I can see a vein throbbing in his temple. He's really mad at me now, but I don't care; I'm mad too. "Thanks to you and that skank that you're not dating, I've had the worst headache all day. So, well done. I've been suitably punished for not bowing down to the great Ryan Jackson. Now leave me the hell alone!" I shout furiously.

I turn to walk away again, but he reaches out and rests his hand on my left hipbone, his thumb gently brushing the bare skin in between the top of my jeans and the bottom of my T-shirt.

I freeze. *What is he doing?* That's way too intimate a place to be touching me. He notices my reaction and glances down at his hand like he didn't realize he'd done it. He immediately drops his hand and looks away.

"I'm sorry you got hurt," he says quietly.

What? Now I feel all flustered and don't know what I'm doing. Oh right, we're fighting.

"I don't care, Ryan. I don't care about any of it," I declare after a pause.

"Yeah, it really sounds like it," he says sarcastically.

I shoot him one last venomous look and turn around to see several students standing in the parking lot gawking at us. Brilliant. Now they'll have that to gossip about too. I hurry back across the parking lot and get into my car. I'm so angry my hands are shaking and I feel dangerously close to tears.

I'm mostly mad at myself, though. I'd started to let him back in, started actually talking to him, not just ignoring him. Started thinking that maybe we could be civil to each other again and maybe one day be friends. I'm an idiot. A complete and utter idiot.

CHAPTER 21

ANY HOPE I HAD OF MINE AND RYAN'S FIGHT not being public knowledge is quashed the second I walk into the cafeteria the next day. I swear the room goes silent, and then as a whole it's as if they look at me and then over to Ryan's table, where he's sitting next to Jessica, who's grinning smugly at me with her arm around his shoulder.

God, she's pathetic. Like I care.

I mean, I'm sure there are some people who couldn't care less, but it definitely doesn't feel like it at that moment. I try to toughen it out and join my table, but I'm in a foul mood and after several attempts by the girls to get me to join in the conversation, they eventually give up. And even though I can tell Erica's desperate to ask about Ryan, the thunderous look I give her warns her off. I only glance up once and, of course, there Ryan is, glaring straight over at me, making it so obvious that his whole table is aware and gawking too. I feel like I'm in a fishbowl and give up. I'm not having this. I leave my untouched tray of food on the table, grab my bag and leave without a word, trying to pretend I don't notice the hush that falls over the room. They probably think I'm going to go crazy and start a fight or something. I guess this is what happens when you fight with the prom king and queen. I haven't been back to the cafeteria this week.

I'm still thinking about this later that week when I pull up outside Jay's house to collect him for my mom. I beep my horn, expecting him to run right out as usual, but there's no sign of him. Awesome. He's probably doing this on purpose and is in one of his brattish moods. I climb out of the car, slamming the door behind me and make my way up the path to the front door. It's only when I've rang the doorbell I realize the driveway is unusually full of cars. I turn back to the door confused and ring the bell again, but I still don't get an answer.

I try the doorknob and it's open. "Hello?" I call.

I step into the house and I'm instantly met with the smell of smoke and is that…marijuana? I make my way down the hallway, calling out to Jay and my aunt. I head toward the kitchen, as I can hear music blasting from that direction. I swing open the door to the kitchen and stop dead.

My aunt is at the kitchen table laughing manically at something one of the three men who are also at the table has said. The table is strewn with beer and empty liquor bottles and there's a haze of smoke hanging over them. The blinds of the room are closed so the whole room is bathed in darkness with the only light coming from a lamp in the corner.

There's aggressive rock music that I don't recognize blasting from the iPod dock.

My aunt looks up and sees me. "Becca!" she shouts loudly.

She jumps up and staggers drunkenly to greet me and tries to throw her arms around me. I let her hug me but actually duck my head back to avoid her breath. She's clearly been drinking for hours. I have no idea who the men are. They're all my aunt's age or older, and from the looks of them, she met them in one of the dive bars she's been hanging out in. They're all covered in tattoos, dressed in scruffy jeans and t-shirts and all look creepy as hell.

Aunt Ruth pulls me over to the table. "This is my niece," she announces.

They look at me with interest, and I can feel their eyes raking up and down my body as I try not to shudder.

My aunt grabs a used glass next to her and tips some whiskey into it before shoving it into my hands. "Here, have a drink!" I look down in surprise at my hands. My mother would flip if she knew my aunt was offering me alcohol.

What is going on? I feel like I've entered a parallel universe. This is not the aunt I know. I know she's been going through a hard time recently, but I had no idea she was drinking to this extent and mixing with these men who are clearly using her for the drinks in her cabinet and whatever else they can get.

"We're about to play strip poker." Oh God, I've got to get out of here. My mom's obviously messed up and Jay's not here.

"Yeah, sugar, take a seat," one of the men leers at me. I glance at him in disgust; he looks older than my dad. I cannot believe these are the kind of people my aunt is mixing with.

"Actually, I'm gonna go," I say to my Aunt. "I thought I was picking Jay up, but I obviously got the wrong day or something."

"Jay's upstairs," my aunt says nonchalantly and I feel sick. Jay is in the same house as all these men while they're drinking like fishes and getting high? And she was just talking about strip poker! What if Jay walked into that? The aunt I know would never, ever do that. She would never put Jay in a situation like this.

"Oh, so should I just grab him, then? Take him back to my house?" I ask, trying hard to keep my voice upbeat and normal.

My aunt shrugs and goes to the kitchen door. "Jay!" she screams at the top of her lungs. "Jay, come down here!"

I feel a hand reach out and brush my leg and I nearly jump a mile. I turn to see one of the men smirking at me and I step away from them toward the door. Jay enters, his eyes wide, looking around nervously. My aunt bends down and picks him up, something he's too big for now and kisses him sloppily on the cheek. Jay doesn't pull away from her, he doesn't move a muscle and lets her do what she wants. I feel my heart starting to beat faster in my chest. I need to get him out of here.

"Hi, Jay," I say, plastering a smile on my face, trying to act like this isn't a horrible situation. "You ready to go?"

He nods slightly, his eyes still wide as my aunt puts him down. She turns and whirls on me. "Why are you here, anyway? Why have you come to get Jay?"

"Mom said she was watching him tonight? I came to get him for her."

Her eyes narrow and she staggers toward me, pulling Jay along by the arm behind her. "Oh did she now? Well isn't my dear sister just so sweet? Always interfering. Sarah is always butting in," she rants. She goes over to the table and picks up her drink, downing it in one gulp. "Well, Jay's my son, not hers, Becca! Did you know that? You tell her that Jay's mine and she cannot keep taking him."

She plops down in her seat and one of the men starts dealing out playing cards while another swigs directly from a bottle of whiskey. She reaches for Jay and pulls him into her lap. He stares at me the whole time, his lips trembling as he tries to stay brave and not cry.

"You don't want to go over to Becca's and see my stupid sister, do you, Jay?" she asks him, hugging him tightly. He looks at his mom and then back to me. I think I can see tears starting to form in his eyes but he blinks rapidly to stop them from falling and shakes his head solemnly at me. I nod, trying to keep calm. I don't know what the best thing to do is. I can't leave him here in this environment, but my aunt does not seem to be in the mood to let him go and I don't want to infuriate her any further.

"Okay, no problem. I'll just go home then," I say. "Can I just give Jay a present first that I got for him?"

She nods and lets Jay down from her lap. He's standing

next to me in seconds, his little body shaking. I can't imagine how terrifying this must be for him, seeing his mom like this. I kneel down beside him and dig around in my bag, pulling out a bag of candy (leftover from the haul Ryan got me), as though that's his gift. "I'm going to come back okay, Jay?" I whisper to him. "I'm just gonna go and get my parents, and they'll come back and look after your mom and get rid of these men. Is that okay?"

He nods back at me, his mouth plastered together in a thin line, trying to stop his lips from trembling.

I plaster a huge smile on my face and give him a quick hug. "Okay. Bye, Aunt Ruth," I call from the door before quickly exiting the house.

I race to my car and jump in, put it in reverse and start driving home as fast as I can. I reach for my phone and dial my mom, but she doesn't answer. I dial my dad instead, but the office secretary tells me he's in a meeting off site and didn't want to be interrupted. I hang up on her before she can continue and call his cell instead; still no answer. I screech around a corner and pray that there are no cops around as I race back to my house. I pull up outside my house and sigh in relief when I see my mom's car in the drive.

I race into the house, leaving my stuff in the car. In my haste, I don't even bother to close the car door. I have this horrible feeling that something bad will happen if I don't get Jay out of that house and get my aunt some help. I don't know what those men are capable of and I don't think she's safe.

"Mom!" I call as loudly as I can, trying desperately not

to panic as I'm scared it will slow me down.

There's no answer and I run through the house, checking every room. When I can't find her, I rush upstairs thinking she's maybe in her bedroom, but that too is empty. "Mom!" I call again, running back downstairs and into the kitchen.

My phone's still in my hand, but when I try her again, her cell starts ringing from its place on the counter behind me.

"Shit." Where could she be? I look out into the garden, hoping she's maybe out there, then I realize there's only one place she'd be nearby without her car. *Ryan's house.*

I take off out of the house and run to Ryan's, hammering loudly on the front door. No one answers so I start banging on the door again, so hard I think I'll probably have a bruise tomorrow. The door swings open and I nearly fall into the house but reach out and grab the frame just in time.

Ryan stares back at me, his arms laden with chips and soda. He raises his eyebrows in surprise.

"I really need to speak to my mom," I tell him urgently, already edging into the house. "Is she here?"

He nods and tells me she's in the backyard. I rush through his house, nearly tripping over the rug in the hallway in my urgency to get to the backyard.

"Mom!" I shout when I see her and she turns in surprise at my voice. I quickly tell her everything that happened at the house and she pales. She turns to Kathy Jackson, and they both instantly rush into the house, grabbing keys and purses. My mom's already on the phone and by the sounds of it she's managed to get hold of my dad and is arranging to meet him at Aunt Ruth's house. I follow them through the house, but my mom stops and turns to me. "I don't want you coming with us, Becca," she tells me.

"No, I'm coming," I protest, but she shakes her head in response. "Mom, please!" I beg her. "I'll follow you in my car and I can bring Jay back. You'll have to stay with Aunt Ruth, but I can get him out of there and out of the way." She pauses and I can see her brain ticking over, weighing up the risk to me.

"Okay, but you don't get out of the car, okay? You wait for him in the car, and then you get out of there." I nod in agreement and follow them to the door but come to an abrupt halt when Ryan reaches out and grabs me.

"I'll come with you," he tells me and I realize he must have heard our conversation.

I shake my head at him. "No, no it's fine."

"I'm coming, Becca," he states while I shake my head, eager to get away and not waste time. I move toward the door, but he doesn't let go of my arm.

"Ryan!" I hear a female voice call from downstairs and realize he must have company in his den.

He groans in annoyance. "It's fine. She can stay here."

"No, Ryan. We don't need your help. Stay here."

"You might need a guy there. To help if things get rough."

I gulp at the thought of something like that happening and then shake my head. "No, my dad will be there and if I need anyone, I'll call Charlie."

I turn to leave again, twisting out of his grasp but he

grabs me again stopping me from leaving. "What can I do? How can I help you?"

I glance at the stairs that lead to his den. "Don't tell them," I say. "Don't tell whoever's down there about my aunt, okay?"

He reels back like I've slapped him. "I would never do that to you. Is that what you really think of me?" He shakes his head at me in disbelief. "I would never do anything to intentionally hurt you." If I'm completely honest, I know he wouldn't do that to me, but I don't have time to feel bad and turn and run out of the house.

By the time I reach my aunt's house, my dad is there and the relief I feel is instant. Kathy Jackson is standing to the side of the gate, her hand on Jay's shoulder. When I pull over, she gently pushes him in my direction and he runs up to the car and jumps in the back seat. I pull away instantly and turn the car around, ready to head home. I look in the rear mirror to check on him, desperate to offer him some sort of comfort. It's only then that he turns to me and I see that he has tears pouring down his face, but he doesn't utter a word.

CHAPTER 22

"**H**EY."

I look up to see Ryan standing in the doorway. I'm in the art room sketching some pictures and trying to forget about the mess from last night and Jay's silent tears. The only remotely positive thing about last night is that I now couldn't give a shit about the fact that I'm still being whispered about over my fight with Ryan four days later. I turn back to my sketches as he makes his way over and sits down next to me.

"How are you?" he asks. I know he's referring to last night. There's no point in pretending he didn't see that drama and his mom's probably told him all about it.

"I'm okay," I tell him, not looking up.

"I came over to your house last night to check on you, but you were already in bed," he tells me. I do look up at him now. He didn't have to do that and when his eyes find mine, I don't see anything except concern in them.

"Jay's going to stay with us for a while," I tell him. "My

parents took Aunt Ruth to rehab today."

He nods and I sigh loudly, raking my hands through my hair and rub my eyes. I feel so drained today. I can't believe I didn't know how bad it had gotten. The signs were all there. I know my mom's been worried sick and I know Jay's been acting up, but I've been so wrapped up in myself I didn't know how bad she'd gotten.

"She's not a bad person, you know?" I tell him. "When I was little, she used to read to me all the time and take me to the beach and play with me the whole time. She had so much time for me." It's so upsetting seeing her like this. She's so different from the loving, caring aunt of my childhood.

"I know that, Becca." And I guess he does. I forgot that he knew Aunt Ruth too. For all I know she's been over at his house when his parents have thrown parties or barbecues. "Sometimes people just go through shit times, but she can get better now. She'll get help."

I nod and manage a small smile. I know he's right; I just wish it hadn't come to this.

"Is this where you've been during lunch all week?" he asks.

I nod.

"Why have you been avoiding the cafeteria?"

I roll my eyes. After last night, I don't really care about my fight with Ryan anymore, but he can't be so dumb as to not notice all the gossip that's been going on since his girlfriend threw a ball in my face.

"Over our fight after dodgeball?" he persists.

"Yes!" He's clearly not going to let this go so I might as

well tell him why I was mad. "You purposely let me get hit in the face just because you were pissed."

He lets out a long sigh. "I really am sorry about that."

I put my pencil down and look over at him.

"It was stupid. Everything just got out of hand, and I'm sorry you got hurt."

"Fine. Whatever."

"Please, Becca. I would never, ever intentionally want you to get hurt."

"Well, it didn't seem like it. You were blocking me and then deliberately moved." I don't mention the part where I insulted him, maybe I shouldn't have done that, but it's not an excuse to let me get physically hurt. "I just don't get it."

"I don't know. I just…" He sighs. "I was in a bad mood and I took it out on you."

"Yeah, you don't say," I say sarcastically. "I'm sorry I didn't come to your game, but I didn't think it was that big of a deal."

"I just…I dunno…" he trails off looking away from me.

"It's fine, I'm over it," I tell him. "Just next time you decide to teach me a lesson, could you do it in private? It's not much fun having the whole school talk about you."

"What do you mean talk about you?"

"Oh come on, Ryan, you know how it works. Anything involving you is big business in this stupid school. The fact that the head cheerleader smacked me in the face with a ball over you was bound to get out. Everyone's been gawking at me all week."

"I don't think she meant to do that."

"Oh, she meant it. She has it pretty bad for you. Obviously she didn't like it that we were on the same team or whatever." I pause. "I blame Jake."

He smiles at this. "Is that why you're skipping lunch? To avoid everyone?"

"No." I pause. "Yes."

Ryan smiles. "Well, if it helps, Mason got caught in a cleaning closet with Julia Simpson just after first period, so I'm pretty sure you'll be forgotten about by now."

"Really?"

He nods. I allow a small smile and go back to my drawing. "It all seems pretty pointless, anyway. After what happened yesterday. Bigger things to think about, you know?"

He nods in agreement. "What are you doing now?"

"Nothing. Have math after lunch."

"Wanna skip?"

My head turns to him. Did he actually just suggest we ditch school? Together? "What?"

"Come on, let me make it up to you, and it'll take your mind off of your aunt."

"You wanna skip together?" I ask.

"Yes. Come on, it's not that weird of a suggestion."

I tilt my head to the side, studying his face. "Just the two of us?"

"Go on, I dare you," he challenges me, his eyes twinkling.

"Um…" I genuinely don't know what to say. I mean, I'd actually really like to ditch for the afternoon, but with Ryan? What on earth would we talk about? I know we've been around each other a lot more recently, but that's more down to circumstance than choice.

"Let me prove I'm not the total asshole you think I am."

His tone is playful, but I can see genuine hope in his eyes and a whole lot of uncertainty. He actually wants to chill together. I guess he has been there for me recently if you ignore the whole dodgeball incident. Maybe we could give this friend thing a shot. I start to nod without realizing it. His eyes widen in surprise that I'm actually agreeing and he smiles. He stands up and I follow him out of the classroom.

We're lying out on the beach, using our bags as pillows and staring up at the sky. I've actually had a really good afternoon. Ryan drove us an hour down the coast and we had lunch at this great seafood shack. He's been making me laugh like we used to back when we were kids, and I feel a lot better about Aunt Ruth and Jay now. He's right. Rehab is the best place for her, and if it weren't for last night, she wouldn't be there now. Now I'm lying out, the winter sun is warm on our skin, and I'm so relaxed I'm close to falling asleep.

"Becca?"

"Sssh, I'm sleeping," I mumble.

"What are you gonna do next year?" he asks.

I turn my head to look at him. "You mean after we graduate?" He nods. "Dunno. College, I guess. Maybe travel for a year first."

"Will you major in art?"

I shrug. "I don't know yet. My dad doesn't want me to limit my options." I chuckle. "I think he's still living in hope that I'll ace my exams and get into Harvard."

Ryan grins at me.

"What about you?"" I ask. I turn over so that I'm on my front, leaning up on my elbows.

"I'm thinking I'll stay in Cali. Well, probably."

"Are you getting a football scholarship?"

He nods and rolls over onto his elbows too, matching my stance. "Yeah, I've had a couple of offers. Just need to decide where."

"Why'd you pick football?" I ask him. I've wondered what made him pick football over basketball ever since my mom told me he was dropping it to focus on football when we went into junior year. "I never got it. You always preferred basketball." He looks at me in surprise and then slowly a wide smile stretches across his mouth, lighting up his whole face. "What?" I ask. He shakes his head, but his smile doesn't budge. "What?" I demand again.

He shrugs. "Nothing, it's just, you spend your whole time acting like you don't know me at all, like we weren't inseparable for the first 12 years of our lives. . .it's nice to know you've thought about me at least in passing over the last five years."

Oh. I turn away and look back out at the ocean. I don't know how to respond. He's right, I do act like we don't know each other, but that was always down to him thinking he was too good for me, at least that's what I always thought. Lately, though, I'm not so sure.

"Sorry," he says and I turn back to face him. He's still looking at me. "I know you don't like talking about before. I shouldn't have mentioned it. I picked football because I'm too short to make it in basketball." I raise me eyebrows in disbelief, the dude's six foot two. Hardly on the short side. "I've got more chance of making it in football."

"Making it?" He's letting me off the hook and I'm grateful. I'd much rather talk about football than drag up the past again. "Like as a professional?"

He shrugs. "Someone has to."

My jaw gapes open. I'd heard he was good but still. "Like to the NFL?"

He laughs at the expression on my face. "You know I'm all state, right?"

"You know I don't know what that means, right?"

He shakes his head, his eyes twinkling. "It means I do okay."

Wow. I had no idea he was aiming so high. But then why would I? I lean toward him and nudge him with my shoulder, something that I wouldn't have dreamt of doing only a couple of weeks ago but now feels totally natural. "Well, remember your old neighbor when you're an NFL superstar."

His eyes find mine and his gaze is so intense I daren't look away. "You really think that's all you are to me? My neighbor?" My mouth opens, but no words come out. He turns to look back out to the ocean. "I'm not likely to ever forget you, Becca."

I clear my throat wondering how it went from relaxed

and comfortable to awkward and tense in about two seconds flat.

"It'll be weird, us not going to the same school, won't
it?" He says suddenly. His tone is lighter and I'm relieved
he's changing the subject. "I mean, we've been at the same
school forever."

I shrug. That's true, we have always been at the same
school since kindergarten, but it's not as if we're friendly
anymore and talk to each other every day or anything. I
wouldn't say it would be weird.

"Are you nervous?" I ask.

He looks at me in surprise. "About college? No, why?"

"I dunno, you just, you know, have it all wrapped up at
MacAllister. Everyone knows you, you can do whatever you
want. I just thought you might be sad to leave it."

"You think I can't survive past high school?"

"Oh come on, Ryan. You know what I mean. You can do
what you want at our school. All the guys have your back,
you can get any girl you want."

He looks out to sea. "Not any girl."

I shrug. I'm not about to start feeding his ego. He knows
the effect he has on the girls at school; he doesn't need it
clarified.

"You know that's all bullshit, don't you?" he asks suddenly.

"What?"

"Popularity or whatever it is that you mean."

"Oh, I'm aware it's bullshit, Ryan. It's just the rest of the
school that seems to care," I say bitterly.

"I'll miss a lot of the guys, but we'll keep in touch, and I think Jake might end up in Cali too."

"You mean you'll still have to deal with Kevin Wilson next year?" I tease.

"Becca, I haven't spoken to Kevin since that day he grabbed you. He's an asshole."

I look at him in surprise. I mean, I know he's an ass, but I thought he and Ryan were friends. Now that I come to think of it, I don't think I've seen them together recently, not that I pay that much attention, but he hasn't been around my locker, or when I saw them at Sal's.

I look around and notice a couple of college age guys looking over at Ryan. I'd seen them looking earlier too. I nod in their direction. "Do you know those guys?" I ask. "They keep looking over."

Ryan turns to look and the guys immediately look away. Ryan smirks. "They're not looking at me, Becca."

I screw my face up, confused. He sighs and rolls his eyes.

"They're looking at you because they think you're hot."

Wait, what? I look over at the guys and they're looking at us again. One of them smiles at me.

Ryan chuckles. "You really don't see it, do you? Look, Kevin Wilson didn't just know who you are because I joke around. He knows who you are because he thinks you're hot. Most of the guys on the team are perfectly aware of who you are. Trust me." My jaw falls open. This is sounding seriously close to Ryan paying me a compliment. I'm almost expecting him to follow it up with an insult or a joke, but he doesn't. "You just don't give anyone the time of day to talk to you."

"Yeah, yeah, whatever," I mumble, suddenly embarrassed.

"That's why it's so annoying that you're with that dick when you could easily get someone else."

My head snaps around to face him, but he's still staring out into the distance.

"Are you talking about Charlie?" I ask sharply.

He looks at me. "Oh come on, Becca. He ditches you at a party when you're wasted, paws all over you in front of us to prove that you're his and won't hang out with your cousin. The guy's a jackass."

My jaw falls open in shock. "What the hell, Ryan? You know nothing about Charlie."

"I just think you can do better is all."

"Oh really? You do? Well, the day you have a successful relationship is the day you can lecture me about mine. What is your record, anyway? Two months?" I sneer.

He doesn't respond, just glares at me angrily. I'm so mad my hands are shaking. *How dare he say these things to me!* "Oh yeah, that's right," I carry on. "They don't have to be your girlfriend for you to treat them like shit, do they? Just use them for sex whenever you feel like it, then move on."

He scowls. "You don't know what you're talking about."

"Oh no? Then why don't you call up Jessica Murphy and ask her how she feels about you, huh? I know you've been hooking up with her but only when it suits you, right? Only when you're bored or at a loose end?" Wow. I *must* be mad if I'm sticking up for Jessica Murphy.

"Shut up, Becca."

"No, you shut up, Ryan! Jesus, you have a go at Charlie for leaving me for a gig at a party and kissing his girlfriend in front of a few people when all you do it treat girls like crap."

I stand up and haul my bag up off the ground, sand flying everywhere.

"You are so self-absorbed, Becca!" he explodes angrily, standing up to face me. "You can't even see what's right in front of you. You can't see anything past Charlie. Do you know how annoying that is? I'm trying to help you!"

"I don't need your help. Charlie and I are fine and even if we weren't, it's none of your damn business."

I turn and start storming away from him as fast as I can, shouting over my shoulder that I'll find my own way home. I'm so angry I reach the sidewalk in record time. Where the hell does he get off saying that stuff to me? Why did he have to do that? I should never have gone with him today. I knew better and I still let him talk me into it. And then he went and ruined it.

Again.

I'm so annoyed with him I could hit him, but I'm annoyed at myself too. It was stupid to think we could be friends again. Stupid to think he could behave like an actual decent human being. And what's really, really annoyed me more than anything else, is realizing that he still has the power to upset me. I still care enough to be upset.

CHAPTER 23

'M IN A BOOTH AT SAL'S WITH CHARLIE, SAM, AND Chris. I personally didn't want to come to Sal's, it's too much of a MacAllister hang out for my liking, and since I'm trying to avoid all the idiots in my school I wanted to go somewhere else, but Chris insisted it's the best pizza in town. So here we are.

I can't help but grin as Sam laughs at some joke that Chris just cracked. She looks so happy. Sam's always been an amazing friend to me. Ever since she sat with me that lunchtime in middle school after Ryan ditched me, she's always been there for me one hundred percent. We've never come right out and said that we're BFF's, we never sat down for that discussion, but she's definitely my best friend, and I don't know what I'd do without her.

She laughs again at something Chris has said, louder this time and she looks over at me to see my reaction. I positively beam at her. She's so happy, so carefree. It wasn't always the case.

Just before Christmas in our junior year, I had walked out of Spanish class after last period one day to see Ryan Jackson leaning against the lockers across from the classroom. I didn't even bother acknowledging him as he pushed himself away from the lockers and moved toward me as I walked down the hall. "Becca," I had carried on walking, ignoring him, thinking that he probably just wanted to send an insult my way. "Becca." He reached out and grabbed my arm pulling me around.

"What?" I demanded, annoyed.

"It's Sam. You need to come with me."

I followed him down the hall, out a side entrance and across the back school fields. We were walking further and further away from the school, down toward the end of the premises toward some sheds where they stored equipment for sports. I was starting to worry. Sam hadn't been herself for a couple of weeks; she was much quieter than usual and had seemed really preoccupied. When I tried to talk to her about it, she'd just dismissed it and disappeared. She'd been skipping lunch and I really hadn't seen her much. Whenever I tried to make plans, she said she was too busy studying.

As we turned the corner by the last shed, I saw a couple of Ryan's friends standing there looking behind them. When I walked past them, I saw Sam sitting on the ground further down, leaning against the wall and curled up in the fetal position. Jake stood awkwardly next to her, touching her shoulder. She was crying uncontrollably.

"Shit," I muttered, dropping my bag and running over to her. I tapped her on the shoulder and when she saw it was me, she started to cry harder. I had sunk down next to her, wrapped my arms around her and pulled her into a hug, letting her get it all out.

I remember being scared. This wasn't like Sam. She was so levelheaded and so calm; something terrible must have happened. I was almost too scared to ask. I tried to calm her down, telling her it was okay and that everything was alright, but she couldn't stop crying.

I looked up and saw Ryan and his friends standing further away, watching us.

"Go away," I snapped. The last thing Sam needed was an audience and with this crowd, Sam's meltdown would be all over the school within an hour. "There's nothing to see. She's fine. Totally fine."

I turned back to Sam and when I looked up again, they'd all left.

"What happened?" I asked her when she seemed to be calming down. There were still tears, but she had her breathing under control now.

"I can't do it, Becca," she whispered. "I can't do it."

"Do what?"

She had reached for her bag and pulled out a few pieces of paper. It was an algebra test. There was a C grade scrawled across the top in red pen.

I got it.

Sam is incredibly intelligent. As in top of our class intelligent and will probably be valedictorian. Her parents are both highly successful. Her mom is a top surgeon at the local hospital and her dad is a professor of literature at Berkeley.

Her oldest brother was valedictorian and got into Harvard and is going on to study at medical school. Her other brother was also valedictorian and got into Georgetown, and he's planning on attending law school after he graduates. Sam is fully expected to be at the top of our class, get into one of the country's top universities, then graduate with a brilliant career ahead of her.

The pressure was immense.

Our SAT's were coming up and I knew that she'd been hammering the books. Turns out, it was much worse than I thought. She'd been studying until two in the morning every night and getting up at five to get in a couple of hours before the start of school. She was physically and mentally exhausted. She had to ace the SAT's, she had to make her parents proud and when she got that C grade, it sent her over the edge. She couldn't cope with the pressure. God, no one could. She just wanted to please her family and make them proud but the expectation on her was huge.

"This doesn't mean anything, Sam. You've got this, okay? Sam? You are going to be okay."

She took a deep breath and nodded at me. I looked around, trying to figure out what the best thing to do was. Sam needed to get out of here and she needed to talk to someone about the pressure she was under and how she was feeling. Unfortunately, that day I didn't have my car, and Sam wasn't in a good enough state to drive herself. I wasn't sure how I was going to get her home.

I helped her stand and wrapped my arm around her, letting her lean on me for support. She was so exhausted it was an effort for her to even walk. We walked around the corner of the shed to head back toward school and standing there was Jake and Ryan. They hadn't left with the others.

I turned to Jake. "Can you give us a ride?" I asked him, ignoring Ryan as usual. "I don't have my car and need to get her home."

He nodded and turned to walk toward the parking lot. We followed him, but then I turned back to Ryan, who was watching us leave. I left Sam to follow Jake and moved toward Ryan.

"Who saw her? Who was with you when you found her?" I didn't even want to know what they'd been doing all the way down here.

"Me, Jake, Mason and John. Bianca and Katie." I nodded. "Sadie Whitaker, too." I screwed my face up at that. "She's a sophomore," he explained.

"Right. I need to go find them then. You can't tell anyone about this, okay? She doesn't need everyone gossiping about her, Ryan, not right now. Don't tell anyone and I'll go tell everyone else."

I turned to walk away and he'd held out his arm to stop me.

"I'll tell them. No one will say anything. I promise." When I turned back to look at him, he looked deadly serious. I nodded, thinking I really should be with Sam rather than tracking down potential gossips and turned to leave, but he grabbed my arm again. "Is she okay?" he asked with genuine concern in his eyes.

I shrugged. "She will be."

Sam was okay. We went home, and when her mom saw the sort of state she was in, she was devastated and assured Sam that she didn't care what score she got or which college she went to as long as Sam was happy. Then she arranged for Sam to go see a doctor and she started going to counseling for a couple of weeks to get her anxiety under control. She took a week off school and when she came back, she was more like her old self.

Ryan was true to his word and no one ever found out about her meltdown, and if they did, they never said anything about it to Sam. And I would know as I double checked with her a couple of times. In fact, Sam said Ryan was great when she got back to school. He got her notes from all the classes she'd missed, even the ones he wasn't in, and he made it clear to her that no one would ever mention what had happened. They were in the same homeroom so they saw each other once a day. I had been a bit annoyed, to be honest. I'd planned on doing that for Sam, but he'd beaten me to it.

After that, they were friendlier, exchanging greetings when they passed in the hall and pausing for small talk every now and again. I, of course, kept on ignoring him whenever she spoke to him when I was there. I was annoyed that he was encroaching on my life. Sam was my friend, not his. But even I couldn't ignore that he'd been good to her and kept his word about keeping her out of our school's pathetic gossip system.

I suppose I was grateful that he came and found me to help her rather than going to a teacher or to one of the guidance counselors. I briefly wondered how he'd known which class I would be in when he was looking for me and decided it must have been coincidence and he had gotten lucky.

Shortly afterward, Sam met Chris, and he's great for her. At first, she wasn't interested, thinking she had too much school work to deal with to date, but he wouldn't take no for an answer and pursued her until she eventually gave in and agreed to a date. They've been together ever since. He's so laid back and carefree and he brings that out in Sam. He really cares about her and anyone with a brain can see that they adore each other. He's a really good caring guy, and I honestly think they might go the distance as a couple. I hope so. They're the best couple I know.

Chris, Sam, and Charlie all start laughing at something and this pulls me out of my daze. Charlie, noticing that I've not been paying attention, playfully reaches out and wraps his hand around the hair from my ponytail and tugs me over to him, planting a sloppy kiss on the side of my head. I laugh at this, but when I glance up, my expression changes when I notice Katie Thompson has walked in followed by her boyfriend John, then Mason, Jake, and Bianca.

I turn back to Charlie, knowing that we're sitting at the back of the restaurant so they probably won't notice us.

"Hey, guys!" Katie Thompson is standing next to our table. She grins down at us and then slides into the space next to Charlie. Unfortunately, we're at one of the massive booths so there is space for them to join us. "I'm Katie," she introduces herself to Charlie and Chris, "one of Becca and Sam's friends from school."

I cock an eyebrow at Sam who smirks back at me. Friend is definitely an exaggeration. I mean, she's been nothing but nice to me since I hung out with her at Ryan's house, but I wouldn't say we were friends. Charlie turns and smiles at her, not looking at all bothered that she's squeezed in next to him. I can't really blame him. Katie's gorgeous.

Chris smiles at her too, then when he turns around, his grin gets bigger as he notices the guys and he jumps up to greet them, looking genuinely happy to see them. My eyes flash to Sam in surprise. I had no idea he knew them. She just shrugs in return and mouths "Mason's party" at me. Ah, Chris went with Sam to the party at Mason's house after that football game. That makes sense then.

Katie carries on introducing everyone to Charlie and they all exchange niceties. Jake squeezes in beside me and I turn to face him, tuning out the conversation going on around me.

"Please tell me you're not here with Bianca Gallagher," I whisper to him. I know they run in the same crowd, but I'd noticed recently whenever I see that group, she's always near him. I know he'd been seeing that Zara girl from the Madison party I went to but didn't know what was happening with that. "I do not approve," I tell him. Bianca Gallagher is Jessica Murphy's number one lackey and, as far as I can tell, doesn't have a brain of her own.

He rolls his eyes at me. "Well maybe I don't approve of your boyfriend," he tells me back and I send him a dirty look. Why on earth would Jake not approve of Charlie? He's only just met him and knows next to nothing about him.

"Maybe you could have a spiritual connection and make love?" I throw back, referring to the last time I saw her in Sal's. Jake laughs at my reaction and reaches out and playfully pushes me away, palm to face. I grin at him and shove him back, but the smile is wiped from my face when I look up and see Ryan walk in holding hands with Jessica Murphy.

I immediately drop my head, hoping they won't see us, and when I look back up, they've stopped to chat with some other students from our school by the door. Of course, I'm not lucky enough that they just go and sit in a booth on their own; the fact that their best friends are currently with us means that they're immediately noticed.

"Hey, Jackson, down here!" John calls.

Ryan looks our way and I swear I see a flash of annoyance in his eyes when he sees me with his friends, which just pisses me off further. *Guess what, Ryan? I don't want to see you either.* We've managed to avoid each other since our fight at the beach. Here I was enjoying pizza and good conversation with *my* friends when his friends turn up, butt in and now bring him over too.

Ryan walks toward us and although I glare at him the whole time, he doesn't look at me once. He tugs Jessica along behind him who happily follows. They stop just behind Chris, who jumps up and greets Ryan like a long lost brother. I can't help sending a scowl in Sam's direction; she just smirks back at me. She knows I'll hate having Ryan here and doesn't even know about our latest fight. I manage to stifle a groan of annoyance at this whole situation.

"And this is Jess," Katie continues to Charlie. Apparently she's decided to be chief introducer for the group. "And that's Ryan, one of Becca's good friends. They're neighbors and grew up together. Were best friends for years, right, guys?" she continues, grinning wickedly at Ryan. I nearly choke on the sip of Coke I've just taken, and it takes Jake banging on my back and Sam shoving some water in my face to get my coughing fit under control.

I have no idea how Katie knew all that stuff, but that was definitely not the time to share. I'm pretty sure Charlie didn't appreciate that information. He didn't really care for it when I told him about the candy Ryan got for me or when I told him he watched Jay play soccer.

Ryan and Charlie barely nod at each other while Jessica glares at Katie in irritation. Charlie reaches his arm out and wraps it around my shoulder, pulling me in toward him. I happily shift in closer.

"So, should we see if we can all fit in around here?" Katie asks, looking like she's enjoying herself.

"No!" I manage to bark out. I can hear Jake snickering to himself next to me and Mason and John are grinning like idiots. I look over at Sam. Surely I'm not the only one who thinks this situation is awkward as hell? I turn to Katie. "We already ate. We'd better go."

"But we only just got here, McKenzie," Jake teases. I send him a dirty look and start fishing around under the table for my purse, eager to get the check and get away from this awkwardness. I glance over at Ryan, and he looks annoyed just to be standing near us.

"What do you guys want to do now?" I ask Sam and

Chris. We'd all planned to hang out together all afternoon.

"Hey, Becca," Charlie interrupts me, not taking his eyes off Ryan. "You've got Jay tomorrow, right? Why don't we take him to go see a movie?"

Surprise crosses my face followed by a smile. "Sure, great," I agree.

I turn to Ryan smugly. *See, Ryan? Charlie does want to hang out with my cousin.* I don't particularly care that he's just doing it to annoy Ryan because he knows he spends time with Jay. He's doing it; that's all that matters. I resist the urge to flip Ryan the finger while he stands there with his jaw clenched, staring at the ground. It looks like smoke is about to blow out of his ears.

I nudge Jake out of the way to stand up, surrendering the booth to them. "You guys want to come back to my house?" I ask Sam and Chris.

"Actually, Becca," Charlie interrupts me again. "You should just come back to mine. My parents are out for the night. No interruptions." I freeze. Did he actually just insinuate to everyone here that we should go back to his house and have uninterrupted sex? How embarrassing! Maybe no one was paying attention and didn't get what he meant. I feel my face go red, but Charlie's looking at me like he's waiting for a response. I nod my head in his direction. "Okay."

Ryan lets out a noise somewhere between a growl of annoyance and a snort of disbelief and he walks away, pulling Jessica along behind him. He sits in an empty booth and somehow she ends up in his lap. She wraps her arms around him and bends her head to kiss him. I pull a face.

That doesn't look very sanitary in an eating establishment.

"Gross," I mutter under my breath as his friends stand and go to join them in the booth.

Jake walks past me as he heads to the booth. "You should cut him some slack, Becca," he says under his breath like he's annoyed with me. "Maybe he doesn't want to know, or any of us, actually, that you're going back to your boyfriends to have sex all night."

Okay, so they definitely got what Charlie was implying. I look at Jake in annoyance, unsure why he's having a go at me again. Great, now all this fighting with Ryan is affecting my friendship with Jake. Fantastic.

I pay the bill and get out of Sal's as fast as I can.

CHAPTER 24

"**B**ECCA!"

I look up from my phone distracted and find Katie Thompson in front of me. I've just finished school, taken a back exit out of the building and have rounded a corner to head to my car and am now standing face to face with Katie. I've had to park further away than usual since I was late this morning. Katie's stood directly in my path and her usual crowd is sitting at a picnic table just up from my car. Katie smiles widely at me. Jessica Murphy scowls over at me and John, Mason and a bunch of other's I've barely spoken to are also there as well. I stifle a groan of annoyance. I could do without this after that scene in Sal's the other day. My eyes flick around them, but thankfully Ryan and Jake aren't there which is a definite bonus.

"Hi," I reply and offer her a quick smile before stepping to the right to get past her.

She moves with me blocking my way. "How are you?" she asks. I frown slightly and look pointedly past her at my car. She completely ignores my not so subtle hint that I want to leave. "How was your day?"

I force myself not to sigh, remembering what Ryan said about Katie liking me and making an effort with me. He's right, she's only ever been nice to me but I don't understand why she's suddenly so friendly. "Um, yeah it was okay," I reply. There's a pause. "How was yours?" I ask awkwardly, mainly to fill the silence. I feel like everyone's watching me.

"Good, really good." She takes a step toward me and before I know it she's linked her left arm through my right and herded me over to her friends and their table. I've got to hand it to her, the girls got skills. Surprisingly the rest of her crowd all smile over at me in greeting and some even wave. Everyone except Jessica.

"So, you're coming to Jake's party, right?" she asks.

"Um, no. I can't that night."

"Seriously? You guys are like best friends and you won't come to his birthday. Why?" My mouth gapes open slightly at how direct she is before I snap it shut. What can I say? I don't want to go because I don't want to see Ryan and all of you? Something tells me that won't go down very well. Besides, Jake knows I won't go, I'll just buy him a pizza one night instead. I just kind of shrug my shoulders and look uncomfortably around. Kate nods suddenly and a small smile appears on her lips. "Because of Ryan, right?" I don't respond. "Okay, in that case…maybe we can work out something else." My eyebrows furrow in confusion at her words.

"Unbelievable!" Jessica suddenly exclaims harshly and stalks off, shooting me a filthy look over her shoulder. I scowl after her.

"What is her problem with me?" I ask confused. For God's sake, she's the one who threw a ball in my face, not the other way around.

"Oh just ignore her," Katie says dismissively. "She's just jealous."

What? "Jealous?" I ask incredulously.

Katie grins. "Yeah, you know?"

"No. What?" I ask, suddenly feeling nervous.

"Because of you and Ryan being," she pauses watching me. When I don't react, she carries on, "...such good friends."

A burst of laughter escapes from me. "Are you kidding me? We are not good friends. He annoys the shit out of me."

The guys around us chuckle and Katie nods, trying to hold back a smile. "Right, sorry."

"Seriously. I mean, we barely talk. She's crazy if she's actually jealous over that," I reiterate. This is turning into one of the most ridiculous conversations I've ever had.

"Yeah, right. I know." She glances over my shoulder. "Well, here he comes anyway."

I turn to the side and see Ryan approaching with Jake and try not to pull a face. He's glancing at Katie and his friends suspiciously. "What are you guys talking about?" he asks as soon as he reaches us.

I wait for Katie to reply, but she just stares back at him smiling.

"Just about how much we can't stand each other," I inform Ryan.

He glances over at me. This is the first time we've spoken since our fight at the beach. I mean, let's face it: we definitely didn't speak in Sal's, we just shot each other dirty looks, and I'm still annoyed at him for the way he spoke about Charlie. I don't understand him. *Was he always this interfering?*

"Oh come on, Becca, he's not that bad," Jake says, slapping Ryan on the back and coming to his defense.

"Well not compared to Adolf Hitler, he isn't," I instantly reply to chuckles from his friends.

"You guys are back to being friends again," Jake continues.

"Please," I scoff. "I'd rather go for a sleepover at Jessica Murphy's."

Ryan snickers and crosses his arms. "Yeah? Maybe you could play dodgeball again?"

My mouth falls open as I hear the laughter from his friends. I can't believe he's just brought that up again. I'm already humiliated enough over that whole incident.

"Fuck you, Ryan!"

"He wishes," someone says from behind me. I swing my head around but I have no idea who said it and they're all looking away, trying not to laugh. I immediately get nervous and have flashbacks to teen movies where the popular kids play a prank on the dork to make everyone else laugh.

Something is definitely going on here.

"I'm leaving," I announce and turn to leave, but Katie reaches out and grabs my arm. "Becca, wait." I stop with a sigh and look at her. "I've been meaning to tell you how much I love your style."

Wait. What? I glance down at my clothes. I'm wearing faded blue skinny jeans that sit low on my hips, a loose fitting white V-neck t-shirt with a hooded sweater thrown over the top. At best my style can be described as laid-back Cali casual, in reality, I grab whatever's clean in my closet.

"Thanks," I answer uncertainly taking in Katie's own outfit. She looks like she's just stepped out of a magazine. She's wearing a green low cut dress which hugs her curves perfectly and compliments her red hair and pale skin, her arms are covered in bracelets and the high heeled boots she's wearing makes her a couple of inches taller than me. The girl looks freaking beautiful. She always does.

"Anyway my cousin's wedding is coming up and I need something new. I was hoping you'd come shopping with me."

My jaw falls open in surprise. *She wants to go shopping? With me?* "Oh, um. I don't know. I'm probably not the best person to ask. . ."

"But you're the perfect person." She smiles sweetly at me. "I have a tendency to go way OTT. You can help me reel it back in." I glance at Jake in confusion. Katie has a ton of friends she can go shopping with, she definitely doesn't need me. Jake just shrugs back at me.

"Um. Maybe Jessica or Bianca could help you?" They're her best friends and I can't imagine Jessica being particularly happy about me hanging with Katie.

"No way. They're like me and I would end up getting the same old thing. I want to mix it up a bit."

"I mean, I don't really go shopping that much."

"What are you doing three weeks from Saturday?" she asks.

I stare at her blankly. Three weeks from Saturday? I don't know what I'm doing tonight. And why on earth would she want to shop with me? We do not socialize.

"Becca, three weeks from Saturday, are you free?"

"Um, I..." I can't think of anything to say and my phone starts ringing, distracting me further. I reach down to my pocket to grab it.

"Leave it," she instructs me, still waiting for an answer. *Wow, she's quite bossy.*

"I don't—" I start to say but John interrupts me. "Just agree to go, Becca." I glance over at him and he's watching Katie with amusement. "She won't give up until you do."

I turn back to Katie feeling a bit bewildered. "Please, Becca. I really need you. Pretty please?"

I sigh and shrug in defeat. "Yeah, I guess I'm free," I say.

She claps her hands in victory and flashes her perfect teeth in a blinding smile. "Great. We'll have so much fun." I nod as Jake comes and stands beside me and I notice Ryan watching us with interest. "What about in the evening? Are you free then too?"

"I guess," I reply lamely. I have no idea what I'll be doing, but something tells me once Katie has decided she wants something, she gets it.

"So you'll shop with me during the day and then hang with me that night?"

"Sure?"

A smug smile crosses her face and then she drops the

bomb she's been setting me up for. "Great, because that night I'm hosting a party at my parent's place at the beach. There's tons of space, everyone can stay over." She raises an eyebrow. "We're all going," she says waving her hand around to include everyone in the vicinity and then stopping and pointing directly at Ryan, "and now so are you."

My jaw falls open in surprise. *She tricked me!* I just stare at her speechless as Jake bursts into loud laughter next to me Katie grins triumphantly at me. She knew I'd never agree to go to a party with this crowd and conjured up that whole shopping scenario so that I wouldn't know this is what she was after. *Liking my style? I should have known!* This is the "something else" she was talking about when I said I wouldn't go to Jake's party. The last thing I want to do is hang around these people all weekend. And why the hell would she want me there?

"I don't think—I mean, I can't," I say backpedaling.

"But you just said you were free, didn't you?" Katie asks sweetly, a mischievous grin on her face. She's got me and she knows it.

I stand there in silence, trying to come up with something to say. I glance at Jake, who looks like he's about to keel over from laughing. "Shut it," I mutter at him. He throws his arm around me good-naturedly. "She's got you there, McKenzie!"

"Oh come on, Becca," Katie continues. "It'll be fun. We're not ogres. You can bring some friends if you want to. Sam's really cool and some of the other girls you eat lunch with."

I narrow my eyes at her. She doesn't know what my other friend's names are, but she's smiling at me with such genuine hope that I can't be mad at her. Apparently she really wants me to come.

"Can I bring Charlie?" I ask and I immediately hear stifled groans of annoyance from Jake next to me and some of Ryan's other friends. Katie's smile wavers just slightly.

"What?" I demand. "He's my boyfriend. He's a really nice guy."

Katie glance over at Ryan, and I immediately know what this is about.

I whirl around to face Ryan. "You better not have been talking shit about him again Ryan!" I snap angrily.

Ryan shrugs. "Bring him along. Let everyone form their own opinion on your perfect boyfriend."

"You have no right to talk about him. You don't even know him."

"Maybe he could bring his guitar and sing to us all?" he suggests mockingly.

"Stop it!"

"Just giving you my opinion, friend to friend," he says sarcastically.

"I don't care about your opinion and you are not my friend" I hiss back vehemently.

"What you getting so worked up about?" he asks smirking, trying to get a reaction out of me.

My blood boils. "YOU ARE SO ANNOYING!" I explode. "You have no right—" I stop suddenly, remembering we have an audience and glance around, embarrassed. Katie looks concerned, but most of the guys are snickering at my expense. Ryan's grinning too, knowing he's riled me up again. He's made me look stupid for his friend's amusement again. I am not going to make a public spectacle of myself. Well, at least not again.

I take a calming breath. "You know what? It's fine. You're entitled to your opinion," I say, my voice back to its normal volume.

Ryan cocks an eyebrow at me, still smirking like an idiot. "Really? That's very mature of you, McKenzie."

"Isn't it?" I reply, my voice dripping with sarcasm. I turn to leave, then face him again. "You can think whatever you want. I couldn't care less about your opinion. You're not even a blip on my radar."

Something in his eyes flashes but he doesn't reply.

"Stay out of my business, Ryan. And stay away from me," I demand.

He nods at me and holds his hands up in defeat. "Hey, no problem. Well, at least for the next couple of hours, anyway."

This stops me from moving. I look at him and the cocky look on his face tells me he knows something I don't. My curiosity gets the better of my want to storm off. "What?" I ask after a pause.

He grins, knowing he's winning whatever stupid fight we're having now. "Didn't you know? I'm coming over to your house tonight for dinner."

My eyes blaze. *He's doing what?* While it's not unusual to see his mom over at our house, and even his dad every now and again, Ryan hasn't been over in years as far as I know. "You're what?"

He raises his eyebrows, looking very pleased with himself. "Jay invited me over. I just got off the phone with your mom. I'll be there by seven."

My jaw drops open. *How dare my mother do this!* She knows how I feel about Ryan. All my good resolve about Jay immediately goes out the window. I don't care how much Jay wanted Ryan there, I'm her child.

Ryan crosses his arms, still with that damn smirk on his face, knowing he's pissed me off.

I narrow my eyes. "Fine. Have fun with my middle aged parents and five-year-old cousin. I'll be out with my perfect boyfriend." His grin falters slightly and I smile back at him sweetly. I glance around at everyone watching us silently and force an even bigger smile on my face. "Bye, everyone," I say waving.

They look between Ryan and me like they're not sure what's going to happen next. This is so embarrassing. This had better not get around school too. Katie looks like she regrets stopping me.

I spin on my heel and walk quickly away, ignoring Jake's shouts for me to hold up. I get in my car and put as much distance between them and me as I can. I have had enough. I am ignoring that entire crowd from now on, rude or not. They're up to something and I have had enough of Ryan Jackson to last me a lifetime. I reach for my phone and call Charlie.

I have some plans to make for the night.

CHAPTER 25

"**S**AM!" I CALL DOWN THE HALLWAY, SPOTTING Sam and hurrying to catch up to her. "I need your notes for English," I say as I reach her.

She furrows her eyebrows at me questioningly.

"I'm failing. I need to get my grades up. Henderson spoke to my mom and she's flipped."

"But you usually ace English."

"I know. I've been ditching a bit though and not getting homework in. I have to pull up Science too by the end of the semester. My parents are pissed."

Pissed is actually a complete understatement. I got back from Charlie's last night to my mom and dad sitting at the kitchen table waiting for me. I tried to breeze past them and go straight to bed, but they made me sit and told me in no uncertain terms that if I didn't get my grades up in both Science and English, they would ground me for the rest of senior year. No car, no phone, no Charlie, and no life. Apparently Henderson had called to tell them about my falling grade in English and he'd even gone to the school office to pull out my attendance records and had reported to my parents how many classes I'd been skipping.

My dad was furious and wouldn't listen to a word I said about senior year being a waste of time on the road to college since I'd already done the hard work with my SAT's. My mom blamed herself for being so wrapped up with Jay and Aunt Ruth and neglecting me. This suited me, thinking it might get me off the hook, but my dad dismissed that completely and said I had to take responsibility for my actions and has given me a month to get my grades up...or else. That's what he actually said. Or else. I dread to think what that means. I can't get around him like I can my mom.

Sam nods at me in understanding. "I'll bring them all in tomorrow."

We keep on walking down the hallway, stopping at her locker. Erica comes rushing over. "Where were you at lunch?" she demands in greeting.

"Library," I reply. She looks a little perplexed at this but not enough for her to stray from her theme.

"Katie Thompson came and sat with us at lunch!" she exclaims excitedly. I nearly laugh out loud. Erica needs to get over this whole popular thing.

"She did," Sam agrees smiling. "She was dining with the common people." I do start laughing at this.

Erica scowls at us, annoyed that we don't agree with the importance of Katie gracing her with her presence. "She told us about that party she's having and invited us!" Erica practically shouts. Of course she did. Sneaky.

"Before you say it, I'm not going."

"Come on, Becca, you have to go," she says, tugging on my arm like a child.

"No."

"But we can't go if you don't."

"Yeah, you can. Katie's nice, she won't care."

Erica glances over at Sam in despair who just shrugs. "She wants us to talk you into going. I kinda think we're invited only if you show up," Sam explains. I shake my head in annoyance. "Oh and Ryan also mentioned Jake's party to us. He came over too. I think he's invited most of our grade. Lunch was pretty eventful," she says smiling as Erica positively beams.

"You should have seen everyone's faces!" she tells me animatedly. "Katie and Ryan both came over at the same time. I thought Paige and Amy were gonna have heart attacks. Ryan is so hot."

I start to laugh. "You're ridiculous."

"Please, Becca," Erica begs. "I cannot miss Katie's party or Jake's. I really need to go and I really want to see Mason."

"Mason?" I ask in surprise. "I thought you were into Matthew Smithy?"

"Well, yeah, but Mason is like top five percent popular in this school."

I grin. "You really are a social climbing whore bag, you know that?"

She smirks back. "I know."

"Well, if you want to go popular, you might as well just go all out and go for Ryan."

She snorts. "Oh come on, I'm ambitious, not delusional." A sly look crosses her face. "Besides from what I've heard there's only one person—"

"Stop!" I interrupt her. "I am so sick of hearing about Ryan Jackson! I don't care who his latest hook up is."

She shrugs. "Y'know, Becca, I don't know what your problem is with him. He's actually a really nice guy."

I whirl on her. What is going on here? She's my friend, not his. She's probably only had two conversations with the guy her whole life. "You don't know him, Erica. I do." I pause, flustered. "I mean, I did." I look over at Sam. "Look you didn't go to our middle school. We were friends, okay? Best friends. We were always together, and then one day he just decided I was too much of a loser for him to be seen with and dropped me. That was it. He was this cool, popular guy now and was too good to be seen with me. Then when I was a freshman? He treated me like shit and let Billy Jameson bet on taking my virginity!"

I take a deep breath following my outburst. I can feel my neck getting warm and for some reason, I can feel tears building in my eyes. What is wrong with me? Thinking about that day back in middle school always riles me and makes me annoyed but never upset. I guess it's because it feels like I constantly have to defend myself where Ryan's concerned these days. I'm so over it.

"That's right, isn't it, Sam?" I say turning to her for clarification. She's watching me carefully, like she thinks there's more to what I'm saying.

She nods slightly in Erica's direction. "Yeah, he was a

jerk."

"Still think he's a nice guy?" I demand.

Erica is looking at me in sympathy now, which is annoying me even further. "Maybe he's changed?"

"I don't care," I insist. "I've barely spoken to him in years, and now he's everywhere I turn."

"Okay, I'll drop it. But think about this party, okay? I had no idea you were so in with that crowd. You are my key to popularity and you would be a very bad friend if you didn't help me out."

I roll my eyes in annoyance. How on earth am I her key to her popularity? I'm friends with Jake—that's it. And she already knew that, but I don't say anything else. I don't want to set her off again.

"Becca!" I turn around and try to stop from sighing when I see Jake walking toward me. I really could do without this right now. "Hey, guys," he says as he approaches.

Erica's face lights up. "Hey, Jake!" she says enthusiastically. He frowns slightly at her, clearly surprised at how happy she looks.

I sigh. "She wants to hook up with Mason," I explain. "Can you help?"

Erica looks mortified, but Jake just shrugs. "Sure, just come over next time I'm with him," he says. Erica goes from mortified to delighted and opens her mouth to say something when Jake jumps in. "I need to talk to you," he says directly to me.

Sam takes the hint and drags Erica away, leaving me with Jake.

"Unless this is about how you can help me get my grade up in Science, I don't care," I say, turning to face him.

He smiles at me. "You've been avoiding me," he states matter-of-factly.

I sigh. "It's not you," I mutter.

"You're avoiding Ryan."

I look away before turning back to him and nodding in agreement. "I don't know what it is lately, he just seems to be everywhere. I don't know why we can't go back to just not speaking like before."

"Come on, Becca. You wouldn't want that."

"He can't keep bitching about Charlie. It's not fair. It's got nothing to do with him."

"I know. I've told him. It's only because he cares."

I scoff in disbelief.

"I know he hates fighting with you, Becca."

"Well, he does a pretty good job of hiding it."

"You guys need to talk."

"No, we don't! Honestly, I need to *not* talk to him, that's what I need to do."

"You guys were so close."

"Oh for God's sake, Jake. That was years ago and you know what he did! You were there! He became too good for me. I was too much of a loser and he ditched me and let Billy Jameson bet on me."

"I've told you a million times that he had nothing to do with that."

"He still ditched me because he was too good to be seen with me."

"Tell me you don't actually believe that, Becca. From what I can see, it's always Ryan that's trying to initiate conversation with you, and I know for a fact he couldn't give a damn who sees you with him." I'm about to retaliate but realize he's actually right. Ryan is the one who talks to me lately and tries to draw me into conversation, regardless of who's there. In fact, sometimes I've even got the impression that he'd rather be talking to me than some of his other friends.

No.

I'm not going to let myself become friends with him again. I have enough friends and God knows he does. Besides, our recent arguments only prove that a friendship between us wouldn't work.

"I don't care, it's done," I tell Jake.

He sighs, frustrated. I don't mean to take it out on him, but he needs to stop acting like Ryan's personal cheerleader.

"Are you still seeing Zara?" I ask suddenly, remembering the party where he hooked up with her and desperate to talk to him about something that doesn't involve Ryan. Plus, if he's hooking up with Zara, then he's not getting with Bianca Gallagher.

He offers me a wry smile but shakes his head. "Nah. Don't think it was me that she really wanted."

I raise an eyebrow. "She hooked up with Ryan?"

"No! Becca, he'd never do that to me. I can't believe you'd even think that."

I scoff and his face goes hard. "He's a good guy, Becca. The best. Just because you choose not to see it—which is what you're doing, by the way—because you're too pig-headed to see past what you think you know."

My jaw falls open. Jake never talks to me like this.

"He's my best friend, Becca. You can't keep running him down and expect me not to say anything. I wouldn't talk about Sam like that to you." He has a point, but still, Sam's not an idiot!

We stand looking at each other awkwardly; this is the closest thing we've ever had to a fight. Jake doesn't fight with anyone.

"Zara's an idiot," I say. "And not because she likes Ryan or anything like that. Because she can't see how great you are. Anyone would be lucky to have you," I tell him. Quite the declaration at three in the afternoon, but I mean it, and it's my way of apologizing.

He grins. "What are you doing now?" he asks and I know he forgives me.

"Uh, standing in the hallway talking to you?

"Smartass. I mean do you have any plans for the next couple of hours?"

"Why?" I ask cautiously.

"Let's go to that new burger joint in town. It's supposed to be good. Even if you're pissed at my boy, you're still my friend, right?"

"Um, okay."

I'm not sure this is the best idea, but Jake and I have always been friends regardless of anyone else and he's trying to make things right between us. Besides, I'm hungry and a burger sounds good. And Charlie has band practice...again!

"Let me just swing by my locker and dump my stuff," I tell him.

"Sweet. We can see if Jackson's there and if he wants to come." This stops me in my tracks. I turn to face him. "Okay, okay I won't ask him. But promise me you'll talk to him? Clear the air?"

I'm about to reply when I look toward my locker and see Ryan standing there with some sophomore cheerleader. They're kissing. *Eww, gross.*

"Looks like he's busy." I snicker. Jake looks to where I'm indicating and annoyance crosses his face. He must not be much of a fan of the girl. He strides toward them.

"Dude, what the fuck?"

They break apart and both turn to look at Jake, who is glaring at Ryan.

"Seriously! You're making out on *her* locker. She's not *not* going to see that!"

"Shut up."

I start to laugh. "Jake, it's fine. It's not like it's the first time."

Jake continues to glare at Ryan, who stares at the floor. The cheerleader links her arm through Ryan's and moves closer to him, watching me the whole time. I almost laugh out loud. Like seriously, Ryan's such a catch any girl would find it hard not to launch themselves at him? Ryan looks distinctly uncomfortable and tries to move away, but she's not having any of it. She stays latched on. I vaguely wonder what happened to Jessica Murphy, but then again Ryan's never really stuck with one girl for too long, so that must be over.

I turn to my locker, open it, shove my books inside and turn back to Jake, who is still glaring at Ryan, who looks equally pissed. His jaw is clenched and everything. *Okay, there's definitely something going on here. Maybe they had a fight over something.*

"Ready?" I ask, already bored with the conversation. Jake nods.

Ryan looks between us. "What are you doing?"

"Going to that new burger joint in Henley. I was gonna see if you wanted to come. Wasn't expecting you to be so busy," Jake says, raising his eyebrows at Ryan, who just scowls back at him.

"Oh, he can't. We're actually just going to the mall. Right, Ryan?" The girl looks up at him, her grip tightens; there's no way she's letting him go. *Ah well, at least I won't have to listen to his shit.*

Jake is still glaring at him. "That's a shame. Just thought you might like to come to a social engagement with me. And Becca." Ryan looks like he's ready to punch Jake.

I look between them both, getting confused. "You're being weird. Come on, I'm hungry." I turn and start walking to the nearest exit. He must still be bitching at Ryan because it's a good couple of minutes before Jake catches up with me.

A couple of hours later, I'm lying on my bed obsessing over why Charlie still hasn't gotten back to me even though his practice should have finished by now and wondering whether Sam will want to do something later when my phone finally beeps. It's a number I don't recognize.

Unknown: How was the burger?

Burger? What?

Me: Who is this?

Unknown: Ryan.

Me: Jackson?

Ryan: How many other Ryan's do you know?

Dick.

Me: How'd you get this number?

Ryan: Does it matter?

Me: Are you stalking me?

Ryan: You wish.

God, he's so freaking arrogant.

Me: Seriously, how did you get this number?

Ryan: Guess.

He is so infuriating! He doesn't even need to be in my general vicinity anymore to piss me off.

Me: Did Jake give it you?

Ryan: Maybe. . .

I am going to kill Jake. I have definitely told him before not to give Ryan my number.

A few minutes pass and he messages me again.

Ryan: Would it make you more or less mad to know I've had your number in my phone for years?

Fucking Jake! I send Jake a quick message bitching at him for giving Ryan my number and then throw my phone down in irritation.

My phone beeps again.

Ryan: I can just imagine your face right now. You've probably gone all red and angry. Wish I was there to see it. . .bet you've already messaged Jake, right?

Despite myself, I let out a small smile at this. *Am I that predicable?*

Me: Shut up.

Ryan: I'm right aren't I? I know you too well, McKenzie.

I shake my head at my phone. I guess he does know me better than I thought that he did. I refuse to give him the satisfaction of agreeing, though.

Ryan: So was the burger place good?

I roll my eyes. What am I, a food blogger? If he cares that much, then he should go read a review online.

My phone beeps again. Seriously, I don't care about the stupid burger. Oh wait, this time it's Charlie.

Charlie: Wanna come over?

Hell yes, I do. I quickly sit up and get changed. It's about time he got back to me. It's only been two days since I saw him but I am definitely ready for my Charlie fix. I quickly check my reflection in the mirror and run outside to my car.

CHAPTER 26

PULL INTO THE STUDENT PARKING LOT THE NEXT DAY in a good mood. Actually, scrap that—I'm in a *great* mood. Last night with Charlie was perfect. He apologized for not being in touch much over the last couple of days and explained that he'd just been really busy with the band and everything.

Then he made it up to me. Nudge, nudge, wink, wink.

I get out of my car and another car door slams just a few spaces away. I look up and see Ryan standing by his car. He's looking over at me. "Hi."

"Hey."

I turn and start walking toward school. I hear footsteps behind me and suddenly Ryan's in front of me, blocking my route. I sigh in annoyance. I look behind him and see his friends are on the steps by the entrance looking over at us, probably waiting for round seven or whatever we're on now.

"I'm sorry," he tells me. This does surprise me. "I'll stop talking about Charlie. You're right, I don't know him and if you like him, then he must be doing something right." I raise an eyebrow and he grins at me. "You know, since you don't like anybody."

I allow a small smile and we stand there awkwardly, neither of us speaking. I start to move, but he blocks my way again.

"So, how was the burger, then? You never text me back."

Seriously? The burger thing again? I turn to face him again. "The burger was good. Really good. You should go."

"Yeah? Well, maybe we could go after school today?"

"Today? I just went yesterday."

"Oh, yeah. Right."

I cock my head in the direction of his friends. "Take someone from your fan club."

"Stop calling them that. You don't even know them."

"I bet Jessica would love to go with you."

"We're not together. I told her a couple of days ago it's not going to happen."

"Okay, so that cheerleader you were with yesterday?"

"That was just…nothing."

"Look, it's none of my business. You can do what you want."

"I just thought, maybe you could get something else on the menu. Try it out? If you want?"

Back to the burger again? Jesus, what is he going on about? He's not even looking at me, just kind of looking behind me, shifting his gaze.

"Look, Ryan, you don't have to do this."

"Do what?"

"Act like we're friends or whatever. You find me annoying and the feeling's mutual. You like nothing more than pissing me off, and I know the last few weeks have been weird, but all we do is argue. It doesn't work, us being friends. We just end up fighting. Let's just leave it, okay? Go back to how it was. In middle school. When we just didn't talk?"

His mouth sets into a line and his eyes finally find mine. Like literally, he looks straight into my eyes. It's a bit distracting. "Right. Sure. If that's what you want."

I don't get him. Why is he being so weird? Whatever. I'm running late now and have to go. I leave him standing there and walk through his crowd into the school. Jessica shoots daggers at me and Mason wolf whistles. I flip them the finger over my shoulder and carry on into the building. I have had way too much interaction with this crowd over the last couple of months for my liking.

CHAPTER 27

RYAN DOES EXACTLY WHAT I ASK AND DOESN'T talk to me. In fact, he barely even looks at me, and I know this because I keep finding myself glancing in his direction more and more. I guess I didn't really notice at first. Life just kind of resumed as it did at the start of my senior year, back before he always seemed to be there. Only now he doesn't try to tease or talk to me. It's not that he's rude or anything, he's just completely indifferent to me being there. I first noticed it about a week after we agreed to go back to not speaking. Henderson passed me back a test from English and to my huge relief, I got an A, which will go a long way to pulling my grade up. I stood just as Ryan walked past. "Hey, I got an A!" I told him happily. He just glanced at me, gave a swift nod and left. I was annoyed at his total rudeness, then remembered he was only doing what I told him to.

I suppose I'd gotten used to him being around more than I realized and when we weren't fighting, I remembered how much I liked him and why we were friends to start with. But then I had to just keep reminding myself that it just wasn't worth the hassle and it was better off this way.

His friends have been giving me a wide berth too. They say hi when they pass, but no one tries to engage me in conversation, not even Katie. Although for some reason, I feel like this is more because she's been told not to talk to me rather than her not actually wanting to speak with me. But that's ridiculous, right? Why would Ryan tell her not to talk to me? Even Jake's being distant. I get the feeling he's annoyed at me for the way I've been with Ryan and even though Ryan and I aren't talking and therefore not fighting, it still feels like he's taken Ryan's side.

Ironically enough, I do end up attending Jake's party after all. Sam, Erica, and a few other friends are going so it's either that or hang out on my own. Everyone is polite enough when they see me, but it feels like his friends all look over at him before acknowledging me, almost as if they're getting his permission. God knows what he's said to them. The party is okay, but I just feel like I can feel Ryan watching me the whole time. Yet when I look over, he never is. He's just talking to whichever girl is next to him at that time.

It does get kind of awkward when Charlie turns up unexpectedly. He had told me he had plans, but when he heard where I was, I get the feeling he changed them. I'm almost worried Jake's going to ask him to leave, but no one says anything. Charlie spends the next half an hour being overly affectionate, always touching me, always kissing me. It reminds me of what Ryan said about him pawing at me to prove I'm his and when Charlie tries to pull me in for a kiss in the middle of a conversation with Sam, I start to think he might be right. I pull away from him and try to laugh it off, but when I turn, I see Ryan looking at me for the briefest of seconds before he turns to the girl on his right and leaves the room with her, clearly having decided on his hook up of the night.

Charlie and I leave soon after that. I'm eager to get away from the weird atmosphere and Charlie is feeling particularly amorous. I've got to admit, this whole Ryan situation is niggling at me, but I just keep reminding myself that I got what I wanted from him and can now focus completely on the person I've wanted all along—Charlie.

CHAPTER 28

"**I**'M SO SORRY, BECCA."

I stare at Sam, unable to speak. Late last night she texted me telling me that she had to speak to me urgently. I'd forgotten all about it and had gotten in late to school so hadn't seen her. She finally tracked me down just before English and pulled me into the girl's bathrooms for some privacy.

I really wish she hadn't.

Charlie has a girlfriend. *Charlie has a girlfriend? I'm not his girlfriend?* It can't be true. It can't be. Sam looks at me anxiously. I know she hates having to tell me this. Apparently Chris found out last night when one of Charlie's friends from his old school spilled. He told Sam right away and now she's telling me. I feel my chin start to wobble and Sam looks horrified. I force myself not to cry.

Oh God.

Charlie has a girlfriend. I'm the other woman. Oh shit. And I had sex with him. I gave up my virginity to some asshole who was completely using me. He didn't like me at all. It was all just bull. I'm desperate for it not to be true, but I know Sam's not lying. I know it's the truth. I guess that's why I couldn't always get hold of him. Shit.

"I'm okay. I've gotta get to class."

I walk quickly out of the girl's bathroom before she can say anything else. I don't believe this is happening. *How could I have been so stupid?* I'm so busy staring at the ground and concentrating on keeping my tears at bay that I don't notice the group standing outside Henderson's room and I walk smack into someone.

"Hey! Watch it!"

I look up in dismay to see Jessica Murphy staring at me like I'm something she's stepped in and I realize that I've knocked her books to the floor.

"I'm sorry," I mutter, my voice barely above a whisper. "I didn't see you there." I duck down and quickly pull together her books before handing them back to her with a shaky hand. "I'm really sorry, I didn't mean to."

I just catch her eyes narrow on my face before my gaze drops back to the ground. The last thing I need is for her to see me like this. I genuinely don't think I can handle another argument right now. I'm so close to losing it that anything could set me off and I really don't want this crowd to be witness to it.

"Whoa, Becca!" It's Jake. I know his voice without having to look. "You apologizing? You mustn't be feeling—" He stops abruptly when I turn to face him. I guess I'm not hiding my emotions very well after all. His eyes widen slightly,

233

"What's happened?"

I shake my head. "Nothing. Everything's fine." My voice cracks just slightly.

Jake opens his mouth to say something else. "She's fine," Sam says from behind me coming up to stand next to me. She takes hold of my arm and pulls me away from their group and further down the hallway, "Come on, Becca."

She walks straight past Henderson's open door and stops a few lockers down from his room where we're out of earshot from the rest of the students that are loitering in the hall.

"Are you sure it's true?" I ask quietly. Deep down I know it is, but I'm desperate for her to tell me that she got it wrong. That there's been a mix-up and the guy that I thought I was in love with hasn't been using me for the last few months.

She nods. "I'm really sorry, Becca. He doesn't deserve you."

"But I only spoke to him this morning. We're supposed to be meeting up after school."

"He probably doesn't know that Chris knows. We wanted to tell you first so you could figure out what you wanted to do."

"How long has he been with her?"

"Becca—"

"How long, Sam?"

She sighs. "They've been together for two years."

I feel like I've been punched in the stomach. This hurts, this really, really hurts. The person who has been my whole world since I met him has got a long term, serious girlfriend.

"He's a fucking idiot, Becca. You are so much better than him. He doesn't deserve you," Sam tells me fiercely.

I reach up to rub my face, trying to make sense of what I'm hearing and notice that my hands are shaking. I can't believe this. I cannot believe this is happening. "Do you think he loves her?"

Sam shrugs helplessly at my words and she reaches out and gently places her hand on my arm in a gesture of comfort. "You're better off without him."

"I slept with him, Sam," my voice trembles again. I gave that bastard my virginity.

Her face softens. "I know."

I shake my head in disbelief. "I am so fucking dumb, Sam. I am so, so stupid." I lean against the locker next to me suddenly drained of all energy and drop my head to rest against it. I feel completely and utterly betrayed. Why is this happening to me? How could he do this to me?

Sam suddenly straightens up, looking down the hall behind me, now that I've slumped against the locker. "Becca, they're looking over here."

I turn my head without thinking and see Jake still standing with Jessica and the rest of their group. The girls and most of the guys are talking amongst themselves, but Jake is standing slightly apart from them with Ryan next to him. Both of their gazes are fixed on me. Unfortunately, it's just when the first of my tears begin to fall and I quickly whip my head back to face Sam, wiping my face furiously.

Jake's by my side in a second, Ryan right beside him. "What's wrong? Why are you crying?"

I shake my head. "Nothing's wrong. I'm fine."

"Becca?"

I turn to glance at Ryan. It's the first thing he's said to me in weeks and this is definitely the closest he's been to me since we agreed to not speak. I quickly turn away from him. The last thing I want is him to know he was right about Charlie all along. I don't need him gloating right now.

"Becs?"

That old nickname is nearly my undoing, but I don't turn back to him. For some strange reason, I feel like if I look at Ryan, I won't be able to hold it together. Instead, I blink rapidly trying to stop anymore tears from falling. "I'm fine," I tell them through gritted teeth.

The bell rings and students up and down the hallway start making their way to class and Jake reluctantly leaves telling me that he'll call me later.

"Do you wanna skip?" Sam asks me and it makes me want to hug her. Sam never skips, she cares too much to do that, but the fact that she'll willingly do it for me makes me feel that little bit better.

"No. Let's go to English," and I turn and walk through Henderson's door before either her or Ryan can say anything else.

I last all of ten minutes before I wish I hadn't bothered with class. All I can think about is Charlie and the way he's lied and cheated on me from the start. I can feel myself getting more and more worked up and I know that I need to get out of there.

I stand up abruptly. "May I be excused?" Henderson

looks up from his desk in surprise, we're supposed to be reading a passage in a book, "I'm really not feeling well," I continue.

He looks at me for a couple of seconds and must see something in my face that stops him from questioning me. He nods and I quickly gather up my stuff and exit the classroom without bothering to wait for a hall pass.

I walk in a daze down the hallway, eyes down, unsure of where I'm even going. I can feel tears well in my eyes and I'm about to lose it. I make a quick detour down to my locker and throw it open, hiding my face inside it while the tears start to fall. I hear footsteps and I know that it's Sam. She's followed me out of English.

"Hey." It's not Sam. It's Ryan. I don't know how he got out of class or why he's here and I don't move, but for some reason the sound of his voice sets me off and my shoulders start shaking violently with sobs while I try to make sure I don't make any noise.

"Becca?" He's standing next to me now and gently touches my arm. I can't hold it in anymore and I let out the breath I've been holding, making a weird sobbing noise. I sound like I'm being strangled, but I can't keep it in.

"What's happened?"

I shrug and look down at the ground.

"Do you want to get out of here?"

I look up and find him looking down at me with concern. I nod slightly. I really don't want to lose it any further at school. He nods quickly, reaches down and picks up my bag, closes my locker and wraps his arm around my shoulder, pulling me into his side. I stare at the ground as he quickly guides me to the nearest exit and out into the parking lot. We reach his car and he opens the passenger door for me. I slide in and stare at the floor while he climbs into the driver's seat and quickly pulls out of the lot.

I stare at the floor the whole way back to his house, unable to stop the tears from falling. I see him glance over at me a couple of times from the corner of my eye, but he doesn't say anything. We pull up outside his house and he comes around and again helps me out of the car, putting his arm around me and leading me into his house. We walk through the house until we get to his den and sink down onto the sofa there. He sits next to me but doesn't say anything, waiting until I'm ready to speak. Finally, I seem to have it under control.

"Charlie has a girlfriend. An actual girlfriend of two years. So it's not even like he's been cheating on me. I'm the other woman." It doesn't feel real saying the words out loud and I can't even look at Ryan, I'm so ashamed. I let out a big sigh. "What is wrong with me? How could I have been so stupid?" Ryan rests his hand on my knee and I look over at him.

"You didn't do anything wrong here, Becs. He's the jackass."

"I really liked him, Ryan. Like *really* liked him."

"I know."

"And I slept with him, Ryan." I'm back to looking at the floor. "I just gave it up to him like it was nothing after only a few weeks. And it wasn't even that good. It hurt like hell and I had to leave right after 'cause his parents were due home." My voice cracks and I know I'm close to breaking down again. "I'm so stupid! I know guys don't care about that sort of thing, but girls do, and it was supposed to be special." This sets me off all over again and my body starts shaking with sobs.

Ryan shifts beside me, and I'm pretty sure I've just made him uncomfortable and he's going to ask me to leave, but the next minute he's slipped his hand under my knees and he's picked me up so that I'm now sitting sideways on his knee. My right shoulder rests against his body with my head on his shoulder and my legs swung over to the other side. It should feel awkward as hell being this close to Ryan but somehow it doesn't. Somehow it feels comfortable and totally natural, like if he stopped rubbing my back right now, I'd miss it.

We stay like this for maybe five minutes until I've calmed down. Then I sit up and wipe my eyes and turn to him. "Thanks."

He's looking at me closely. "Anytime."

I smile at him. "Why are you being so nice to me? I'm such a bitch to you."

He smiles good-naturedly and shrugs. "I usually deserve it."

"I guess you were right about him after all."

Ryan doesn't break my gaze. "I'm sorry he's hurt you, but I'm not sorry you've broken up."

We're both just sitting like this, with me on his knee, his arm resting on my back and we're watching each other. My eyes scan his face and it's like I'm seeing him for the first time and maybe it's because I've just found out about Charlie, or maybe I'm just not thinking straight, but before I know it, I'm leaning forward and I'm kissing him.

And oh my God does it feel right.

He freezes for just a second before he reacts, pulling me into him and kissing me back with such force it actually makes me dizzy. We adjust ourselves so that as much of our bodies are pressed against each other as possible and my body reacts to him, wrapping my legs tighter around him. That's right, somehow I'm now straddling Ryan. We're both getting breathless, but we don't stop. There's something frantic about the way we're kissing, something desperate about it. His hands are in my hair, on my back, and I'm grinding my hips into his groin.

Holy crap! Grinding my hips into his groin? I suddenly come to my senses. I am making out with Ryan, and if it carries on like this, it won't end there. Ryan Jackson, *the* Ryan Jackson. The guy all the girls at school melt over, the guy who loves to embarrass me and humiliate me in any way possible. This would give him enough ammunition to last until the end of the year! I have got to move.

I break away suddenly, prying his hands off my hips and clambering off him.

"Oh my God, I'm sorry."

Ryan looks up at me dazed, like he can't quite figure out what's going on. My heart is hammering so hard in my chest I'm sure he can hear it. "I am so, so sorry. I shouldn't have done that. I wasn't thinking properly. Please don't tell anyone," I plead.

"Becca—"

I cut him off before he can say anything else. "I've got to go. Let's pretend this never happened. Shit, I'm sorry." I turn and literally run out of there, not being able to get away fast enough.

Great, Becca. Well done. Like my life wasn't complicated enough.

CHAPTER 29

S O FAR I'VE DONE PRETTY WELL AVOIDING RYAN. It helps that he's always surrounded by people. My mom didn't believe me when I said I was sick for the second day running so I had to come to school. No one seems to know about what happened, which is a relief, but he might just be biding his time and waiting for the perfect moment to humiliate me. Every time he's called me, I've sent his calls to voicemail. I've deleted any texts without opening them and I've been skipping English so I don't have to deal with that. He even came over to my house last night, but I was in my room and pretended to be asleep when my mom came upstairs. I am not going to discuss the other day with him; not for his or anyone else's amusement. As far as I'm concerned, it never happened.

◆

Jay and I are on the sofa in my front room. The TV's on but

I'm trying to concentrate on the Science homework that's spread across my knees while Jay is using markers to color in a Superman coloring book. I glance over at him and although he's concentrating intensely, he's definitely not staying within the lines.

"Mom called me every day this week," he tells me suddenly, looking up. I smile at him and nod in encouragement. "And I'm going to get to see her again really soon!" he tells me excitedly. I grin at his enthusiasm. I know that my parents spoke to my aunt about her responsibilities and it looks like it may have worked. She definitely seems to be making more of an effort with Jay and apparently rehab is working really well. "And my dad is coming to see me next weekend. Auntie Sarah showed me the email where it said he's paid for the flights so he's definitely coming!" He's grinning at me from ear to ear, clearly delighted.

"That's great, Jay," I tell him. I really hope they are getting their act together. I go back to my homework and we're quiet for a few minutes.

"Can we go see Ryan?" he asks.

My head snaps up to face him, but he's still staring at his picture. "No," I say instantly, probably a bit more forcefully than necessary.

"Why?" he asks.

"Because we don't like him."

"I do." He pauses. "And he likes you."

"Why do you say that?" I ask quickly, again, probably too quickly. My heart starts beating faster.

Jay shrugs nonchalantly, clearly having no idea how I'm

now hanging off his every word. "Because when I'm there, he always asks where you are and what you're doing."

"He does?"

Jay nods. "Yeah, and who you're with." He pauses, looking at me hopefully. "So can we go see him?"

"No," I reply. My heart's still beating a mile a minute. *He asks Jay about me? What does that mean? Nothing. It means absolutely nothing,* I tell myself. He's just being nice, but for some reason I feel like I want to ask him about it, why he wants to know where I am. But I'm being ridiculous. Knowing Ryan, he's probably trying to find out information he can use against me at a later date.

Yes, that's what is it I tell myself.

"Why not, Becca?" Jay's voice is taking on that whiny tone that I hate.

"I'll give you five dollars and take you for ice cream if you stop asking to go to Ryan's," I tell him.

"Deal!" he shouts back at me excitedly. The kid will do anything for ice cream.

My phone beeps next to me. I glance at it, expecting it to be another text from Ryan, which I can delete immediately, but freeze when I see it's from Charlie.

Charlie: I'm outside your house.

I stare at the phone for five seconds in surprise. I text him right after I left Ryan's the other day and told him never to contact me again. He'd tried to call me right away, but when I didn't answer, he didn't try again. I have to admit, that hurt. He didn't even care enough to push me on it. I didn't tell him I knew about his girlfriend, but I guess he knew the reason. I cried when that reality hit, but I pulled myself together and realized he really wasn't worth it. The asshole didn't deserve anymore of my time or attention, and I refused to let myself wallow in it. To be honest, I've been thinking about Ryan a whole lot more that I've been thinking about Charlie in the last couple of days.

My phone beeps again.

Charlie: I know you're at home. I can see your car. Come out.

I stand to look out the window and sure enough, his car is there. He's looking at the house and has probably seen me. My heart's suddenly beating fast again. *Shit.*

"Stay here," I tell Jay. "I'm just going outside for two minutes and then we'll go get ice cream." He nods and I smooth down my hair, hoping I don't look too much of a wreck. Then I stop myself. I do not need to impress Charlie anymore. I don't owe him anything.

I leave my house and walk down the drive toward his car. I stop several feet away and he gets out of the car to face me. I cross my arms and look away; I have no idea what to say.

"I'm sorry, Becca," he tells me.

I shake my head and finally look at him. Only this time when I look at him, he doesn't make my heart flutter. Instead, I see that his hair looks greasy and his slim build looks scrawny rather than sexy.

"Why?" I ask him and instantly hate myself for it. I don't want to show him that I care.

He shrugs. "Because you're hot?" he says, cocking a

grin.

I look at him in disgust and resist the urge to slap him. Is he actually trying to make this into a joke? His expression turns somber at my obvious disgust, like he realizes he can't joke with me and make this go away. "I never meant for it to go this far," he carries on. "Things weren't going great with Catherine. That's her name."

"Your girlfriend?"

He nods. "Yeah."

"That girl we saw at the gig that time?"

"She went to my old school. She knows Catherine."

I shake my head in disgust, remembering how I thought that was weird at the time, how he didn't introduce me but all it took was for him to pull me into a dark corner and show me a bit of attention and I'd been too distracted to think about it again. I'm such a fool.

"Look, Becca, you're awesome and I'm sorry. Catherine and I broke up. The distance was too hard and I should have done it ages ago."

"You mean she found out about me and dumped your ass?"

He looks away and I know I'm right. *Total dick.*

"I would have picked you anyway. I'm sorry I lied to you, but we could try again? I like you so much, Becca. We're so good together."

I can't believe what I'm hearing. He actually thinks I could forgive him for something like this? For such a be-trayal? And only because his actual girlfriend dumped him first and now he doesn't want to be alone. I look at him—

this guy I was infatuated with, this guy that I thought I was in love with—and I feel nothing. Absolutely nothing.

I think back over our whole relationship and remember how he made me feel. Like I couldn't question him about things, how I had to accept whatever he gave me, however much time he chose to give. How I felt that if he didn't contact me, it was my fault. I'd done something wrong, I was to blame. I wasn't good enough.

"Go away, Charlie." I look him straight in the eye. "Don't contact me again."

He looks confused at my response, which I suppose is because all I ever did was be there for him whenever he wanted, for whatever he wanted. But I'm still me. I won't put up with this bullshit no matter how much I like someone, or in Charlie's case, *think* I like someone.

He opens his mouth to say something but the look I send him stops him. He looks away and climbs back into his car, driving out of my life for what I hope is the last time.

I stand and watch him go and don't feel anything. Tears don't even come close to my eyes. I can't believe I wasted so much of my time on him to begin with.

CHAPTER 30

I T'S MID-MORNING AND I'M HEADING TOWARD MY
locker, knowing I left my math book in there. As I get closer,
I sigh in annoyance. Ryan's there and he's surrounded as
usual. I'm going to have to start planning ahead and only
come at lunch or when I'm certain he's in class. He looks up
and our eyes meet. He steps toward me, but I spin on my
heel and rush away. Who needs books anyway? There is no
way I'm having that conversation with him. Not now, not
ever.

―――――――◆―――――――

"Becca, are you okay? You seem a little nervous." Sam looks
at me quizzically. I bite down on my lip and push my tray of
food away, I have no appetite. I'm at lunch and anxious because I can feel him watching me. I'm grateful that he hasn't
come over and spilled everything in front of everyone. At
least he's trying to catch me on my own. I just have to make

sure that I'm never on my own.

"I'm fine. Totally fine." I lie. I haven't told her about the kiss with Ryan. I'm too embarrassed, but she obviously knows there's something wrong.

"Is it Charlie?" she responds. I nearly laugh out loud. The one good thing about this whole Ryan situation is at least I've not been thinking about Charlie. At all. That lying, cheating bastard.

"No, it's not Charlie. Do you want to get out of here?"

She nods agreeably and stands. I follow suit and try and steer her out of the cafeteria conspicuously. She looks at me in surprise. "Don't you have Anatomy next? You're going the wrong way. I'm going that way too."

Oh shit, this means I'm going to have to walk directly past Ryan's table. Oh well, at least I've got Sam with me so he won't say anything and his table is so full maybe he won't notice me.

I quickly smile at Sam and reverse directions. I pick up the pace and think I've almost made it.

"Becca!"

Jesus, he says it loud enough so that half the cafeteria hears him. Sam stops walking and turns to face him, leaving me with very little choice but to do the same. His whole table's staring at me with unveiled curiosity. Oh my God, what if he's already told them and they're just waiting for the show to begin? If Jessica could shoot daggers from her eyes, I'd be dead right now.

He's laid back slouched in his chair, arms crossed and he's staring at me directly. I don't dare look him in the eye.

"What?" I mutter.

"I want to talk to you."

I glance around desperately; it's not just his table watching me. I feel myself blushing. Oh God, please don't out me in front of all these people, I'd die. The whole school would know about it by the end of the day. I'll be a complete laughing stock.

"What about?"

"You know what about." His voice is loud and clear. *Oh fuck, everyone really is listening.*

My eyes find Jake, who's sitting next to him. He's watching me, glancing back at Ryan every so often. Jake will rescue me; he won't let Ryan do this to me. I plead with my eyes, but he just sits there waiting. Yup, he knows. Clearly Ryan's told him and he wants to see this pan out. Great, my last hope is gone.

Ryan sighs loudly and abruptly stands, picking up his bag. He cocks his head toward the nearest exit. "Are you coming? Or are we gonna have to do this in front of everyone?"

There's literally not a sound in the room. I'm going to die of shame. My heart is beating loudly in my chest, but I freeze. I don't know what the best thing to do is. I really don't want to have this conversation with him. When I don't react, something flashes in his eyes and he drops his bag back onto the floor.

"Fine," he bites out. His voice isn't particularly loud but to me in the silence of the room, it feels like he's shouting. "Are you back with Charlie?" he asks me.

Blood rushes to my head. Why the hell is he talking about Charlie? What is he doing? Oh God, this is it. He's going to tell the whole school I jumped him after finding out about Charlie. I glance around desperately looking for some teachers or lunch staff that might stop this, but I can't see anyone. It's just face after face of students staring back at me, waiting for my moment of humiliation. My hands start to tremble at my sides.

When I don't respond, he scoffs at me. "You're back with him after what he did to you?" he continues. "When he was fucking someone else behind your back?"

I hear gasps from the watching students, but I don't look at them. I only stare at Ryan and the look of disgust on his face. I'm actually shaking now. *Why is he doing this? And why does he think I'm back with Charlie? Does he actually think that little of me?*

My silence seems to infuriate him further. "No, wait. Actually, it was you he was fucking behind *her* back, wasn't it?"

Oh my God. He did it. He told everyone what Charlie did to me. He just told the whole damn school. There are shocked gasps, murmurs, and snickers around me. I bite my lip to try to stop it from trembling. My stomach starts churning and I actually think I might throw up.

I see Jake stand and say something to him, trying to get him to move away, but Ryan ignores him, not looking away from me. All I can hear is the blood rushing to my ears.

"And you're back with him." This time, it's not a question and he sounds bitter. Really bitter. I don't know why he thinks this, why he's just told everyone this. I was right all along—he just wants to make me look a fool and ruin my life.

He opens his mouth again and I know this is it, the moment he tells the whole school that I kissed him after finding out my asshole ex-boyfriend was cheating on me, that I was that desperate and pathetic after being betrayed I thought I could jump him. But Sam cuts him off. "No she's not back with that idiot," she snaps at Ryan. I look at her and can tell she's pissed. Sam doesn't get angry, but she looks angry now. "But thanks for telling everyone that. Nice, Ryan, real nice," she continues, her voice is cold and she's looking at him in disgust. "Is there anything else you want to announce to the whole student body?" Her words cut through the silence of the room and that's when he glances around and seems to notice for the first time that everyone is watching us. "Nothing to say now?" she asks, staring him down. "Shame you weren't this quiet a few minutes ago," she mutters. "Now we're late so…" She lets the sentence linger, sending him a death glare. I glance back at him still shaking and find his eyes are back on me. She touches my arm and I look at her like she's given me a lifeline. She turns toward the door and I follow her on trembling legs. We exit and make our way down the hallway, away from the silence of the cafeteria and the total humiliation I've just suffered in there.

She glances at me sideways. "Are you okay?"

I nod but feel anything but okay.

"What was that about?"

I swear I'm still shaking. From terror, from adrenaline,

I have no idea. I shake my head. "I have to go. I'll talk to you later." I turn and rush from school, all my good intentions of not ditching gone. I need to get the hell away from this school. Now.

CHAPTER 31

'M LYING ON MY BED WHEN THERE'S A KNOCK ON my door. Sam sticks her head in; clearly she's come straight from school. "Hey. Can I come in?" I nod in response.

She comes and sits down in front of me. "Okay, spill. What is going on between you and Ryan Jackson?"

I just groan in response.

"Becca!"

"Do you know what happened after we left?"

"Erica said he kicked over a chair and then disappeared with Jake."

Oh God. "Did everyone see?"

"Yup. Everyone's been talking about it all afternoon."

I groan again. "Shit!"

"He came and found me after school. Told me to tell you he was sorry. I told him to tell you himself, but he said that he couldn't because you've been ignoring him all week. That you're refusing to talk to him."

I look away from her and stare at the ceiling.

"He seemed, I dunno, pretty worked up. Annoyed. Upset, even." I still don't say anything; she sighs loudly. "Are you gonna tell me?"

I can feel myself going red, and for the millionth time I wish I didn't always blush like a ten-year-old. "I kissed him," I practically whisper the words.

Her jaw nearly hits the floor. "You did what?" Her face lights up with excitement.

"I know, I know, it's so stupid. It was just after I found out about Charlie. I was really upset and he was being nice to me, and I just..." I break off. She's grinning from ear to ear.

"This is awesome!"

"Are you kidding me? This is Ryan Jackson I'm talking about. The guy who loves to torture me. He's gonna tell everyone how I launched myself at him in desperation, and I'll never be able to set foot in school again." I look up at the ceiling in despair. *Why me?*

Sam's brow furrows in confusion. "Don't you think if he was gonna do that, he'd have done it already? It's been, what, four days?"

"He's probably just biding his time. He would have done it in the cafeteria in front of everyone if you hadn't cut him off."

"It all makes sense now. To me, it looked like he just wanted to talk to you. Then got mad when you wouldn't."

I sigh. "Trust me, Sam. He's waiting for the right moment to humiliate me. I should have just got out of there, but I froze."

"What was all that stuff about Charlie? You're not getting back with him, are you?"

"No! I have no idea what that was about."

"Have you even spoken to him?"

"No. Well, he came around here a couple of days ago, but I told him to leave. I don't want anything to do with him."

"Maybe he saw him outside your house? Maybe that's why he said it?"

Maybe that's right, maybe that's why he thought I was getting back with him. That would explain it. Still, that's no reason to humiliate me in front of everyone. What does it matter to him anyway?

"I hate him," I tell Sam. I don't hate him, I know that. But to be honest, I'm not exactly sure what I feel about Ryan right now. Everything is so confusing.

Sam looks at me for a moment, then crosses her legs like she's about to make an announcement.

"Did you ever wonder why Fran Cunningham never came after you when you confronted her over Kylie?"

I pause thinking back to that day in freshman year. I'd been so angry at the way she had treated Kylie and for the way she mocked her that I reacted and called her out for the bully she was in front of all her friends, all the most popular kids in school. Sam had been with me. She'd been furious and had actually lunged at me, but Ryan had at some point moved to stand next to me and stepped in front of me, stopping her from getting to me before Jake pulled me away. Later that night when the adrenalin had worn off, I'd started to worry. Fran wasn't a girl that you messed with and I knew she'd find a way to get back at me, to make me miserable but nothing ever happened. She looked at me like I was dirt but that was it and then she graduated later that spring. Of course, I'd wondered at the time why she hadn't come after me, but I hadn't thought about it in years and figured she'd just suddenly grown a conscience. I shrug at Sam.

"Well, I did. I swear I was waiting for months for her to come at us. So I asked Jake at the start of sophomore year. When Jake was dragging us away from her that day and Ryan stayed and we saw him talking to her?" She pauses to make sure I'm listening. There's no need; I'm hanging on every word. I remember that day clearly, while Jake had been trying to get me to calm down and go home we'd turned to find Ryan standing with Fran in deep conversation, the rest of the crowd also listening to him. "Well, apparently he was making it crystal clear to her and everyone else there that if she went after you, she'd be going after him."

She pauses while she lets this news set in. All I can do is stare back at her.

"Then he told her that if she did go after you, he'd go after her. Think about it, Becca. Ryan was a freshman. Yeah, he was popular, but it's not like it is now. Fran was this senior and he didn't know who'd take his side, if everyone would turn against him and go after you regardless, but he didn't care. He made it clear that you were to be left alone and he made sure you were. That's why Ryan and Jake and all those guys were there the next day when we got to school. Not to watch Fran kick your ass but to make sure she didn't."

I let this sink in for a moment, thinking back to that day and the anger I'd felt and the fury that I knew was coming my way from Fran. I'd gotten to school and found her waiting for me, along with what looked like half the student body probably waiting to see me get my ass kicked, but Ryan and all his friends were there too. They'd been watching her, waiting for her to react. At the time, I'd thought it was because they were there to watch a fight. Sam couldn't be right, could she? Ryan had been there with all his friends to protect me and make sure I was safe? It makes sense now, why Fran never said anything. I try telling myself that Fran went too far and that's why nothing ever happened afterward. Everyone was too disgusted by her actions, and even though I know part of that is true, I can now see the other side. Ryan laid down the law. He came to my rescue, back when I refused to even look in his direction.

"Why didn't he say anything?" I eventually ask.

Sam shrugs. "I don't know. I guess he didn't want you to feel indebted to him. It's no secret the way you feel about him. He probably didn't want to make you uncomfortable."

I open my mouth to respond. Then close it again. I have no words right now.

"Look, don't kill me, but have you ever wondered why he goes out of his way to mess with you? Like you're on the other side of the room, nowhere near him, and he's surrounded by people and the center of attention, yet he singles you out, trying to get your attention?"

I screw my face up. "I'm just lucky, I guess."

"I mean it, Becca. Look, remember I went to that football game a while back? Well, I swear he kept looking up at us in the stands throughout the game. I think he was waiting for you to show up. Then at the party afterward we walked in and knew no one. I mean, we knew people, but that's not our crowd and no one really spoke to us. We just stood there like idiots until he noticed us, and even though he was surrounded by people, he came right over to say hi and introduce us to people."

"Yeah, I'm not saying he's not friendly Sam. At least not to other people," I mutter.

"It was weird. As soon as he came over, it was like it was okay for everyone else to talk to us and suddenly we were socially acceptable. That guy has some serious power."

"Yeah and he's about to use that against me," I point out.

"He stayed with us for a while, kept looking at the door. He didn't say anything, but I knew he was waiting for you."

"Oh come on! Wasn't that the night he first hooked up with Jessica?" I say incredulously.

"He didn't even look at her until Erica let slip that you were out with Charlie. I dunno. After that, he seemed pissed, started drinking and then disappeared with her."

"You're way off Sam," I insist.

"And that's the reason you guys had that huge fight after dodgeball, isn't it? He was mad at you for not showing up?"

"Who told you about that?" I ask quickly.

She rolls her eyes at me. "Come on, Becca, everyone knows about it. I just didn't say anything because I knew you wouldn't want to talk about it."

I groan again. I didn't think it was public knowledge

that Ryan was mad at me for not going to the game. But of course, everybody knows about it. It involves Ryan, doesn't it?

"You're wrong," I state decisively.

She sighs. "Fine. But think about it, okay? He protected you from Fran, he took you home after Charlie ditched you, he bought you all that candy just 'cause he remembered you like it, and he's literally always at your locker."

"What are you saying?"

She looks at me like I'm stupid. "He likes you, Becca. I've thought that for a long time now, but I never said anything because I thought you hated him."

I nearly laugh out loud. "You're crazy. I know Ryan, and that is not what this is about."

"He asks me about you," she tells me, smiling. "He has for years. Whenever we're in homeroom. He thinks he's being all subtle asking about my weekend and casually asking who I was with. Sometimes he drops your name, thinking I won't notice. Sometimes I tell him stuff about you just to put the poor guy out of his misery."

"Are you being serious?" She nods. My jaw falls open in surprise, but then I shake my head. "No, Sam. You're wrong." She can't be right, the whole idea is ridiculous.

She nods and stands. "Okay, if that's what you say. But I don't think I'm the only one who thinks he's into you. Especially not after today." She grins at me before walking toward the door. "I've gotta go. Will you be at school tomorrow?"

I nearly snort. "What do you think?"

She just rolls her eyes at me and leaves the room. I bury

my head in the pillow, trying to get today's events out of my head and work out how I'm going to tell my parents that I have to switch schools. But what I focus on more than anything is trying to get that damn kiss out of my head.

CHAPTER 32

MY MOM HAS HER "NO ARGUING FACE" ON. I bite my lip. She can't make me do this.

"Rebecca Louise McKenzie! I do not know what's been going on with you this week. I know you've not been sick, even though you've taken two days off school, but you will go upstairs right now, put some makeup on and the dress I have bought for you and you will come to this party with us. Kathy and Bill are very dear friends of ours and I will not insult them by leaving you here at home."

Shit, shit, shit.

I turn hopefully to my dad, but he looks even more annoyed with me. "Now, Becca."

Oh God, how could I have forgotten about Bill Jackson's fiftieth birthday party? It's all mom and Kathy have talked about for weeks. If I'd remembered, I could have just made sure I was out at Sam's and not come back for it. Crap!

I slowly stomp back upstairs, cursing the day I was born. Oh man! It's not just going to be Ryan I have to deal with tonight, but his whole freaking fan club will be there. His mom said she'd told him to bring friends. This is not going to end well.

◆

I finally make my way downstairs, my dad looking pointedly at his watch. My mom turns to me in annoyance but breaks out into a smile when she sees me. "Becca, you look beautiful." My dad grins in agreement with something like pride in his eyes.

"Thanks," I mumble. Okay, so I made an effort. A big effort. I curled my hair and pulled it over to the side. I've made my eyes look all smoky by lining them with kohl eyeliner and the dress my mom bought for me is stunning. It's a shimmery silver color that clings in all the right places, and the green of my jewelry brings out my eyes. Finally, I've added platform heels to give me some extra height. If Ryan's going to ruin my life tonight, I might as well look good while he does it.

We exit our house and walk the hundred yards or so to the Jackson residence. You can already hear the music playing. There's a huge tent built in their backyard and tons of people milling around. I lag behind my parents, still hoping for some sort of miracle that will excuse me from this party. The look my mom shoots me tells me I'd better get moving.

We enter through the front door, a man in a waiter's uniform smiling and holding the door for us. Wow, they really are going all out. I look up and the entire Jackson family is standing just inside greeting everyone. My mother and father rush forward to hug Bill and Kathy. Ryan looks up and does a double take when he sees me. Clearly he wasn't expecting me to come. *You and me both, Ryan.*

Lisa looks over at me and practically squeals. She rushes over to hug me. "Becca, you look absolutely stunning." She gives me a tight hug and turns to her brother grinning. "Doesn't she look great, Ry?"

He looks over blushing and mumbles something under his breath before turning away. Lisa grins at me wickedly and gives me a wink. *What was all that about?*

Bill and Kathy come over to say hi, each gushing about how good I look, and Bill makes me promise to dance with him later. Hey, maybe I should make an effort with my appearance more often.

Kathy smiles at me warmly. "We're actually almost ready to eat. You missed cocktail hour so we'll have to go straight to the tables." I nod in agreement and follow my parents through to the tent, their friends smile and greet them, and I almost feel bad for making them late. Almost, not quite.

I'm standing around waiting for them when Kathy comes and wraps her arm around me. "Don't worry, sweetie, we haven't put you with us oldies. You're at Ryan's table." I inwardly groan and face the direction she's pointing to, but there's only Jake sitting over there.

Okay, weird. I sigh and make my way over.

Jake whistles when he sees me approach. "You look smoking, Becca. Has Ryan seen you?"

I glare at him in response. He chuckles. "I'm guessing you're still pretty pissed about that scene in the cafeteria?"

"You mean him telling the entire school my private business?"

Jake whistles at my tone. "Yeah, he shouldn't have done that. But then you shouldn't have ignored him all week after hooking up with him." Yup, of course, he knows all about our kiss.

I glare at him and Jake holds his hands up in defeat. "Hey, I'm staying out of this from now on, but you guys should definitely talk tonight. Sort out your shit. He's been like a caged bull all week."

Ryan comes over and sits down. I don't even glance at him, but my heart starts beating faster, especially when Jake gets up and leaves us alone, trying to give us some privacy or whatever.

"I didn't think you'd come," he tells me.

I shrug in response. There's not really much I can say to that.

"I'm sorry. I shouldn't have said that stuff about Charlie in front of everyone."

"No shit."

"I thought you'd gotten back with him."

"Clearly. You told the whole freaking school."

He looks away, glancing around the tent and then turns back to me. "I saw him outside your house." *Ah, so he did see us.*

"I was telling him to go and not to come back."

"So you're not getting back with him?" he asks again,

like he needs it reiterated.

"No, Ryan. I am not getting back with Charlie." He opens his mouth to speak again, but I cut him off. "Let's just leave it, Ryan, okay? If we talk, we argue. Let's just get through tonight, then we can avoid each other for the rest of our lives."

His jaw clenches and his mouth sets into a straight line. He looks pissed at me. Again.

"I'm gonna go get a drink," I tell him, standing to move away. I'm not thirsty, but I need to get away from him, because right now he's causing all kinds of mixed up feelings within me that I do not want to have to deal with.

I return to the table just as the first course is being served and concentrate on the plate in front of me while Ryan glares at me the whole time. *Great, this isn't awkward at all.*

Jake gets bored of us by the end of the salads and disappears for a couple of minutes. He comes back with a couple of Ryan's cousins who were clearly seated elsewhere. I nod hello but don't get involved in the conversation. Whatever, at least now there's not complete silence at the table. I look around wondering when I can make my escape. I turn back and catch Ryan looking at me with such anger I sink a bit lower in my chair. This night can't be over fast enough.

Ding, ding, ding!

A fork is clinking against a champagne glass and I realize it must be time for the toasts. A champagne glass has appeared next to me, but I've been too busy staring at my plate to notice. I turn to face Mr. Jackson, glad for an excuse to face away from the table.

He looks around the room and asks his family to join him. Lisa jumps up, but Ryan doesn't move. It takes another request from his father to get him out of his seat and to the front of the dance floor. I smirk. It's quite funny watching him squirm for a change. He looks so awkward at the front.

His father starts by saying how lucky he is to have such a wonderful family but I'm barely listening. All the effort I've made in avoiding Ryan has meant that I haven't really looked at him tonight and he looks good. Really good. It's the first time I've ever seen him in a tux and standing up there, he's even taller than his father. His broad chest fills out the shirt, his hair is shining but still slightly messy, which I like. It makes him still Ryan. He's looking down at the floor waiting for the speech to end, hands shoved in his pockets.

Suddenly he looks up at me and I can't turn away. His blue eyes pierce mine. My heart starts beating a mile a minute and I lose my breath.

Oh God, I think I want him. I want Ryan Jackson. This will not end well for me.

Okay, I need to get a grip. I turn back to Jake just as the speeches end and the dancing starts. Ryan's dancing with his sister so I still have a few minutes before he gets back here.

Jake's watching me smirking.

"What?" I demand.

He holds his hands up. "Nothing. Nothing at all."

I glance around at our nearly empty table. "So, why are

we sitting here by ourselves? Where's the rest of your friends from school?"

Jake shrugs. "Ryan called them up today and told them not to bother coming. I think his mom was pretty pissed and the girls have been bitching about it all day."

Right. Now I'm confused. "Why would he do that?"

He lets out a deep sigh. "Because, Becca, he knew that if you came and they were here, you'd feel uncomfortable."

My jaw drops. "But I wasn't even gonna come. My parents forced me."

"Exactly and he still did it anyway."

He stares pointedly at me. I'm really confused.

"Oh for God's sake Becca! For someone who's usually pretty smart, you're being incredibly stupid. Ryan likes you, okay? He's always liked you."

"Likes me? Like he wants to be friends again?"

"No, Becca. He does not just want to be your friend."

I'm speechless, just staring at Jake with my mouth hanging open.

He rolls his eyes and sighs, clearly disappointed with my stupidity. "Come on, Becca, think about it, *really* think about it."

"But all he does it try to piss me off and make me look stupid and embarrass me."

"Because it's the only way he could get you to talk to him! Look, I'm not saying it was the smartest move, but he just wanted you to talk to him. Even if it was you shouting at him."

"But he's always with a different girl?"

"He might have messed around with other girls, but he's never cared about any of them like he has about you. He didn't think you gave a damn, so I dunno, all the other girls were a distraction or something. That Jessica Murphy thing was all her."

I'm shaking my head. Is this a joke? Sam was right and Ryan was actually jealous of Charlie? This can't be right. I can tell Jake's getting exasperated with me.

He leans forward intently, like he's trying to get through to me. "He cares about you, Becca. He really, *really* cares about you. Kevin Wilson is done at school as far as Ryan's concerned. You should have seen what Ryan was like after he grabbed you. He wanted to kill Charlie for hurting you. When we bumped into you at that party that time, he couldn't concentrate knowing you were there, drunk and with another guy. He remembers things about you that I wouldn't even know about myself. Why do you think I've been pushing you to hang around with us so much? I'm sick of hearing about it so I've been trying to help it along."

"But we argue all the time."

He sighs deeply. "I think they call that chemistry, Becca. I think at this stage you're the only person in school who doesn't know how he feels." He glances up and throws his napkin down, standing up. "Just work it out, one way or another." He turns and walks away.

I panic. "Hey, wait!" I'm not sitting here at an empty table by myself, I stand quickly to follow him.

"Stop!" I turn back around and Ryan's returned to the table. "We need to talk, Becca."

269

I nod. He's right. I need to sort this out. I'm feeling really confused. Like *seriously* confused right now.

I look around. "Yeah, okay. Now's probably not the best time. Maybe tomorrow?"

His gaze doesn't budge from me. "No, right now," he says firmly.

He starts walking quickly toward me, and without breaking stride and before I have time to do anything, he's grabbed my hand and is pulling me along behind him. I almost trip up and am practically running to keep up with him. I catch Lisa looking at us and whispering to Ryan's mom before he pulls me out of the tent.

He walks straight into his house and directly up the stairs, pulling me with him. He opens his bedroom door and pushes me in, following and closing the door behind him.

"God, Becca! You're driving me crazy."

I nod, rubbing my arm. It hurts a bit from him pulling so hard and I'm a little out of breath from the running, but I don't think this is the best time to mention it.

He walks past me toward his desk, his back to me. Suddenly he turns around and looks me dead in the eye. "Why have you avoided me all week? After we kissed?"

I blush and look around the room. This is so weird.

"Becca?" he coaxes me.

"Because I thought you were going to tell everyone about how I threw myself at you and turn me into a laughing stock. You know, embarrass me."

Ryan sighs and shakes his head at me. "You actually think I'd be embarrassed about what happened?"

I shrug. "I was. I don't know what came over me. I know everyone would find it hilarious, me kissing you."

Ryan sighs loudly, shaking his head at me. "You are so clueless, Becca." He squares his shoulders and takes a deep breath. "I'm gonna speak and for once you're just going to listen to me. Okay? No interruptions."

I nod slightly. I suddenly feel awkward. This is the first time in years I've been in his room and I don't know what to do with myself. I look back at Ryan, who is studying me intently and decide I'd prefer to look at the floor.

"Look, I stopped talking to you in the seventh grade because the guys were giving me shit, saying I liked you. By the time I figured out that I didn't care what they thought, you were done with me. Like, that was it. I was gone from your life and you didn't want to know me. And I missed you, Becca, a lot. You act like I don't even know you, but I know you a lot better than you think. I'm always aware of you. Whenever you're in the room, I know exactly where you are. Jesus, when I get to the cafeteria at lunch, I look to your table first to see if you're there before I look at mine. I notice when you miss a day off school. I know what times in the day you go to your locker and I try and be there too. I pick up on anything my mom ever says in passing. I know the only subject you care about is Art, but you're smart enough to ace every class if you wanted to. I know your first kiss was in a game of spin the bottle and it was with Mason. You have no idea how much that pissed me off. I wouldn't speak to him for a week. I said those things to Billy Jameson that time because I was crazy jealous that you were out on a date with him. It should have been me that took you on your first date and I couldn't handle that you were there with him. I swear on my mom's life, though, Becca—I would have stopped that bet about him sleeping with you. I never, *ever* would have let that happen to you." He pauses. "I give you shit at school 'cause it's the only way you notice me."

He pauses. I don't dare look up. *Is he telling me that he likes me?* He lets out a sigh of frustration.

"Then these last few weeks you actually started talking to me again and it wasn't about me pissing you off and you snapping back. We were actually becoming friends again. You're literally all I can think about, and then you tell me I've got it wrong and there's not a chance we'll ever be friends. Then that jackass makes you cry, and it makes me want to kill him. And you kiss me. You kiss me Becca, and I think *yes, something is going to finally happen between us*, and then you freak out. You ignore me all week, refuse to speak to me, make me look like a complete dick in the cafeteria, and then you turn up here looking like *that*."

There's a pause. My body's shaking.

"And you are just so fucking annoying!"

My eyes snap up at this and he's staring straight back at me. Bright blue eyes pinning me still, forcing me not to move.

"And you're infuriating. And exasperating and moody. And shitty and stubborn. And kind. And funny. And clever and talented. And beautiful." He pauses. "You're so freaking beautiful, Becca."

I'm about to start hyperventilating now.

"And I love you."

I officially cannot breathe. Ryan is watching me, waiting for me to react and I can barely remember my own name. *Ryan Jackson just said he loves me.*

I don't believe this is happening, but his eyes tell me he meant every word. Ryan Jackson, the popular boy at school, my old friend, my total nemesis.

"You love me?" My voice is actually trembling.

He nods, his eyes focused on mine, his hands clenching nervously like he's not sure he made the right decision to tell me.

"But you're always with a different girl?"

He shrugs. "I thought you hated me and was trying to forget about you. It didn't work. None of them are you. It's only ever been you, Becca."

"Are you being serious?"

He nods his head and a wry smile crosses his face. "I am so in love with you, Becca. Always have been." He pauses, studying my face for my reaction. "Everyone knows it too and I couldn't care less. I'm sick of pretending I don't think you're the best person I know. That I don't think about you the whole time. I think you're the only one who hasn't picked up on it."

I think back and it all starts to make sense. I remember how he always seemed to be there, how he was always watching me if I was talking to someone. How Jake was always trying to push us together, how when we're not fighting it's so easy to be around him, how its comfortable and relaxing, like being with my best friend. Then I think how

Ryan is capable of pissing me off more than anyone else I've ever met, and how I've not been able to stop thinking about him or our kiss since it happened.

Oh my God. I'm stupid. I love him too!

A huge smile crosses my face. I can't help it. I'm literally beaming.

Ryan lets out a breath he's been holding and tentatively returns my smile. I take a step toward him and he meets me halfway. He takes my hand and I feel a shiver run up my spine. We stand like this for a few minutes, just grinning at each other like idiots, soaking each other in, seeing each other in a different way.

Then he hesitantly leans forward to kiss me, slowly, giving me the chance to pull away if I want to. I step forward, pressing my lips to his and wrapping my arms around him and pulling him into me.

Everything just feels right.

We should have done this year's ago.

EPILOGUE

Ryan

I WALK OUT OF MY COACH'S OFFICE STILL GRINNING like an idiot. There's no hiding it; I'm crazy happy. I never thought it would ever happen with Becca. I've wanted her for as long as I can remember and now she's finally mine. I can't even believe it.

I remember the moment I realized that I loved her. We had just started high school and I knew I liked her. I knew her ignoring me gave me a weird ache in my stomach, but I didn't recognize it as love.

I had been sitting at a table in the cafeteria along with some of the guys from the football team. The older guys had been checking out the new "talent," as they called it. Seeing which girls in the incoming freshmen class were the hottest and who would be worth talking to. They'd already seen a dozen girls that they were interested in when Billy Jameson, this arrogant junior, whistled under his breath and demanded, "Who is that?"

I knew just by looking at him he'd spotted Becca. I already knew where she was sitting—I looked for her the minute we walked into the cafeteria—and he was looking that way. Becca had always been pretty, but she had changed over the summer, grown taller, had a tan, her hair was longer and was impossibly shiny and she had started to gain some curves. She was generally looking incredibly hot. I'd been dreading anyone but me noticing it.

Jake, Mason, and John turned to see where he was looking and then as a group turned to look at me. Even back then they had an idea of how I felt about her. Billy noticed and glanced at me. "You know her, Jackson?"

I just shrugged and took a bite out of my burger.

"So who is she then?"

"Becca McKenzie," I replied.

"Is she yours?" God, he was a prick. Like anyone could own anyone, especially Becca. And no matter how much I wanted her to be mine, I knew that she wasn't.

I had shaken my head, refusing to look at Jake. At that moment, Becca jumped up and I could see she had knocked her juice all over herself. She picked up some napkins and started dabbing at her shirt, lifting it up to inspect it. I swear, I think I audibly swallowed, catching a glimpse of her flat stomach, and I know I wasn't the only one looking. She glanced up and caught us all looking, instantly dropped her shirt, and sat back down looking away.

"Dibs!" Billy announced making everyone laugh, although I could feel people looking at me too, wondering what the story was there.

I then spent the next few weeks watching him make his move on her. She never looked particularly interested, but when I saw her by her locker laughing at something he had said, it had made me feel sick. He announced a few days later at the end of practice that he had a date with her that Friday.

I was surprised when they showed up at the cookout and as she walked up next to him holding his hand, I felt a jealousy so intense it shocked me. When she excused herself, I headed over to him and the few people he'd been standing with. I didn't care what I said, I just wanted him to be put off, so I insulted her as best I could, not knowing she was listening in. I actually didn't know about the bet they had made and there is no way I would have let them go through with it, but then she stepped out of the shadows and I knew she'd heard everything.

I could see that she was trying to control her emotions, that what she'd heard had hurt and humiliated her. I thought for a second she was going to crack, that she was going to lose it, but of course, she didn't. Becca is so good at hiding her emotions, at pulling it together, that she just calmly made it clear that she would never speak to Billy again. Then she looked at me with utter loathing and walked away.

Jake went crazy when he heard what happened. He hadn't been there, but Mason filled him in on the details and told him exactly what had been said.

"What the hell, Ryan? Why would you do that to her?

This is Becca we're talking about. Not some random girl," he demanded.

"Yes, I know. I didn't know she was listening," I fired back, getting irritated. I didn't need reminding of how badly I had acted.

"This is how you think you're going to get her to like you again? You would actually have let them bet on sleeping with her? Fuck, Ryan, what is wrong with you?"

"Shut up," I growled back, stepping closer to him, my fists were actually clenched at my sides. "I didn't know about the stupid bet. What do you care anyway? I know you like her, just come out and admit it."

He had shaken his head in disgust at me. "Yes, I like Becca, she's my friend. We've been friends for years and years. But why don't we talk about how you feel about her? You think I don't see you staring at her? Why don't you just grow up and admit how you actually feel and not treat her like shit."

I just glowered at him before he brushed past me and left the room without another word.

"Why don't you just tell Becca that you love her?" A voice said from behind me. I turned to see Lisa standing there, leaning against the doorframe of my bedroom. She had just graduated from college and was home for a couple of months. She clearly heard the whole fight.

"I don't love Becca," I scoffed at her.

She cocked an eyebrow at me and smirked. "If you say so little brother." Then she turned and walked away.

I had sat down and tried to think about something else.

Tried to think about anything but Becca McKenzie. But I couldn't. I couldn't get her out of my head. The way she looked, the way she laughed, the way she rolled her eyes. She kept playing on a loop over and over in my head.

I had gotten up and made the twenty minute walk over to Jake's house where he was shooting hoops. When he saw me, he passed the ball over, and I took aim and watched it fly through the hoop. I turned to him. "I think I love her."

He rolled his eyes at me. "Well, yeah. Duh."

After that, I tried to apologize to her, but she just ignored me and kept on ignoring me. The only good thing about that whole mess was that it seemed to put her off dating for a long time because I didn't see her with anyone else.

She still totally ignored me, but she didn't ignore Jake, and that was how I pushed my way back into her life, even if only fleetingly. When she was talking to Jake, I would be there and make a cocky joke. She couldn't wait to get away from me, but at least it was some interaction with her. I could see how frustrated she grew when I was near her, how her walls came up, but I didn't care. At that stage, I would do anything just to talk to her, but she would just stare blankly back at me or flat out ignore me.

I even turned up where I knew she'd be once or twice, but it never worked out how I hoped. One time I overheard Sam saying she was going to the beach with Becca, and I couldn't resist the urge to turn up, the temptation of seeing her in a bikini too much for me. Sam had just smirked at me—I think she's always known how I feel about Becca, but she's too nice to call me on it—and Jake had laughed out loud when he realized Becca was at the beach and that was why I dragged him down there. Becca just sat there, ignoring me, letting the three of us have a conversation around her. Unfortunately, she was wearing a tank top and shorts rather than the bikini I had pictured her in but I was just enjoying being away from school with her and after an hour of Jake's teasing and jokes she eventually relaxed just slightly and even said something directly to me at one point. But then Mason and John and a bunch of other's from school turned up and she tensed up again. I didn't even know how they knew where we were, but after the girls laid their towels out and I started throwing a ball around with the guys I turned back to them to find Becca and Sam rolling up their towels, getting ready to leave. Sam had waved goodbye in my direction and Becca said a few words to Jake and then they were gone. That's kind of what always happened. Becca always got away from me as fast as she could.

I remember at the end of junior year telling myself that I had to get over it. I had to stop thinking about her the whole time. She really was not interested in me, she couldn't stand me and I was only hurting myself by having this dumb, constant hope that she would change her mind about me. I wasn't even letting myself think about her being my girlfriend. All I wanted was for her to talk to me again, to be civil to me, to have her back in my life in whatever small way I could get, instead of the looks of disgust and disdain I always got when I tried talking to her.

I thought I managed it. She was away the whole summer and I told myself I was over it. I dated over the summer, stayed busy working and playing ball, hanging with the boys the whole time. But then on the first day of senior year, I saw her get out of her car all the way from across the lot and that same old feeling was there, that same old hammering of my heart and that longing that's only seemed to grow since she stopped talking to me. I saw her greet her friends as she walked to the main entrance, smiling and laughing at something someone said. I know the exact second that she saw me because her face turned into the mask she's used on me since the day I fucked up our friendship when we were twelve years old. She didn't even glance at me. Of course, I wolf-whistled as she passed, anything to get her attention, but she didn't even look in my direction. The guys saw it though, and although they didn't say anything, I knew they knew how I felt about her. It was getting harder and harder for me to hide it. Jake's the only one who knew how deeply I really felt about her, the only one I'd talk to about her.

As she passed us on the steps, Jake reached out from the end of our group to grab her for a welcome hug, and I tried not to grimace in annoyance. Jake's my best friend in the whole world, but I hated how she was with him. She was herself with him; she always relaxed when she saw him and let down that wall she puts up with everyone but her close friends. I was jealous—really damn jealous. I mean, I know their relationship is purely platonic and they're just good friends who have known each other for years, but I'd give anything for her to genuinely smile just at seeing me. She walked on and Jake saw me looking at them and rolled his eyes. He'd been telling me for years just to talk to her, to tell her how I felt. I didn't want another lecture about it.

I remember seeing her at that party. I spent the majority of high school hoping she would show up at a party, that maybe she would be more relaxed outside of school and maybe let those walls down. Hell, I even made sure I invited my entire grade to my sixteenth birthday, literally everyone, hoping that if some of her friends came, she'd be more likely to turn up. All it got me was a trashed house and a month's grounding for letting the party get out of hand.

I was so shocked when I saw her standing there in that corner. When she didn't turn away immediately, I figured she was drunk. She probably thought she was hiding it pretty well, but I could see her swaying. She gave me her usual attitude, but when she said Kevin groped her because of the way I treated her, Id felt sick. I still couldn't believe he'd been dumb enough to try that shit with her. As soon as she left, I thrown him into the nearest lockers and made it clear he was done as far I was concerned. He told me he was sorry, that he didn't know I cared. The idiot practically begged, but I was done with him. And I made it clear to the rest of the guys too. I know Becca thinks I have some stupid power at school, and maybe I do, and for once I was happy to use it to destroy Kevin Wilson. I didn't want anything to do with him.

I hadn't even wanted to go to Zara's party that night, but I had promised Jake a couple of days before and he definitely wasn't letting me change my mind. The only thing I'd been able to think about all day was Becca's face after Kevin had grabbed her, the look of pure disgust and actual panic as she gathered her things. The look she shot me when I tried to help her was of pure hatred, but I could see she was trying to hold it together; her hands were shaking slightly and she was blinking really fast like she was trying to stop tears. I was so angry at him that he would do that to her, and I just wanted to help her, to reassure her, but she didn't want me near her. When she nailed him in the dick, I actually felt proud of her. I hadn't been able to get her out of my head all day, though. At lunch, I was watching her to see if she'd look at me. She glanced my way once and I caught her eye, but she just looked through me like I wasn't there at all.

When I walked in on her with that dick, with her legs wrapped around him, I felt like I'd physically been punched in the gut. I'd gone looking for her, hoping to talk to her and instead I saw some fucking loser who was in no way good enough for her with his hands all over her. When I found out he was her boyfriend, it was like a second punch to the gut, this time from Floyd Mayweather. I shouldn't have been surprised, really. I'd known how amazing she was for years, and it was only a matter of time before she finally let one of the many guys I knew would be interested in her into her life. Billy Jameson definitely put her off dating for a while, but I knew it wouldn't last forever.

When she followed him out of the room and up the stairs, it took all my resolve not to grab her and take her home. The thought of her having sex with someone made me want to punch the wall, again and again, preferring the pain of a broken hand to the pain of knowing she was with someone else.

I went back to Jake and had just stood there, glowering across the room, not speaking. I could see Jake sending me curious glances wondering what was going on, but I ignored him and all attempts by Zara and Katie to draw me into the conversation. All I could think about was Becca, and that creep with his hands all over her.

Mason had come over. "Hey, did you know Becca McKenzie is here?" he said to me directly, knowing how I felt about her and knowing I would want to know if she was at the party. "I just saw her heading upstairs with some guy."

I sent him a look which meant I clearly didn't want to talk about it. He held his hands up and instantly backed off.

Jake glanced over at me. "She's with a guy?"

I nodded. "Her boyfriend," I bit out.

Sympathy crossed Jake's face, which just pissed me off more. I didn't want to be pitied. "Aww, man, I'm sorry. I didn't know she was with anyone."

"Why would you care who Becca McKenzie's with?" Katie asked me curiously.

John had sent her a warning glance and shook his head, indicating that I wouldn't want to talk about it. You see, that was the thing. It was the worst kept secret between my male friends that I liked Becca. Everyone knew, but I just wouldn't talk about it. That was why I couldn't believe Kevin Wilson thought he could pull that crap and grope her. Didn't he know I was willing to destroy anyone over Becca? I thought they all knew that.

Katie looked over at me and the tension that was radiating off me in waves and nodded in understanding. "You

284

like her?"

I didn't respond, but I heard John snort and mutter "understatement" underneath his breath. I scowled over at him.

"Does she know?" Katie continued.

"No. And she's not going to either," I told her. Katie nodded. I didn't care that Katie knew. She was one of my good friends and unlike some of the others girls in our group, she wasn't a gossip. But I didn't want Becca to know. I knew the way she felt about me and didn't want her to feel uncomfortable. And who was I kidding? As long as I didn't say anything, I could still have this dumb hope that maybe one day she'd change her mind about me rather than shoot me down completely.

I think that was the moment that Katie decided to try and help me with Becca. After that, she was always asking me about her and trying to talk to Becca when she saw her, but she soon learned getting Becca to open up to a new person wasn't as easy as she thought.

"I need some air," I muttered. I turned and walked out the back door into the yard, and when I found her later drunk and alone, I was furious that her boyfriend had just left her, even though it did mean that I got to spend some one on one time with her for the first time in years. Even if she did spend the whole journey insulting me before throwing up on the sidewalk.

She still didn't want to know me, she would still rather have talked to anyone over me, but she was still there when my grandmother died. She still chilled with me; she still wouldn't let me be alone. Because that's Becca. She's prickly, she's snarky, but she's kind.

After that, I dunno, I figured I had nothing to lose. I started taking more chances, showing up where she was, talking to her more, and I could almost see the internal battle she was fighting. She didn't want to let me back into her life—she's nothing if not stubborn—but she was slowly letting her walls down, relaxing around me.

Then she ditched me for Charlie and I lost it. I know I was a dick for letting Jess hit her during dodgeball, but I was so mad at her. I was pissed with Charlie, anyway. Luke had told me what had happened at that gig. He had seen Charlie pull her into the middle of the crowd then just leave her when it turned into a mosh pit. Luke said you could tell just by looking at her how stressed she was getting and Charlie didn't even notice because he was off doing his own thing. But I couldn't say anything, no matter how much I wanted to, because as Jake pointed out, she wasn't my girlfriend, she was his. And he was right. When I mentioned it when we were outside, I could tell how pissed she was with me just for bringing it up. But then she said she'd come and watch my game and I'd thought that was going to be the night, the night she finally just hung with me and would just be there again. I would take any time she would spend with me. I didn't even think about kissing her. I mean, of course, I thought about it, but I just wanted her to be there for me. I was distracted the whole game, scanning the crowd for her when I could. I'm lucky I didn't screw the whole thing up, but she never came. At the party afterward, I stood like an idiot watching the door waiting for her to show, but then

Erica told me she was with Charlie and I felt like such a fool. I saw Becca's look of surprise when Mason invited her and her friends to his party. After she'd looked away, he caught my eye and winked at me. He knew I'd want her there, and despite what Becca might think, Mason would never be exclusive about who he invited to his parties. At this stage, everyone was trying to help me with her. They were so sick of my crush (I mean, come on, that tutoring shit they came up with?) and I honestly thought that she would come, but she didn't even give me a second thought when she went off with Charlie.

Enter Jess. I'm not proud of it, but Jess is cool and she's hot and she wanted me, so I went with it. I had known that Jess had been into me for a while, but I always avoided hooking up with her in the past because I knew she'd want something serious rather than just a casual hook up. Because that's the thing—I don't do girlfriends. Yeah, I dated around—a lot—but I always kept it casual, kept it simple, and that was because of Becca. The only girlfriend I wanted was Becca McKenzie. I've always known everyone else was a distraction, but I knew Jess would want more than that. After Becca ditched me, I figured I'd give it a shot with Jess, thought she'd be the perfect person to help me get over this stupid thing with Becca, but it didn't happen. It didn't change anything. God, even when I fight with Becca, it excites me. I enjoyed it way more than I would ever admit. Watching her get all flustered and angry and knowing it was me who made her so mad, I realized she did care at least a little bit, even if she'd never admit it. She cared enough to be pissed at me.

So I kept trying, kept trying to be there, and then she told me to stop hanging around her and I had to take it. I had to listen to her and I kept my distance. I tried to stop thinking about her, tried to stop looking out for her, but it didn't make any difference. I still wanted her. When I saw her crying over Charlie, I wanted to go and ruin the guy. I hated that he had the power to upset her like that, hated that he was lucky enough to have her, yet still treated her like that, hated him for doing that to her. I mean, how stupid could he be?

And then she kissed me, and I've never been so surprised or happy about anything in my life.

I thought that was it, that was finally it, but then she stopped suddenly, like she'd only just realized what she was doing, and she freaked. She ran away and left me feeling lower than I've ever felt before in my life. Then she ignored me, wouldn't look at me. If she saw me, she walked in the other direction. Ignored all my calls and texts, even when I plucked up the courage to go to her house, she wouldn't come downstairs. Then I saw her with Charlie outside her house and I thought they were back together. So I confronted her, in front of everybody.

I could see she was shaking, could see she was mortified, but she had been driving me crazy since our kiss and I wanted to get back at her. I know now it was a shitty thing to do, but can I help the way our school works? Gossip spreads like wildfire, and in all honesty, I wasn't thinking about anyone else when I confronted her. I just wanted to sort things out with her. Then when Sam cut me off and Jake pulled me away, I realized how unfair that was, how tough that would have been for her. I was pretty sure she'd never, ever speak to me again.

Then she turned up at my dad's birthday and she looked the most beautiful I'd ever seen her. And that's saying something since I think she looks beautiful every time I see her. I couldn't tear my eyes away from her at first and when she confirmed she wasn't back with Charlie, my heart literally fucking soared. I decided to do it. Decided to go all out and make her listen to me. Tell her how I felt once and for all. At least then I could say I tried everything.

And I did. And she didn't run away, she didn't tell me to get lost. She looked shocked to the core, but then I could almost see the wheels in her brain turning, working things out and I knew she was starting to figure it out. Understand why I was always where she was, understand why I always had something to say, understand the way I felt about her and she smiled. She actually smiled, and that was it. That was the best moment of my life. The moment when I got my best friend back and the girl that I've been in love with ever since I can remember.

I walk into the cafeteria still grinning like an idiot. I can't stop. I walk to my lunch table, past Becca, who is already sitting down at hers. She glances up at me and her face lights up. I'll never get tired of seeing that. I've waited so long for her to look at me like that. She gives me a knowing smile and it takes all the self-control I have not to pick her up and drag her back to my house. I can't stop thinking about her. I cannot get enough of her. I can't believe she's finally mine.

I reach my table and slide into my seat. Mason glances up at me and screws his face up when he sees me smiling. I've not exactly been the happiest person in the world recently.

"What are you so happy about?" he asks.

I shrug but can't wipe the smile from my face.

Jake on my left glances over at me and chuckles. "Yeah, Ryan, what could possibly have made you so happy?"

Confusion crosses Mason's face and the rest of the table quiets down, tuning into our conversation. Realization dawns on Mason, and he breaks out into a huge grin. "You nailed McKenzie, didn't you?"

I smirk back at him and look around to see that the rest of the table doesn't really look too surprised at the news and are grinning back at me, looking genuinely happy for me. Wow, I guess everyone really did know how I felt about her.

I think originally everyone enjoyed watching me getting roasted by Becca. It's not usually the way it works, but they soon changed their minds when the way she treated me made me into the world's moodiest asshole. And the thing is, I know they all like her too. That thing Becca thought about us being the popular kids and looking down on her is crazy. I know most of the girls think she's funny and I know for a fact that everyone is in awe of her for standing up to that psycho Fran Cunningham when we were freshman. Becca was fearless that day, and I was so fucking proud and impressed by her. Katie's made an effort with her recently and would be BFF's with her if Becca would let her, and I'm pretty sure if my male friends didn't know how obsessed I was with her, at least a couple of them would have tried to have hooked up with her by now. In fact, I know that's true. I've caught a few of the guys checking her out over the years, but they all knew she was off limits. Even though I never said anything, never admitted to anyone but Jake how I felt about her, they all knew.

"Finally!" says John while the others echo his sentiments. Only Jessica rolls her eyes in annoyance and I feel a pang of regret about using her as a distraction, but then remember she's already been on a few dates with a college guy her sister introduced her to. The guys start to slowly clap their hands, giving me a round of applause.

I start to laugh and look over at Becca, who is listening to her crazy friend Erica. "Actually, I think I'll ditch you losers today and go sit with my girlfriend," I say still grinning.

This really sets them off and they start laughing, banging on the table and stamping their feet on the floor. Becca looks up in surprise at the noise and when she sees me grinning at her and the rest of my table looking over, she turns slightly pink but doesn't look away. It's probably for the best that she doesn't look away because most of the students in the cafeteria are looking over now; my friends are making that much of a racket. She'd die of embarrassment.

I start walking over to her and the cheering and whistles start; my friends obviously find this very entertaining. I couldn't care less. Becca shakes her head slightly, but she's smiling and doesn't look away from me. I drop into the seat beside her, throwing my arm over her shoulder and ignore the astonished looks from her friends. Only her friend Sam is looking at me like she's not surprised and winks in my direction.

Becca turns and looks me straight in the eye, raising an eyebrow. "So you told them?" she asks.

I lean over quickly and kiss her right on the mouth. She freezes in surprise and then shocks me by leaning into me and kissing me right back.

This sends my friends into overdrive, making them even louder, if possible, whooping and yelling over at us. My grin gets so wide I feel like my face is going to split in two. Becca just kissed me back, in front of everyone. She wasn't ashamed or trying to hide it. She claimed me just as much as I claimed her.

Becca looks over at my friends and the scene they're making and flips them the finger, but she's laughing. I know she hates being the center of attention, but I'm not going to pretend we're not together and now everyone knows. And they can get used to it, because if I have anything to do with it, we'll be together for a very long time.

Want to see what happens to Becca and Ryan? Look out for

FOUR YEARS LATER

coming soon…

Enjoy this book? Please consider leaving a review online or recommending to a friend.

ACKNOWLEDGMENTS

This is the first book I've ever written and it wouldn't have been possible without a bunch of people.

First of all, huge thanks to Leah for being my first reader (of anything I've ever written), and for her instant encouragement and enthusiasm. Your response made me think this may be something worth pursuing.

A big thank you to Beth for reading it in the early days, helping me iron out the issues and for always being willing to re-read the chapters I've worked on. You've been a great cheerleader.

Humongous thanks to Sara Ney (you should all check out her books), who showed me the way in this scary world of self-publishing and was so kind in her advice and encouragement. Sara also introduced me to Christine who I'm so grateful to for Beta reading for me. Thanks for your suggestions and pointing out when my writing gave away my Britishness.

Thanks to Murphy for a brilliant cover and for answering all my endless questions for me. Also big thanks for helping me find Megan who did such a fantastic job at editing the novel. Something it was in desperate need of. Megan, I truly appreciate all your hard work.

Thanks to Laura for proofreading and all her advice on how to promote my book. It was greatly appreciated and thank you to Stacey for formatting. . .I wouldn't have known where to start.

Big thanks to all my brilliant family and friends – you guys are amazing.

Finally, to anyone who has read this book, posted a review or recommended it to a friend. Thank you, thank you, thank you! It means the world to me.

ABOUT THE AUTHOR

Emma Doherty grew up in Yorkshire, England. She attended Northumbria University in Newcastle, and then bummed around the world for a bit. She now lives in London, UK.

Emma loves to hear from readers. You can get in touch with her on twitter (@Em_Doh) or Facebook (Emma Doherty Author).

Made in United States
North Haven, CT
16 October 2022